S0-BBN-847

Edited by Peter Weston

Andromeda 1

An original SF anthology

ST. MARTIN'S PRESS   NEW YORK

HOUSTON PUBLIC LIBRARY

79-083932-8
HUM

Copyright © 1979 by Peter Weston
All rights reserved. For information, write:
St. Martin's Press
175 Fifth Avenue
New York, N.Y. 10010
Manufactured in the United States of America

RO1616 50698

Library of Congress Catalog Card Number: 78-21400

ISBN 0-312-03649-3

INDEXED IN  SSI 79-83

CONTENTS

Appearance of Life by Brian W Aldiss
© Brian Aldiss 1976

Starthinker 9 by Michael G Coney
© Michael G Coney

Waltz of the Bodysnatchers by Bob Shaw
© Bob Shaw

Travellers by Robert P Holdstock
© Robert P Holdstock 1976

Valley of the Bushes by Naomi Mitchison
© Naomi Mitchison 1976

An Infinite Summer by Christopher Priest
© Christopher Priest 1976

Doll by Terry Greenhough
© Terry Greenhough

A Beast for Norn by George R R Martin
© George R R Martin

The Giant Killers by Andrew M Stephenson
© Andrew M Stephenson 1976

Seeing by Harlan Ellison
© Harlan Ellison 1976

ANDROMEDA ONE

INTRODUCTION

EXACTLY fifty years ago, in April 1926, the very first science fiction magazine was born. How the world has changed in that time! So, today, what do we mean by 'good science fiction'?

It's impossible to describe yet we all feel sure we'll recognise it when we see it. Is there some mysterious common factor, some special ingredient that makes an occasional story stand out from the crowd? And if there is, can it be captured, pinned down and analysed, and the secret utilised to fill a whole book with nothing *but* top stories?

Alas, in six months of searching I've found nothing so clear-cut. Some stories are strong on plot but lacking in characterisation; others are fascinating in technical detail at the expense of writing style. Each one is different, leaving me no alternative but to fall back on just one Golden Rule: every single story in ANDROMEDA is here because in my judgment I think it is a winner.

Many times I've been surprised and delighted by the audacity of science fiction writers, amused and entertained, occasionally shocked or given entirely new understandings. I *care* for our literature; at its best it can do so much, so well, that I find myself wanting nothing but the best, in flat contradiction to a basic law of the Universe which states that no more than 50% of anything can be above average.

The ten stories here have been selected to try and put that best before you, carefully distilled from more than three hundred manuscripts submitted for this first ANDROMEDA volume. I believe you will enjoy them. I think they are a good reflection, in their different ways, of some of the directions in which modern science fiction is going.

A word about ANDROMEDA itself. It is intended to be a showcase of the very finest original stories, from both established writers and up-and-coming newcomers. No taboos or prejudices, no barriers against the newest of new writers who have never before sold professionally. The only requirement is quality, and a certain originality, for after fifty years some of the stock situations of science fiction have just about been worn into the ground.

It's highly unlikely, for instance, that there is anything left to say about mad professors, reincarnation, or Adam and Eve. Maybe it's also time we took a hard look at our much-loved Galactic Empires, clinking robots, and those many worlds-after-the-Bomb, for they too have grown stale. I love the way in which my good friend Dr Jack Cohen dismisses the archetypal *bad* SF story, 'It turns out the flying saucers are piloted by evil telepathic mutants from Atlantis.'

And I don't believe a word of it!

It seems to me that there is no shortage of bright new ideas; so much is happening in the real world, today, which simply begs for the razor-keen extrapolation which science fiction can provide. Have you looked in the scientific journals lately? They're crammed with all sorts of discoveries that, in one way or another, will affect the lives of us all. As for current events, well, would you have believed that Aberdeen, Scotland's granite city, would turn into an oil town?

These are just a few ideas of what, to me, science fiction can be about. Above all it should be fresh, wide-eyed (as opposed to *wild*-eyed!), and fun to read. That's what I hope you'll see in ANDROMEDA.

— PETER WESTON

APPEARANCE OF LIFE

by Brian W Aldiss

AFTER NEARLY twenty years I can still clearly recall my first Brian Aldiss story. 'T', a passive, near-mindless creature racing back through space-time to the very dawn of life on Earth, to destroy the human race before it even was born.

There I sat in my schoolboy's cap on the top deck of a 'bus, entranced, fascinated by this new book with the strange title, Space, Time and Nathaniel. *This, I knew immediately, was Good Stuff!*

In the light of what has since followed that may now seem rather primitive Aldiss, but even then revealing a certain lightness of touch, a fresh new insight that has subsequently made Brian the finest of all science-fiction short-story writers. 'Appearance of Life', like 'T', is fascinatingly ingenious, and also oddly autobiographical. Like Brian Aldiss himself the role of our narrator is to search for insights, to put together the most unlikely constructs and to see what new meanings emerge.

Something very large, something very small: a galactic museum, a dead love affair. They came together under my gaze.

The museum is very large. Less than a thousand light years from Earth, countless worlds bear constructions which are formidably ancient and inscrutable in purpose. The museum on Norma is such a construction.

We suppose that the museum was created by a species which once lorded it over the galaxy, the Korlevalulaw. The spectre of the Korlevalulaw has become part of the consciousness of the human race as it spreads from star-system to star-system. Sometimes the Korlevalulaw are pictured as demons, hiding somewhere in a dark nebula, awaiting the moment when they swoop down on mankind and wipe every last one of us out, in reprisal for having dared to invade their territory. Sometimes the Korlevalulaw are pictured as gods, riding with the awfulness and loneliness of gods through the deserts of space, potent and wise beyond our imagining.

These two opposed images of the Korlevalulaw are of course images emerging from the deepest pools of the human mind. The demon and the god remain with us still.

But there were Korlevalulaw, and there are facts we know about them. We know that they abandoned the written word by the time they reached their galactic-building phase. Their very name comes down to us from the single example of their alphabet we have, a sign emblazoned across the façade of a construction on Lacarja. We know that they were inhuman. Not only does the scale of their constructions imply as much; they built always on planets inimical to man.

What we do not know is what became of the Korlevalulaw. They must have reigned so long, they must have been so invincible to all but Time.

Where knowledge cannot go, imagination ventures. Men have supposed that the Korlevalulaw committed some kind of racial suicide. Or that they became a race divided, and totally annihilated themselves in a region of space beyond our galaxy, beyond the reach of mankind's starships.

And there are more metaphysical speculations concerning the fate of the Korlevalulaw. Moved by evolutionary necessity, they may have grown beyond the organic; in which case, it may be that they still inhabit their ancient constructions, undetected by man. There is a stranger theory which places emphasis on Mind identifiable with Cosmos, and supposes that once a species begins to place credence in the idea of occupying the galaxy, then so it is bound to do; this is what mankind has done, virtually imagining its illustrious predecessors out of existence.

Well, there are many theories, but I was intending to talk about the museum on Norma.

Like everything else, Norma possesses its riddles.

The museum demarcates Norma's equator. The construction takes the form of a colossal belt girdling the planet, some sixteen thousand kilometres in length. The belt varies curiously in thickness, from twelve kilometres to over twenty-two.

The chief riddle about Norma is this: is its topographical conformation what it always was, or are its peculiarities due to the meddling of the Korlevalulaw? For the construction neatly divides the planet into a northern land hemisphere and a southern oceanic hemisphere. On one side lies an endless territory of cratered plain, scoured by winds and bluish snow. On the other side writhes a formidable ocean of ammonia, unbroken by islands, inhabited by firefish and other mysterious denizens.

On one of the widest sections of the Korlevalulaw construction stands an incongruous huddle of buildings. Coming in from space, you are glad to see that huddle. Your ship takes you down, you catch your elevator, you emerge on the roof of the construction itself, and you rejoice that – in the midst of the inscrutable symmetrical universe (of which the Korlevalulaw formed a not inconsiderable part) – mankind has established an untidy foothold.

For a moment I paused by the ship, taking in the immensity about me. A purple sun was rising amid cloud, making shadows race across the infinite-seeming plane on which I stood. The distant sea pounded and moaned, lost to my vision. It was a solitary spot, but I was accustomed to solitude – on the planet I called home, I hardly met with another human from one year's end to the next, except on my visits to the Breeding Centre.

Wind tugged me and I moved on.

The human-formed buildings on Norma stand over one of the enormous entrances to the museum. They consist of a hotel for visitors, various office blocks, cargo-handling equipment, and gigantic transmitters – the walls of the museum are impervious to the electromagnetic spectrum, so that any information from inside the construction comes by cable through the entrance, and is then transmitted by second-space to other parts of the galaxy.

'Seeker, you are expected. Welcome to the Norma Museum.'

So said the android who showed me into the airlock and guided me through into the hotel. Here as elsewhere, androids occupied all menial posts. I glanced at the calendar clock in the foyer, punching my wrisputer like all arriving travellers to discover where in time Earth might be now.

Gently sedated by alpha-music, I slept away my light-lag, and descended next day to the museum itself.

The museum was run by twenty human staff, all female. The Director gave me all the information that a Seeker might need, helped me to select a viewing vehicle, and left me to move off into the museum on my own.

Although we had many ways of growing unimolecular metals, the Korlevalulaw construction on Norma was of an incomprehensible material. It had no joint or seam in its entire length.

More, it somehow imprisoned or emanated light, so that no artificial light was needed within.

Beyond that, it was empty. The entire place was equatorially empty. Only mankind, taking it over a thousand years before, had turned it into a museum and started to fill it with galactic lumber.

As I moved forward in my vehicle, I was not overcome by the idea of infinity, as I had expected. A tendency towards infinity has presumably dwelt in the minds of mankind ever since our early ancestors counted up to ten on their fingers. The habitation of the void has increased that tendency. The happiness which we experience as a species is of recent origin, achieved since our maturity; it also contributes to a disposition to neglect any worries in the present in order to concentrate on distant goals. But I believe – this is a personal opinion – that this same tendency towards infinity in all its forms has militated against close relationships between individuals. We do not even love as our planet-bound ancestors did; we live apart as they did not.

In the summer, a quality of the light mitigated any intimations of infinity. I knew I was in an immense enclosed space; but, since the light absolved me from any sensations of clausagrophobia, I will not attempt to describe that vastness.

Over the previous ten centuries, several thousand hectares had been occupied with human accretions. Androids worked perpetually, arranging exhibits. The exhibits were scanned by electronic means, so that anyone on any civilised planet, dialling the museum, might obtain by second-space a three-dimensional image of the required object in his room.

I travelled almost at random through the displays.

To qualify as a Seeker, it was necessary to show a high serendipity factor. In my experimental behaviour pool as a child, I had exhibited such a factor, and had been selected for special training forthwith. I had taken additional courses in Philosophicals, Alpha-humerals, Incidental Tetrachotomy, Apunctual Synchonicity, Homoontogenesis, and other subjects, ultimately qualifying as a Prime Esemplastic Seeker. In other words, I put two and two together in situations where other people were not thinking about addition. I connected. I made wholes greater than parts.

Mine was an invaluable profession in a cosmos increasingly full of parts.

I had come to the museum with a sheaf of assignments from numerous institutions, universities, and individuals all over the galaxy. Every assignment required my special talent – a capacity beyond holography. Let me give one example. The Audile Academy of the University of Paddin on the planet Rufadote was working on an hypothesis that, over the millennia, human voices were gradually generating fewer phons or, in other words, becoming quieter. Any evidence I could collect in the museum concerning this hypothesis would be welcome. The Academy could scan the whole museum by remote holography; yet only to a rare physical visitor like me was a gestalt view of the contents possible; and only to a Seeker would a significant juxtapositioning be noted.

My car took me slowly through the exhibits. There were nourishment machines at intervals throughout the museum, so that I did not need to leave the establishment. I slept in my vehicle; it was comfortably provided with bunks.

On the second day, I spoke idly to a nearby android before beginning my morning drive.

'Do you enjoy ordering the exhibits here?'

'I could never tire of it.' She smiled pleasantly at me.

'You find it interesting?'

'It's endlessly interesting. The quest for pattern is a basic instinct.'

'Do you always work in this section?'

'No. But this is one of my favourite sections. As you have probably observed, here we classify extinct diseases – or diseases which would be extinct if they were not preserved in the museum. I find the micro-organism beautiful.'

'You are kept busy?'

'Certainly. New exhibits arrive every month. From the largest to the smallest, everything can be stored here. May I show you anything?'

'Not at present. How long before the entire museum is filled?'

'In fifteen and a half millennia, at current rate of intake.'

'Have you entered the empty part of the museum?'

'I have stood on the fringes of emptiness. It is an alarming sensation. I prefer to occupy myself with the works of man.'

'That is only proper.'

I drove away, meditating on the limitations of android thinking. Those limitations had been carefully imposed by mankind; the androids were not aware of them. To an android, the android umwelt or conceptual universe is apparently limitless. It makes for their happiness, just as our umwelt makes for our happiness.

As the days passed, I came across many juxtapositions and objects which would assist clients. I noted them all in my wrisputer.

On the fifth day, I was examining the section devoted to ships and objects preserved from the earliest days of galactic travel.

Many of the items touched me with emotion – an emotion chiefly composed of nosthedony, the pleasure of returning to the past. For in many of the items I saw reflected a time when human life was different, perhaps less secure, certainly less austere.

That First Galactic Era, when men – often accompanied by 'wives' and 'mistresses', to use the old terms for love-partners – had ventured distantly in primitive machines, marked the beginnings of the time when the human pair-bond weakened and humanity rose towards maturity.

I stepped into an early spaceship, built before second-space had been discovered. Its scale was diminutive. With shoulders bent, I moved along its brief corridors into what had been a relaxation room for the five-person crew. The metal was old-fashioned refined; it might almost have been wood. The furniture, such as it was, seemed scarcely designed for human frames. The mode aimed at an illusionary functionalism. And yet, still preserved in the air, were attributes I recognised as human: perseverance, courage, hope. The five people who had once lived here were kin with me.

The ship had died in vacuum of a defective recycling plant – their micro-encapsulation techniques had not included the implantation of oxygen in the corpuscles of the blood, never mind the genetosurgery needed to make that implantation hereditary. All the equipment and furnishings lay as they had done aeons before, when the defect occurred.

Rifling through some personal lockers, I discovered a thin band made of the antique metal, gold. On the inside of it was a small but clumsily executed inscription in ancient script. I balanced it on the tip of my thumb and considered its function. Was it an early contraceptive device?

At my shoulder was a museum eye. Activating it, I requested

the official catalogue to describe the object I held.

The reply was immediate. 'You are holding a ring which slipped on to the finger of a human being when our species was of smaller stature than today,' said the catalogue. 'Like the spaceship, the ring dates from the First Galactic Era, but is thought to be somewhat older than the ship. The dating tallies with what we know of the function – largely symbolic – of the ring. It was worn to indicate married status in a woman or man. This particular ring may have been an hereditary possession. In those days, marriages were expected to last until progeny were born, or even until death. The human biomass was then divided fifty-fifty between males and females, in dramatic contrast to the ten-to-one preponderance of females in our stellar societies. Hence the idea of coupling for life was not so illogical as it sounds. However, the ring itself must be regarded as a harmless illogic, designed merely to express a bondage or linkage—'

I broke the connection.

A wedding ring . . . It represented symbolic communication. As such, it would be of value to a professor studying the metamorphoses of nonverbality who was employing my services.

A wedding ring . . . A closed circuit of love and thought.

I wondered if this particular marriage had ended for both the partners on this ship. The items preserved did not answer my question. But I found a flat photograph, encased in plastic windows, of a man and a woman together in outdoor surroundings. They smiled at the apparatus recording them. Their eyes were flat, betokening their undeveloped cranial reserves, yet they were not unattractive. I observed that they stood closer together than we would normally care to do.

Could that be something to do with the limitations of the apparatus photographing them? Or had there been a change in the social convention of closeness? Was there a connection here with the decibel-output of the human voice which might interest my clients of the Audile Academy? Possibly our auditory equipment was more subtle than that of our ancestors when they were confined to one planet under heavy atmospheric pressure. I filed the details away for future reference.

A fellow-Seeker had told me jokingly that the secret of the universe was locked away in the museum if only I could find it.

'We'll stand a better chance of that when the museum is complete,' I told her.

'No,' she said. 'The secret will then be too deeply buried. We

15

shall merely have transferred the outside universe to inside the Korlevalulaw construction. You'd better find it now or never.'

'The idea that there may be a secret or key to the universe is in any case a construct of the human mind.'

'Or of the mind that built the human mind,' she said.

That night, I slept in the section of early galactic travel and continued my researches there on the sixth day.

I felt a curious excitement, over and above nosthedony and simple antiquarian interest. My senses were alert.

I drove among twenty great ships belonging to the Second Galactic Era. The longest was over five kilometres in length and had housed many scores of women and men in its day. This had been the epoch when our kind had attempted to establish empires in space and extend primitive national or territorial obsessions across many light-years. The facts of relativity had doomed such efforts from the start; under the immensities of space-time, they were put away as childish things. It was no paradox to say that, among interstellar distances, mankind had become more at home with itself.

Although I did not enter these behemoths, I remained among them, sampling the brutal way in which militaristic technologies expressed themselves in metal. Such excesses would never recur.

Beyond the behemoths, androids were arranging fresh exhibits. The exhibits slid along in transporters far overhead, conveyed silently from the museum entrance, to be lowered where needed. Drawing closer to where the new arrivals were being unloaded, I passed among an array of shelves.

On the shelves lay items retrieved from colonial homes or ships of the quasi-imperial days. I marvelled at the collection. As people had proliferated, so had objects. A concern with possession had been a priority during the immaturity of the species. These long-dead people had seemingly thought of little else but possession in one form or another; yet, like androids in similar circumstances, they could not have recognised the limitations of their own umwelt.

Among the muddle, a featureless cube caught my eye. Its sides were smooth and silvered. I picked it up and turned it over. On one side was a small depression. I touched the depression with my finger.

Slowly, the sides of the cube clarified and a young woman's

16

head appeared three-dimensionally inside them. The head was upside down. The eyes regarded me.

'You are not Chris Mailer,' she said. 'I talk only to my husband. Switch off and set me right way up.'

'Your "husband" died sixty-five thousand years ago,' I said. But I set her cube down on the shelf, not unmoved by being addressed by an image from the remote past. That it possessed environmental reflexion made it all the more impressive.

I asked the museum catalogue about the item.

'In the jargon of the time, it is a "holocap",' said the catalogue. 'It is a hologrammed image of a real woman, with a facsimile of her brain implanted on a collapsed germanium-alloy core. It generates an appearance of life. Do you require the technical specifics?'

'No. I want its provenance.'

'It was taken from a small armed spaceship, a scout, built in the two hundred and first year of the Second Era. The scout was partially destroyed by a bomb from the planet Scundra. All aboard were killed but the ship went into orbit about Scundra. Do you require details of the engagement?'

'No. Do we know who the woman is?'

'These shelves are recent acquisitions and have only just been catalogued. Other Scundra acquisitions are still arriving. We may find more data at a later date. The cube itself has not been properly examined. It was sensitised to respond only to the cerebral emissions of the woman's husband. Such holocaps were popular with the Second Era woman and men on stellar flights. They provided life-mimicking mementoes of partners elsewhere in the cosmos. For further details, you may—'

'That's sufficient.'

I worked my way forward, but with increasing lack of attention to the objects about me. When I came to where the unloading was taking place, I halted my vehicle.

As the carrier-platforms sailed down from the roof, unwearying androids unloaded them, putting the goods in their translucent wraps into nearby lockers. Larger items were handled by crane.

'This material is from Scundra?' I asked the catalogue.

'Correct. You wish to know the history of the planet?'

'It is an agricultural planet, isn't it?'

'Correct. Entirely agricultural, entirely automated. No humans go down to the surface. It was claimed originally by Soviet India

17

and its colonists were mainly, although not entirely, of Indian stock. A war broke out with the nearby planets of the Pan-Slav Union. Are these nationalist terms familiar to you?'

'How did this foolish "war" end?'

'The Union sent a battleship to Scundra. Once in orbit, it demanded certain concessions which the Indians were unable or unwilling to make. The battleship sent a scoutship down to the planet to negotiate a settlement. The settlement was reached but, as the scout ship re-entered space and was about to enter its mother-ship, it blew up. A party of Scundran extremists had planted a bomb in it. You examined an item perserved from the scoutship yesterday, and today you drove past the battleship concerned.

'In retaliation for the bomb, the Pan-Slavs dusted the planet with Panthrax K, a disease which wiped out all human life on the planet in a matter of weeks. The bacillus of Panthrax K was notoriously difficult to contain, and the battleship itself became infected. The entire crew died. Scout, ship, and planet remained incommunicado for many centuries. Needless to say, there is no danger of infection now. All precautions have been taken.'

The catalogue's brief history plunged me into meditation.

I thought about the Scundra incident, now so unimportant. The wiping out of a whole world full of people – evidence again of that lust for possession which had by now relinquished its grip on the human soul. Or was the museum itself an indication that traces of the lust remained, now intellectualised into a wish to possess, not merely objects, but the entire past of mankind and, indeed, what my friend had jokingly referred to as 'the secret of the universe'? I told myself then that cause and effect operated only arbitrarily on the level of the psyche; that lust to possess could itself create a secret to be found, as a hunt provides its own quarry. And if once found? Then the whole complex of human affairs might be unravelled beneath the spell of one gigantic simplification, until motivation was so lowered that life would lose its purport; whereupon our species would wither and die, all tasks fulfilled. Such indeed could have happened to the unassailable Korlevalulaw.

To what extent the inorganic and the organic universe were unity could not be determined until ultimate heat-death brought parity. But it was feasible to suppose that each existed for the other, albeit hierarchically. Organic systems with intelligence might achieve unity – union – with the encompassing universe through knowledge, through the possession of that 'secret' of which my friend joked. That union would represent a peak, a flowering. Beyond it lay only decline, a metaphysical correspondence to the second law of thermodynamics!

Breaking from this chain of reasoning, I realised two things immediately: firstly, that I was well into my serendipitous Seeker phase, and, secondly, that I was about to take from an android's hands an item he was unloading from the carrier-platform.

As I unwrapped it from its translucent covering, the catalogue said, 'The object you hold was retrieved from the capital city of Scundra. It was found in the apartment of a married couple named Jean and Lan Gopal. Other objects are arriving from the same source. Do not misplace it or our assistants will be confused.'

It was a 'holocap' like the one I had examined the day before. Perhaps it was a more sophisticated example. The casing was better turned, the button so well concealed that I found it almost by accident. Moreover, the cube lit immediately, and the illusion that I was holding a man's head in my hands was strong.

The man looked about, caught my eye, and said, 'This holocap is intended only for my ex-wife, Jean Gopal. I have no business with you. Switch off and be good enough to return me to Jean. This is Chris Mailer.'

The image died. I held only a cube in my hands.

In my mind questions flowered.

Sixty-five thousand years ago . . .

I pressed the switch again. Eyeing me straight, he said in unchanged tones, 'This holocap is intended only for my ex-wife, Jean Gopal. I have no business with you. Switch off and be good enough to return me to Jean. This is Chris Mailer.'

Certainly it was all that was left of Chris Mailer. His face made a powerful impression. His features were generous, with high forehead, long nose, powerful chin. His grey eyes were wide-set, his mouth ample but firm. He had a neat beard, brown and streaked with grey. About the temples his hair also carried streaks of grey. His face was unlined and generally alert, although not without melancholy. I resurrected him up from the electronic distances and made him go through his piece again.

'Now I shall unite you with your ex-wife,' I said.

As I loaded the holocap into my vehicle and headed back towards the cache of the day before, I knew that my trained talent was with me, leading me.

There was a coincidence and a contradiction here – or seemed to be, for both coincidences and contradictions are more apparent than real. It was no very strange thing that I should come upon the woman's holocap one day and the man's the next. Both were being unloaded from the same planetary area, brought to the museum in the same operation. The contradiction was more interesting. The woman had said that she spoke only to her husband, the man that he spoke only to his ex-wife; was there a second woman involved?

I recalled that the woman, Jean, had seemed young, whereas the man, Mailer, was past the flush of youth. The woman had been on the planet, Scundra, whereas Mailer had been in the scoutship. They had been on opposing sides in that 'war' which ended in death for all.

How the situation had arisen appeared inexplicable after six hundred and fifty centuries. Yet as long as there remained power in the submolecular structure of the holocap cells, the chance existed that this insignificant fragment of the past could be reconstructed.

Not that I knew whether two holocaps could converse together.

I stood the two cubes on the same shelf, a metre apart. I switched them on.

The images of two heads were reborn. They looked about them as if alive.

Mailer spoke first, staring intensely across the shelf at the female head.

'Jean, my darling, it's Chris, speaking to you after all this long time. I hardly know whether I ought to, but I must. Do you recognise me?'

Although Jean's image was of a woman considerably younger than his, it was less brilliant, more grainy, captured by an inferior piece of holocapry.

'Chris, I'm your wife, your little Jean. This is for you wherever you are. I know we have our troubles but ... I was never able to say this when we were together, Chris, but I do love our marriage – it means a lot to me, and I want it to go on. I send you love wherever you are. I think about you a lot. You said – well, you know what you said, but I hope you still care. I want you to care, because I do care for you.'

'It's over a dozen years since we parted, my darling Jean,' Mailer said. 'I know I broke up the marriage in the end, but I was younger then, and foolish. Even at the time, a part of me warned that I was making a mistake. I pretended that I knew you didn't care for me. You cared all the time, didn't you?'

'Not only do I care, but I will try to show more of my inner feelings in future. Perhaps I understand you better now. I know I've not been as responsive as I might be, in several ways.'

I stood fascinated and baffled by this dialogue, which carried all sorts of overtones beyond my comprehension. I was listening to the conversation of primitive beings. The image of her face had vivacity; indeed, apart from the flat eyes and an excess of hair she passed for pretty, with a voluptuous mouth and wide eyes – but to think she took it for granted that she might have a man for her own possession, while he acted under similar assumptions! Whereas Mailer's mode of speech was slow and thoughtful, but without hesitation, Jean talked fast, moving her head about, hesitating and interrupting herself as she spoke.

He said, 'You don't know what it is like to live with regret. At least, I hope you don't, my dear. You never understood regret and all its ramifications as I do. I remember I called you superficial once, just before we broke up. That was because you were content to live in the present; the past or the future meant nothing to you. It was something I could not comprehend at the time, simply because for me both past and future are always with me. You never made reference to things past, whether happy or sad, and I couldn't stand that. Fancy, I let such a little matter come between our love! There was your affair with Gopal, too. That hurt me and, forgive me, the fact that he was black added salt in my wound. But even there I should have taken more of the blame. I was more arrogant then then I am now, Jean.'

'I'm not much good at going over what has been, as you know,' she said. 'I live each day as it comes. But the entanglement with Lan Gopal – well, I admit I was attracted to him – you know he went for me and I couldn't resist – not that I'm exactly blaming Lan ... He was very sweet, but I want you to know that that's all over now, really over. I'm happy again. We belong to each other.'

'I still feel what I always did, Jean. You must have been married to Gopal for ten years now. Perhaps you've forgotten me, perhaps this holocap won't be welcome.'

As I stood there, compelled to listen, the two images stared raptly at each other, conversing without communicating.

'We think differently – in different ways, I mean,' Jean said, glancing downwards. 'You can explain better – you were always the intellectual. I know you despise me because I'm not clever, don't you? You used to say we had non-verbal communication ... I don't quite know what to say. Except that I was sad to see you leave on another trip, going off hurt and angry, and I wished – oh well, as you see, your poor wife is trying to make up for her deficiencies by sending you this holocap. It comes with love, dear Chris, hoping – oh, everything – that you'll come back here to me on Earth, and that things will be as they used to be between us. We do belong to each other and I haven't forgotten.'

During this speech, she became increasingly agitated.

'I know you don't want me back, Jean,' Mailer said. 'Nobody can turn back time. But I had to get in touch with you when the chance came. You gave me a holocap fifteen years ago and I've had it with me on my travels ever since. When our divorce came through, I joined a fleet of space-mercenaries. Now we're fighting for the Pan-Slavs. I've just learnt that we're coming to Scundra, although not with the best of motives. So I'm having this holocap made, trusting there'll be a chance to deliver it to you. The message is simple really – I forgive anything you may think there is to forgive. After all these years, you still mean a lot to me, Jean, though I'm less than nothing to you.'

'Chris, I'm your wife, your little Jean. This is for you wherever you are. I know we have our troubles but ... I was never able to say this when we were together, Chris, but I do love our marriage – it means a lot to me, and I want it to go on.'

'It's a strange thing that I come as an enemy to what is now, I suppose, your home planet since you married Gopal. I always knew that bastard was no good, worming his way in between us. Tell him I bear him no malice, as long as he's taking care of you, whatever else he does.'

She said: 'I send you love wherever you are. I think about you a lot ...'

'I hope he's made you forget all about me. He owes me that. You and I were once all in all to each other, and life's never been as happy for me again, whatever I pretend to others.'

'You said – well, you know what you said, but I hope you still care. I want you to care, because I do care for you ... Not only do I care, but I will try to show more of my inner feelings in future. Perhaps I understand you better now.'

'Jean, my darling, it's Chris, speaking to you after all this long time. I hardly know whether I ought to, but I must.'

I turned away. At last I understood. Only the incomprehensible things of which the images spoke had concealed the truth from me for so long.

The images could converse, triggered by pauses in each other's monologues. But what they had to say had been programmed before they met. Each had a role to play and was unable to transcend it by a hairsbreadth. No matter what the other image might say, they could not reach beyond what was predetermined. The female, with less to say than the male, had run out of talk first and simply begun her chatter over again.

Jean's holocap had been made some fifteen years before Mailer's. She was talking from a time when they were still married, he from a time some years after their divorce. Their images spoke completely at odds – there had never been a dialogue between them ...

These trivial resolutions passed through my mind and were gone.

Greater things occupied me.

Second Era man had passed, with all his bustling possessive affairs.

The godly Korlevalulaw too had passed away. Or so we thought. We were surrounded by their creations, but of the Korlevalulaw themselves there was not a sign.

We could no more see a sign of them than Jean and Mailer could see a sign of me, although they had responded in their own way ...

My function as a Prime Emplastic Seeker was more than fulfilled. I had made an ultimate whole greater than the parts. I had found what my joking friend called 'the secret of the universe'.

Like the images I had observed, the galactic human race was merely a projection. The Korlevalulaw had created us – not as a genuine creation with free will, but as some sort of a reproduction.

There would never be proof of that, only intuition. I had learned to trust my intuition. As with those imprisoned images, the human

23

species was gradually growing fainter, less able to hear the pro-grammed responses. As with those imprisoned images, we were all drifting further apart, losing definition. As with those imprisoned images, we were doomed to root through the debris of the past, because copies can have no creative future.

Here was my one gigantic simplification, here my union with the encompassing universe! This was the flowering before the de-cline.

No, my idea was nonsense! A fit had seized me! My deductions were utterly unfounded. I knew there was no ultimate 'secret of the universe' – and in any case, supposing humanity to be merely a construct of the Korlevalulaw: who then 'constructed' the Korlevalulaw? The prime question was merely set back one step.

But for every level of existence there is a key to its central enigma. Those keys enable life-forms to ascend the scale of life or to reach an impasse – to flourish or to become extinct.

I had found a key which would cause the human species to wither and die. Ours was merely an umwelt, not a universe.

I left the museum. I flew my ship away from Norma. I did not head back to my home world. I went instead to a desolate world on which I now intend to end my days, communicating with no one. Let them assume that I caught a personal blight instead of de-tecting a universal one. If I communicate, the chance is that the dissolution I feel within me will spread.

And spread for ever.

Such was my mental agony that only when I reached this barren habitation did I recall what I neglected to do in the museum. I forgot to switch off the holocaps.

There they may remain, conducting their endless conversation, until power dies. Only then will the two talking heads sink into blessed nothingness and be gone.

Sound will fade, images die, silence remain.

STARTHINKER 9

by Michael G Coney

DO ALL the best people come from my native Birmingham? Science fiction and fantasy writers in particular; like J R Tolkien, John Wyndham, and now Michael Coney, before he emigrated (by way of a night-club in Antigua) to British Columbia, where he is employed by the Forestry Commission.

But in many ways I find Michael Coney still a very 'English' writer despite his geographical separation; perhaps this is the reason why so many of his dozen or more novels have first appeared in this country. Novels like Mirror Image, Winter's Children, *and his latest,* Charisma. *Like another British author in* Andromeda *he studied as an accountant, like that same contributor his piece here is a love story, but be warned; this one carries a sting!*

Starthinker thought to me.

Her thoughts were coming through much more strongly now. It wasn't just that we were closer; it was as though the very idea of my approach was enhancing her powers. *Together*, she seemed to be saying, *we can work miracles* . . .

As though Starthinker's powers aren't miracle enough.

Alone on Earth she is capable of flashing thought-messages to the stars, faster than light; instantaneous, so far as our crude instruments can establish. Hers is a rare gift. Throughout the inhabited Galaxy there are only thirty Starthinkers, although there are thousands of lesser worldthinkers, like myself.

And she sits in that strange, old-fashioned little cottage at the end of the road where the trees hang over, and the sea glitters through from the rocky inlet below.

On a warm September (Earth months) afternoon I walked along that road to meet Starthinker. The area around Fay Ness is a Recreational Reserve and the trees are old and knotted, the houses older. These stone cottages squat on the steep hillsides overlooking the inlet 'with that same watchful tenacity which has endured for centuries, closing their eyes each night on a scene which is unchanged, which will never change. Maybe that's why Starthinker likes it here, because of the timeless serenity. In her work she experiences the concept of immense distances, incredible speeds which lead, on occasions, to bewildering apparent transpositions of events in the Galaxy, seeming switches of cause and effect as her messages are relayed by the worldthinkers.

We worldthinkers aspire to be Starthinkers – and never make it, because Starthinkers are born, not trained. And having been born, they must be sheltered and protected from the corrosive effects of society, for their gift is a delicate thing, easily destroyed.

Starthinker thought to me, 'Where are you now, my love? What can you see?'

'There's a bend in the road, with a cottage on the left. An old woman is wishing autumn wasn't coming. She's sitting in her window, see?'

I opened my mind, wide open, and Starthinker saw what I saw.

That's the sort of thing Starthinker can do.

And what can I do? Little enough, to have earned the love of one like Starthinker. I can sit in my room, receive messages from Starthinkers attuned to my wavelength, and relay them to another worldthinker anywhere in the world, or on the planets and moons in our little System. But I can't send my thoughts *out*, across Deep Space. I don't have the power.

The old woman waved to me. A pretty girl walked by, short pleated skirt and long legs; she smiled at me tentatively. I grinned back but passed on without slackening pace. This was not difficult with Starthinker so close, filling my mind with love for her alone. Down on the water below a yacht passed, sails straining to catch the fitful winds which gusted in between the rocky headlands. The yacht went about, nosing out into the middle of the inlet to catch more wind. The sails fell slack, then quickly filled on the other tack. The sight was beautiful and efficient, like a seagull. I showed Starthinker the boat, and I showed her a seagull too.

She thought, wistfully, 'It's wonderful to have you so near, my darling. I don't get out much. There's so much to do, so much work ...' And she was gone, flashing a message to some star. I couldn't catch it, of course. But soon I felt her warmth in my mind again. 'The leaves are turning brown,' she said. 'Show me some more.'

But she was gone again before I could concentrate. I didn't concern myself unduly. I'd soon be meeting her for the first time, face to face.

Jane had gotten unpleasant when I told her I was going to see Starthinker.

'What?' she said incredulously.

'I said I'm leaving. Look, what else can I say? I've just got to go, that's all.'

'My God, do you know what you're saying? You leaving me for this ... this *freak*, whose name you don't even know? What the hell has gotten into you?'

'Names don't mean anything in Thinking, Jane,' I tried to tell her. 'It's the image that counts. The person, the mind.'

'What? How can you be in love with someone you've never seen, tell me that? And you so interested in sex ... You must be insane!'

'Starthinker's made me realise how pointless sex is,' I said.

'What!'

'Starthinker and I never say *what*,' I said.

I'll never forget that day I first *met* Starthinker.

A message came in, routine stuff. 'The Supreme Council of the Galactic Empire has passed a resolution deploring the repeated violation of Alcidian space by Khalim armed vessels. The Supreme Council further resolved that, should the said violations continue, the Supreme Council will put the following motion to the vote: to wit, that the Government of Khalim be severely censured for its unlawful actions.'

It was simple; I relayed it without thinking, all over. Instantly, there was not a Thinker in our System who was not aware of the Alcidian v. Khalim situation.

Not that it mattered to them. Not that it mattered to anyone except the Alcidians who were being fried on their own planet. And, quite frankly, the resolution didn't matter much to *them*, either.

I thought.

'What can you expect from the Supreme Council,' came the reply from afar. 'Action?'

I felt as though a jolt of voltage had been passed through my Thinking chair. 'Who the hell was that?' I thought.

27

'Starthinker 9. You're a very unusual worldthinker, you know that?'

You see, Starthinkers cannot pick up the emanations of world-thinkers. They operate on a different plane altogether. It's said that they can only pick up the thoughts of another Starthinker – which makes them very lonely people. Mostly, they have to rely on speech, with all the misunderstandings that implies.

'And you're a very unusual Starthinker,' I thought back.

We were in tune. Incredibly. At first I experienced a wild surge of stupid pride, thinking that I'd become a Starthinker myself – but of course I hadn't. I experimented, but soon gave up. No other Starthinker could pick me up.

And Starthinker 9 could pick up no other worldthinker.

It was just she and I.

We're busy people in Intergalactic Thinkways, but there are times when the political news slackens, and the stockmarket clos-ings coincide, and nobody wants to send personal messages for a while – and at such times Starthinker and I got together. We con-versed about people and animals and life, about love and morals and boats and biology, about love and beans and sculpture and love. We entered into the deepest corners of each other's minds, we probed and discovered and laughed and looked.

And we came out loving each other.

Jane said, 'I hope she's as ugly as sin, you bastard!'

Her epithet was inappropriate. I can't think where she got it from. She cried a lot when I left, and told me not to come back, ever.

Of course I'd visualised what Starthinker looked like. This visualisation was not for any purpose I could easily explain; it was just a sort of *curiosity*, like wondering what time it is on a lazy afternoon. I imagined Starthinker to have blonde hair hanging almost to her waist. She had blue eyes, I thought, and a very wide smile. Her face would be plump but not chubby, just nicely rounded so that the bones didn't stick out like a ballerina's. She would be quite tall, with high full breasts and long legs. Some-how I always saw her wearing white.

Once I thought to her, 'Stand in front of a mirror and project!'

But all I got back was amusement. I felt a little ashamed, as though I'd looked into a private diary.

Yes, I often used to wonder what Starthinker looked like. If Jane had known that, she'd have placed entirely the wrong construction on my motives in leaving. She had a knack for that.

That's why Jane said, 'I hope she's as ugly as sin, you bastard!'

I remember saying, 'Can't you understand? Love isn't a physical thing. Love is a blending of minds, a meeting of souls.'

Jane brayed with laughter. It was not a pleasant sound, but it was the last time I heard her laugh. I had to admit that my explanation of love sounded trite – but how can you explain such a thing to a sceptic, when all the best phrases have been used too many times?

Actually, I think Starthinker herself was naïve.

She's been placed under strict security from the moment her talents had been discovered at the age of Standard six. From that time on she had been allowed contact with very few people, all carefully trained in their job. She had never been punished, rewarded, or taught. She had been allowed total self-expression, and such learning as she achieved was entirely of her own volition; a library (carefully selected) and scanner were available but no suggestion was made that she use it.

Due to the selection of the library tapes, she knew nothing which we might call 'bad' – and precious little we might call 'good'. But she knew a hell of a lot about zoology, biology, sculpture and other matters which had caught her interest.

It seemed that puberty had not caught her interest, since she was now Standard nineteen but had expressed no curiosity to me in the workings of her body.

However, I had my suspicions about this apparent peculiarity. I suspect that Starthinker's mentors had gently told her that the body was not quite *nice*; a thing not to be spoken of or even thought of. This would fit in with all the stories we'd heard about Starthinker training: that sex drained the talents, and was avoided. It also fitted in with my own feelings. Somehow I didn't want to think of my Starthinker in terms so crude as sex.

My Starthinker was a virgin all in white, and would remain that way.

But her mind; oh, her *mind* . . .

*

She was with me again, soft and gentle, so kind and loving.

'Hey, where's that boat now?'

Funny that they should have forgotten the obvious.

Funny that they should have gone to all this trouble to shelter Starthinker from the possibility of physical attraction – yet forgetting that ninety per cent of the attraction is in the minds of the lovers; and Starthinker travels with her mind, sees with her mind, hears with her mind. So why did they miss the possibility that she might love with her mind?

I showed her the boat beating out to sea, rocking in the wake of an incoming hovercruiser. I showed her the autumn heather on the opposite hillside, streaked with pale trails where the animals and the people had walked. I showed her the sky, and the deep water below.

I think I loved what I saw, and this love went out with my thought-pictures.

'You like my place.' She was pleased. I could imagine her smiling with that generous mouth of hers, patting her golden hair into place as she waited for me. 'Not much further, now. Just around the corner. Why didn't you bring a car?'

'Uh ... I don't know.' But I did. It was nervous about the meeting; there was no point in kidding myself. I'd left the car way back among the houses, and I was walking because it was easier, that way, to keep my emotions and my apprehensions in check.

'No, don't be nervous,' Starthinker thought.

'Are you sure they'll let me see you? I mean, you said they didn't allow you visitors. They told you it was a ... distraction, didn't they?'

She hesitated. 'Well, they vet people pretty carefully. I see the old doctors, the psychologists, the nurses, the ... guards sometimes, the old lady who cleans.'

The jealousy was there again, suddenly. 'And you don't ... like these people?'

She laughed with her mind. 'You mean do I love them, any of them? Of course not. They're old, my darling.'

My mouth was dry. Why was I torturing myself, so close to Starthinker? 'But love is a mind thing,' I said. 'It has nothing to do with age. You could still love a physician. A physiotherapist. Couldn't you?'

She smiled into my body. 'I'm a Starthinker. How could I love anyone I couldn't converse with? How would I know what a doctor really thinks, behind all the sympathetic talk? But you and I, we *know* each other. We know everything there is to know about each other, and yet we love – or maybe that's why we love. So stop

30

worrying. Your eyes are looking at my house, and you don't see it!'

I had come across seventy-five light years to this place.

It had taken me a long time, relatively speaking; ships cannot travel quite as fast as thought – but here was my destination.

It was a stone cottage like the others, built into the hillside like a granite outcrop, surrounded by masses of trees and shrubs. There was an old stone wall surrounding a garden where late flowers bloomed. I heard bees, the sea lapping at the rocks below, the sad yell of a gull.

I heard a generator humming somewhere.

A gaunt concrete structure loomed beside the cottage, painted grey.

A uniformed man watched me from a door.

I was scared. The place looked suddenly forbidding. I glanced at the windows, wondering if I might catch a glimpse of Starthinker. I saw a face, but it couldn't have been her. She was gone from my mind, spiriting some message to the other end of the Galaxy.

The gate lurched and squealed as I opened it and I realised this wasn't the proper way in. There was a hovertruck parked around the back, beside the concrete building. The main entrance was probably there. Seen close to, it was apparent that the more recent structure was much bigger than the cottage.

'What do you want?' somebody shouted.

I looked around. I was inside the walled garden now, half-way up the path to the front door, feeling like a trespasser. The guard was watching me from the other side of the stone wall.

'I've come to see Starthinker,' I said.

'You've what?'

'I've come to see Starthinker.'

'You're kidding. Come on out of there. This is a restricted area.'

I left the garden and approached him, trying to see into his mind. There was nothing there – or was there just a suggestion . . . ? No. Nothing. A deadness of the mind, of the soul; an imperviousness to Thinking. The man was a guard and had been chosen for unreceptiveness, so that the messages wouldn't leak out. The other people; the doctors and so on, were probably the same.

Starthinker asked suddenly, 'What's the trouble?'

'There's a guard.'

31

'Oh, that's no problem. Tell him I say he must let you in.'

I stood in front of the guard. 'Starthinker says you must let me in.'

'She spoke to you?' He looked surprised, disbelieving, hesitant, 'Uh ... Come with me,' he said finally. He led me around the back where, as I had thought, the main entrance was. It looked like a hospital entrance; I caught the flash of someone in white walking past. The guard told me to wait then disappeared with a backward, puzzled glance.

'I'm inside,' I told Starthinker.

What she projected was not clear; just a confused babble of happiness, love and anticipation.

'You,' the guard beckoned. 'In here.'

The room was small and bare; just a desk, a few chairs, a calendar with a beautiful nude girl holding a flower in her mouth, hangers with a row of dingy coats. There was another door opposite.

Somehow I *knew* Starthinker was through there.

I wondered if she looked like the girl on the calendar.

I walked towards the door. A guard caught me by the arm; 'Sit here,' he said. A man with thick features watched me from the other side of the desk.

'You allege you've had contact with Starthinker.'

'Yes. Can I see her now?'

He smiled. I couldn't see into his mind either; but I sensed that the smile was not honest. 'I'd rather you answered some questions.'

'Go ahead.'

Hurry up, darling, thought Starthinker.

'Just how the hell did Starthinker contact you?'

'I'm a worldthinker. We contacted in the usual way.'

'But we understand *you've* contacted *her*, as well.'

'Yes. That's not so unusual ... Can I see her now?' The urgency was unbearable; Starthinker's thought were shouting hunger in my mind.

'That's impossible. You haven't been cleared through security.' I could tell he was losing interest, that he wanted to shrug me off, to get rid of me. It was there in his face.

'What are you talking about, security?' I asked. 'She can tell me anything she likes.'

He leaned forward, staring into my face. He spoke slowly, as though to a child. Hell, I'm twenty-two Standard years old. He said, 'This is a restricted area. Starthinker is a valuable piece of property.' (That's what he said, *property*.) 'Nobody is allowed to see Starthinker unless they've been cleared. You'll have to go through the proper channels. If I just let anyone in, we'd gets nuts in. And Starthinker might get herself killed.'

I heard him, but I couldn't believe him. 'Are you trying to tell me you're frightened I might kill Starthinker?'

'That's what I'm trying to tell you.'

'But I couldn't kill her. I've come seventy light-years to see her!'

'A goddamned alien,' the man grunted. 'I might have known.'

'I love her. She loves me. You don't kill someone you love!' They weren't going to let me see her. They weren't going to. 'Let me in there!' I commanded.

I sensed the puzzlement from Starthinker, near by.

The man was flushed, pop-eyed. 'I'll take none of that crap from you,' he blustered. 'No goddamned . . .' he searched for some epithet '. . . alien comes in here and starts talking about Starthinker like that. Get the hell out!'

He stared at me as though he was looking for tentacles and I remembered, from way back, unhappy tales I'd heard about the prejudices of Earth people.

'You shouldn't have told him . . .' Starthinker cried in distress.

I shouldn't have told him. Now he thought I had scales under my clothes. Yet my ancestors were from Earth . . .

'Get that freak out of here!' the heavy man shouted.

The guard was beside me, gripping my arm as though expecting me to make a fight of it. 'Starthinker must be kept pure,' he murmured, excusing his superior's action . . .

'My darling!'

I wheeled round; the voice came from the mind and from the lips.

A lovely girl stood in the doorway, twisting desperately as a female guard hung on to her arm, and another grasped her around the waist. She had blue eyes and her face was oval, pale. She was very beautiful.

She was Starthinker.

And she looked at me with love. And she held her arms out to me, and the guards fought to hold us apart.

'Oh, my God,' said the big man.

Starthinker thought, as the door slammed between us and the guard wrestled me away, 'I'm so sorry, my love. I never thought they would act like this. They've always been so . . . kind.'

I thought back, 'Maybe I should have known. Maybe it's my fault. I should have made allowances for them. I've heard that Earth people take time to get used to anything they think is unusual . . .'

She interrupted me with soft, sympathetic images. 'These people are the abnormal ones; you've shown me that. I've lived with them all this time, and never realised it. Please don't go back home, not yet. We must try again. I'll refuse to work any more, unless they let us be together. And . . . even if that doesn't work . . . at least I've seen you . . .'

And I'd seen her. I'd *seen* Starthinker.

The guard had led me outside. He still held my arm; I was concentrating on Starthinker too hard to think of resisting and I was surprised, when I looked around, saw the trees, felt the wind. The guard let me go. I stood there, wondering what to do. Starthinker was not thinking straight; just jumbled emissions of despair and sorrow.

The guard was looking at his watch. He hesitated. 'Uh . . . Look, I go off duty now. I'm sorry about what happened, real sorry. Can I.give you a ride back to the town?'

In the car, I asked him, 'Why do you Earth people hate aliens?'

He glanced at me. 'Look, you've gotten the wrong idea. We don't hate you. It's just that Starthinker has to be kept . . . uh, quiet. She won't be able to transmit for days after this upset. She mustn't get, uh, excited, you know what I mean?'

'You mean love.' After all this, I could feel the anger begin to rise in me. Had I come all this way to meet a planetful of people who thought love was bad? 'How the hell do you *know* love is bad for her?' I asked loudly.

The sunlit water flickered as the trees went past. The guard glanced at me, but said nothing.

I thought about the innocence of Starthinker, that wonderful innocence of a girl who has never known the world and its people; their connivings and quarrellings and fightings; a girl who knows only the good things, because evil has been carefully filtered out of her living. What a pity that such innocence must inevitably lead to disappointment, when the people around her show themselves for what they really are. I would have liked that innocence to be preserved for ever.

34

The guard spun the wheel, the hovercar swayed and swung up a hill. He said, 'Hell, there's nothing wrong with love.' I sensed that he was becoming more friendly now. The vehicle glided to a stop and sank to the ground with a sigh of expelled air. We were on a high knoll, overlooking the ocean. The view was breathtaking.

I thought to Starthinker: 'I'll come again tomorrow. They'll have had time to think it over by then. I'm sure everything will be all right, darling . . .' Her reply was calmer; she was recovering. I was still near.

Love is a mind thing.

'There's love, and there's love,' said the guard.

I found myself wondering what love was like, here on Earth. It was a strange concept; you know, men and women – virtually two different species to our way of thinking – in *love*, with *each other*. . . . Earth is a strange place, but I was glad I'd come. It's interesting to learn that there are other methods of reproduction, besides ovular coelescence.

The guard was smiling at me now; he rested his hand on my knee in the friendliest fashion.

'Hey . . .' he said softly. 'You're not a bad-looking chick, you know that?'

I smiled back. He seemed to be accepting me for what I was. I was glad.

On my home planet of Whileaway, we too can accept that other worlds might have such creatures as *men*. We are very tolerant.

WALTZ OF THE BODYSNATCHERS

by Bob Shaw

BOB SHAW is widely known as the creator of the famous 'Slow Glass' stories, assembled in the excellent novel, Other Days. Other Eyes. *He might almost have built a critical reputation on just that one concept, yet he has also published something like a dozen other books of equal ingenuity. (My own favourite is probably* Night Walk, *to appear soon in hardcover for the first time in the U.K.)*

A native of Belfast, Bob is by training an engineer, but he first began to write in the early 1950s, one of a triumvirate of young enthusiasts who amused themselves and their friends through the pages of various amateur magazines. Little did they realise what an excellent training ground this would be for the time when it came to turn to professional storytelling. (James White was another founding member of this 'Belfast Triangle'.)

For a time Bob moved to Canada, but now resides in the English Lake District with his wife Sadie and family. Until recently, he was Public Relations Manager for a well-known engineering company but he is now writing full-time.

'I think I can be of service to you,' the pale stranger said. 'I want to commit suicide.'

Lorimer looked up from his drink in surprise. Even in the half-light of the bar, it was obvious that the dull-voiced man who had come to his table was ill, shabby and tired. His thin shoulders were bowed within his cloak, making him appear as slight as a woman, and his eyes smouldered with broody desperation in a white triangular face. *What a wreck!* Lorimer thought contemptuously. *What a pitiful bloody mess!*

'I want to commit suicide,' the stranger repeated, his voice louder but still lifeless.

'Don't shout it all over the place.' Lorimer glanced around the cavern-like bar and was relieved to see there was nobody within hearing distance. 'Sit down.'

'All right.' The man sagged into a chair and sat with his head lowered.

Looking at him, Lorimer began to feel a furtive pounding elation. 'Do you want a drink?'

'If you're buying I'll have one; if you're not, I won't. It doesn't really matter.'

'I'll get you a beer.' Lorimer pressed the appropriate button on the order display, and a few seconds later a beaker of dark ale emerged from the table's dispensing turret. The stranger seemed not to notice, and Lorimer pushed the cool ceramic over to him. He drank from it without relish, automatic as the machine which had served him.

'What's your name?' Lorimer asked.

'Does it matter?'

'To me, as a person, it doesn't matter a damn – but it's more convenient when everybody has a label. Besides, I'll need to know all about you.'

'Raymond Settle.'

'Who sent you, Raymond?'

'I don't know his name. A waiter down at Fidelio's. The one with the rosewood hair.'

'Rosewood?'

'Brown and black streaks.'

'Oh.' Lorimer recognised the description of one of his most trusted contacts, and his sense of elation grew stronger. He stared at Settle, wondering how any man could let himself get into such a leached-out state. Something about the way Settle spoke suggested he was intelligent and well educated, but – Lorimer drew comfort from the thought – intellectuals were usually the ones who folded up when the going got a little tough. For all their so-called brains, they never seemed to learn that strength of body led to strength of mind.

'Tell me, Raymond,' he said, 'what relatives have you got?'

'Relatives?' Settle stared down at his drink. 'Just one. A baby girl.'

'Is that who you want the money to go to?'

'Yes. My wife died last year, and the baby is in Our Lady of Mercy's Hostel.' Settle's lips stretched in what ought to have been a smile. 'Apparently I'm considered unfit to bring her up by myself. The Office of the Primate would overlook my various character defects if I had money, but I'm not equipped to earn money. Not in the conventional manner, anyway.'

'I see. Do you want me to set up a trust fund for the kid?'

'That's about the best thing I could leave her.'

Lorimer felt an uncharacteristic chill of unease which he tried to ignore. 'Just our luck to be born on Oregonia, eh?'

'I don't know much about luck.'

'I mean, life's a lot simpler on planets like Avalon, Morgania, or even Earth.'

'Death's a lot simpler, too.'

'Yeah, well ...' Lorimer decided to keep the conversation businesslike. 'I'll have to get more details from you. I'm paying twenty thousand monits, and I have to be sure nothing goes wrong.'

'No need to apologise, Mr. Lorimer. I'll tell you everything you want to know.' Settle spoke with the calm disinterest of one whose life had already ended.

Lorimer ordered another drink for himself, making a determined effort not to become contaminated by the other man's despair. The important and positive thing to concentrate on was the fact that Settle – in dying – would open up rich new lives for two other human beings.

Next morning the double suns were close together above the eastern horizon, merging into an elongated patch of brilliance which imprinted peanut-shaped after-images on the retina. Lorimer floated up from the city through flamboyant forests of gold shading into tan. On the crest of the hill, surrounded by vistas of complicated shoreline and small islands, he steered his skimmer off the road and allowed it to sink to the ground in the gardens of the Willen house. He got out of the vehicle, stood for a moment, appreciating the luxury of his surroundings, then walked the short distance to the patio at the rear of the house.

Fay Willen was seated on a bench with her back to him, busy stretching canvas over a wooden frame. She was wearing a simple white dress which enhanced the lustrous blackness of her hair. Lorimer paused again, drinking in the vision of what was his already by natural law and which was soon to come into his legal possession. He made a sound with his feet and Fay whirled to face him, startled.

'Mike!' she said, getting to her feet. 'What are you doing here so early?'

'I had to see you.'

Fay frowned a little. 'Wasn't that a little risky? You didn't even call to check if Gerard was still away.'

'It doesn't matter.'

'But he's bound to get suspicious if you . . .'

'Fay, I told you it doesn't matter.' Lorimer was unable to suppress the triumph in his voice. 'I found one.'

'You found what?' Fay was still displeased, unwilling to relax or warm to him.

'The thing you said I'd never find in a hundred years – a man who wants to commit suicide.'

'Oh!' The small hammer she had been holding clattered on the patio with a curious ringing sound. 'Mike, I never thought . . .'

'It's all right, sweetie.' Lorimer took Fay in his arms and was surprised to feel that she was trembling. He held her tightly, remembering all the times he had got his way in disagreements simply by making her aware of the pent-up strength in his body.

'You won't even have to be there when it happens,' he murmured. 'I'll take care of everything.'

'But I never really expected to be mixed up in a murder.'

Lorimer experienced a flicker of impatience, but was careful not to reveal it. 'Listen, sweetie, we've been all over this before. We won't be *murdering* Gerard – we'll just be dispossessing him.'

'No, I don't like it.' Fay looked up at him with troubled eyes.

'Just dispossessing him, that's all,' Lorimer coaxed. 'It isn't your fault that the Church and the Law somehow got rolled into one on this planet. On any other world you'd be able to get a divorce for the things Gerard has done – or on account of what he doesn't do – but here the system forces you to take other steps. They don't even permit emigration. It's the system's fault, not yours.'

Fay disengaged herself from his arms and sat down again. Her oval face had lost its colour. 'I know Gerard is old. I know he's cold . . . but, no matter what you say, he'd still have to be killed.'

'It doesn't even have to hurt him, for God's sake – I'll get a cloud gun for the job.' The meeting with Fay was not working out as Lorimer had planned it, and he could feel his self-control slipping. 'I mean, how long would he be clinically dead? Just a couple of days in an open-and-shut case like the one we're planning.'

'It isn't right, Mike.'

'As far as Gerard would know, he would close his eyes and waken up in a different body.' Lorimer sought for ways to strengthen his argument. 'A *younger* body, too. This guy I've got lined up doesn't seem very old. We would even be doing Gerard a favour.'

Fay hesitated then slowly shook her head, with fixed eyes, as though following the sweep of a massive pendulum. 'I've decided against it. If I agreed before, it was only because I thought it could never happen.'

'You're making this difficult for me,' Lorimer said. 'I can't really believe you've changed your mind. I mean, if you had I'd almost be tempted to blackmail you into it – for your own good.'

Fay gave a short laugh. 'You couldn't blackmail me.'

'I could, Fay, believe me. The Primate doesn't like anybody to engage in adultery, but I'm just a man – with a tendency to venal sin built into him – and I'm not married. I'd probably get a month's suspended sentence. You, on the other hand, are a woman who has betrayed a faithful husband . . .'

'Gerard *has* to be faithful! He isn't equipped for anything else.'

'The Primate won't hold that against him. No, sweetie, all the money and fancy lawyers in the world wouldn't save you from going up for a year. At least a year.' Lorimer was relieved to see that Fay looked suitably horrified. She had the advantages of being rich and beautiful, but when it came to emotional or intellectual in-fighting a certain passivity in her nature guaranteed him victory every time. He paused for a few seconds, long enough to let the threat of prison have maximum effect, then he straddled the bench beside Fay.

'You know, this is the craziest conversation I've ever heard,' he said soothingly. 'Why are we talking about blackmail and prison when we could be talking about our future together? You hadn't really changed your mind, had you?'

Fay stared at him in sad speculation. 'No, Mike, Not really.'

'That's great – because this character I found yesterday is too good to waste.' Lorimer squeezed Fay's hand. 'It turns out he's an unsuccessful artist. I thought you could sell anything in the art line these days, but if there were any garrets on Oregonia this guy would be starving in one of them. That reminds me, can you let me have the pay-off money now?'

'Twenty thousand, wasn't it?'

'Yes.'

'I think there's more than that in the downstairs safe. I'll get it for you now.' Fay turned to leave, then paused. 'What's his name?'

'Raymond Settle. Have you heard of him?'

Fay shook her head. 'What sort of paintings does he do?'

'I don't know.' Lorimer was slightly taken aback by the question. 'Who cares, anyway? The only thing that matters is that he's determined to kill himself.'

On the way back down the gilded hill and into town Lorimer reviewed his plan. Its elements were simple. Gerard Willen was an industrious and moderately successful businessman, so nobody could really say he had married Fay for her money. He had seen her once, had fallen in love, and had courted her with a desperate ardour to which Fay – always liable to manipulation by anyone with strong motivations – had easily succumbed. The trouble with their marriage was that Gerard, as though having expended the dregs of his vitality on the chase, had almost immediately become paternal rather than passionate. He demanded no more of Fay than that she be seen on his arm at Church functions and formal dinners.

The biological pressures had built up within Fay for more than a year, and Lorimer – fencing coach at an exclusive gymnasium – counted himself lucky to have appeared on the scene at precisely the right time to act as a release mechanism.

In the beginning, for about a month, he had been content just to possess Fay's body, then had come the conviction that he had earned all the things which went with it. He wanted the money, the splendid houses, the status, and – above all – the escape from the hopeless daily chore of trying to impart grace to plump matrons who used their foils like flyswatters. But Gerard Willen stood squarely in the way.

On Earth, or one of fifty other planets, there would have been the twin possibilities of divorce or straightforward murder. On Oregonia, neither of these options was open. The dominance of the Mother Church meant that divorce was impossible, except in very extreme circumstances. It was certainly out of the question for a minor thing like sexual incompatability. And murder – due to the fact that Oregonian law prescribed Personality Recompense as a punishment – was much too risky.

It was dark when Lorimer parked his floater at the prearranged meeting point on the northern outskirts of the city. For an uneasy moment he thought Settle had failed to make it, then he noticed the thin figure emerging from the blackness of a clump of trees. Settle was moving slowly, weaving a little, and he had difficulty in getting into the vehicle.

'Have you been drinking?' Lorimer demanded, scanning the dimly-seen triangular face.

'Drinking?' Settle shook his head. 'No, my friend, I'm hungry. Just hungry.'

'I'd better get you something to eat.'

'That's very kind of you, but ...'

'I'm not being kind,' Lorimer interrupted, unable to conceal his disgust. 'It would ruin the whole thing if you died on us. I mean, if your body died.'

'It won't,' Settle told him. 'It hangs on to life with a tenacity I find a little disconcerting – that's my whole problem, after all.'

'Whatever you say.' Lorimer boosted the floater up off the ground and drove it forward. 'We can't afford to be seen together, so keep your head down. I'm taking you up to the Willen house.'

'Are we going to do it tonight?' A rare note of animation had crept into Settle's voice.

'No. Gerard Willen is out of town, but you'll have to see the layout of the place in advance, to make sure nothing goes wrong on the big night.'

'I see.' Settle sounded disappointed. He tightened his cloak around himself, huddled down in the passenger seat and remained quiet for the rest of the journey up to the house. Lorimer did not mind the silence – talking to the other man made him feel cold and, in a way he failed to understand, threatened. He made his way up the hill, choosing roads he knew would be deserted, and parked in the lee of the big house. The night air felt crisp as he stepped out of the floater, and the starlight lay like an unseasonal frost on the lawns and hedges. They went through to the patio at the back, where yellow radiance from the windows of the house provided enough illumination for them to see clearly. Lorimer took the cloud gun from his pocket and handed it to Settle, who gripped it with a thin reluctant hand.

'I thought you said it wasn't tonight,' Settle whispered.

'Just get used to the feel of the gun – we can't afford for you to miss.' Lorimer urged his companion forward. 'The plan is that you're supposed to be sneaking into the house to steal something – the fact you're a down-and-out will make the story sound even better. You go in through this french window, which is never locked, and you start looking around for valuables.' Lorimer turned the handle of the window frame and pushed it open. Warm air billowed around them as they went inside the long unlit room.

'What you don't know is that right next to this room is Gerard Willen's study where he has a habit of working late at night, when he should be in bed with his wife. You move around in here for a while, then you knock something over. This would do.' Lorimer pointed at a tall vase on a shelf.

'Willen hears the noise, and comes in through that door over there. You panic and smoke him a couple of times with your gun. Do it as many times as you want – just make sure he dies.'

'I've never killed anybody,' Settle said doubtfully.

Lorimer sighed. 'You're not killing him – you're killing yourself. Remember?'

'I guess so.'

'Don't forget it. When Willen goes down, you stand looking at him – stupefied – until Fay Willen appears in the doorway. You let her get a good look at you, then you throw the gun down and make a run for it, back out the way you came. The police pick you up in less than an hour. Fay identifies you. You confess. And that's it!'

'I didn't realise it would be so complicated.'

'It's *simple*, I tell you.' The hopeless monotone of Settle's voice had angered Lorimer to the point where he felt like throwing a punch. 'Nothing could be easier.'

'I don't know . . .'

Lorimer gripped Settle's shoulder and was appalled at how frail it felt beneath the cloak. 'Listen, Raymond, you want your kid to get the money, don't you? Well, this is the only way you can fix it.'

'What will happen to me . . . afterwards? Will it hurt?'

'The experts say it's absolutely painless.' Lorimer poured warm encouragement into his voice, clinching his victory. 'There'll be a very brief trial, possibly on the same day, and you'll be found guilty. All they'll do then is put a kind of helmet over your head and another one on Willen's head. They'll plug you both in to the cerebral coupler, throw a switch, and it will be all over.'

'I'll be gone for ever?'

'That's right, Raymond. The transfer process takes about a millionth of a second – so there isn't time to feel pain. You couldn't get a better way out.' Lorimer spoke convincingly, but in his heart there were doubts. Advanced neuro-electronics had made it possible to punish a killer – and, to a large extent, recompense his

44

victim – by transferring the mind of the dead person into the body of the murderer. It was a neat, logical system; but, if it was as humane as its proponents claimed, why was it not practised universally? Why was Personality Compensation banned on a number of progressive worlds?

Lorimer decided not to distract himself with needless speculation. All he had to remember was that displacement of identity was one of the very few grounds upon which the Oregonian Mother Church would grant a divorce. Gerard Willen would live on in Settle's body – but, because it was a different body to the one which he had mouthed the holy vows and shared Fay's matrimonial bed, the marriage would automatically be annulled. Lorimer thought it ironic that the Church, which regarded a marriage as an eternal union of souls, should be so anxious to dissolve the bond at the first hint of physical promiscuity. *If it suits His Holy Highness*, he thought, returning his attention to the matter at hand, *it suits me*. He went over the plan twice more with Settle, rehearsing him carefully for his part, ducking out of the way each time the inexperienced Settle allowed the gun to swing in his direction.

'Watch where you're pointing that thing,' he snapped. 'Try to remember it's a lethal weapon.'

'But you wouldn't be dead – you'd only be displaced,' Settle said. 'They'd put your mind into my body.'

'I'd rather stay dead.' Lorimer stared at Settle in the dimness of the room, wondering if there had been a hint of amusement or malice in his last remark. 'You'd better give the gun back to me before there's an accident.'

Settle compliantly handed the weapon over, and Lorimer was in the act of dropping it into his pocket when the door to the room was thrown open. Lorimer spun, instinctively levelling the gun at the figure in the lighted doorway, then he saw the intruder was Fay. His forehead beaded with sweat as he realised he had almost been startled into pulling the trigger.

'Mike? Are you there?' Fay turned on the room lights and stood blinking in the sudden brilliance.

'You bloody little *fool*!' Lorimer snarled. 'I told you to stay upstairs if you heard anybody in here tonight.'

'I wanted to see you.'

'You nearly got yourself smoked! You nearly ...' Lorimer's voice failed him as he thought of what might have happened.

'I'm in on this thing, too,' said Fay unconcernedly. 'Besides, I wanted to meet Mr. Settle.'

Lorimer shook his head. 'It's better that you don't. The less previous association there is, the less chance of somebody being able to prove collusion.'

'There's nobody in the house but the three of us.' Fay looked past him at Settle. 'Hello, Mr. Settle.'

'Mrs. Willen.' Settle gave an absurdly dignified bow, his eyes fixed on Fay's face.

Lorimer became aware that Fay was wearing a rather insubstantial black nightdress, and he felt a surprising pang of annoyance. 'Go back upstairs,' he said. 'Raymond and I were just about to leave. Isn't that right, Raymond?'

'That is correct.' Settle smiled, but his face was paler and more desperate than ever. He swayed slightly and caught a chairback for support.

Fay started forward. 'Are you ill?'

'It's nothing to be concerned about,' Settle replied. 'I seem to have forgotten to eat anything for a couple of days. Careless of me, I know . . .'

'You must have something before you leave.'

'I offered him a meal, but he turned it down,' Lorimer put in. 'He doesn't like eating.'

Fay gave him a look of exasperation. 'Bring Mr. Settle through to the kitchen. He's going to have some milk and hot steak sandwiches.' She strode ahead of them, switched on the sonic oven, and in little more than a minute had served Settle with a litre of cold milk and a platter of aromatic toasted sandwiches. Settle nodded his gratitude, untied his cloak and began to eat. Watching him devour the food under Kay's approving gaze, Lorimer got a feeling that in some obscure way he had been cheated. He developed an inner conviction that if Fay had not been present Settle would have continued refusing to eat, which seemed to indicate he was now playing for sympathy . . .

When the realisation came to him that he was beginning to consider Settle as a rival for Fay's affections, Lorimer gave a low chuckle. If there was one thing he knew for certain about Fay it was that – after Gerard Willen – she had no room in her life for yet another tired, thin and sickly man. He moved over beside Fay and put his arm around her shoulders, holding her securely within the aura of his own physical strength. He watched Settle with a kind of proprietory amusement.

46

'Look at him eat,' he whispered. 'I told you he was a starving artist.'

Fay nodded. 'I wonder why he wants to die.'

'Some people let themselves get that way.' Lorimer decided against mentioning the existence of Settle's daughter in case it made Fay go soft. 'If you ask me, it's the best thing for him.'

A few minutes later Settle raised his eyes from the empty platter. 'I would like to thank you for the . . .' His words faded away and he sat staring at something on the opposite side of the large room. Lorimer looked in the same direction, but could see nothing there except for one of Fay's meaningless paintings, incomplete and still on the easel, which she must have dragged in from the patio and forgotten to put away.

Settle looked at her and said, 'Is this your work?'

'Yes, but I'm sure it won't mean anything to you.'

'It looks to me as though you were painting light itself. With no containment. With no reference whatsoever to restrictive masses.'

Lorimer began to laugh, then he felt Fay make an involuntary movement. 'That's right,' she said quickly, 'but how did you know? Have you tried the same thing?'

Settle gave a sad, hopeless smile. 'I wouldn't have the courage.'

'But surely . . .'

'Let's break this up,' Lorimer said impatiently. 'Raymond has been here too long already, and if somebody sees him the whole plan is wiped out.'

'How could anybody see him?' Fay said.

'An unexpected visitor could drop in.'

'At this time of night?'

'Or somebody could call you on the seephone.'

'That's hardly likely, Mike. I can't think why anybody in the . . .' Fay had been speaking with a firmness which Lorimer found slightly disconcerting, but she allowed the sentence to tail off uncertainly as the kitchen filled with a gentle chiming. It was the call signal from the seephone in the corner.

'I'd better see who it is.' Fay spoke in a low voice as she moved towards the screen.

'Wait till we get out of here,' Lorimer said urgently, feeling his nerves vibrate in time with the insistent signal.

'It's all right – I'm accepting the call in sound only.' Fay touched a button on the communications console, and the image of Gerard Willen appeared on the screen. He was a frail-looking

47

man in his fifties, with a long serious face and pursed mouth, and dressed in sombre business clothes.

'Hello, Gerard,' Fay said. 'I wasn't expecting a call from you.'

'Fay?' Willen's eyes narrowed as he peered at his own screen. 'Why can't I see you, Fay?'

'I'm getting ready to go to bed, and I'm not properly dressed.'

Willen nodded his approval. 'You are wise to be careful – I've heard of Godless individuals who intercept domestic calls in the hope they will be able to practise voyeurism.'

Fay gave an audible sigh. 'The Devil is always learning new tricks. Why did you call me, Gerard?'

'I have good news. I have completed my business in Holy Cross City and will be flying out tomorrow morning. That means I shall be with you before noon.'

'I'm so glad.' Fay shot Lorimer a significant glance. 'You've been away too long.'

'I am looking forward to being back,' Willen said in his precise, neutral tones. 'I have a difficult report to write and will be able to concentrate much better in the peace of my own study.'

That's what you think, Lorimer chanted to himself, feeling an upsurge of confidence and joy. He listened intently to the rest of the conversation, despising Willen and at the same time feeling grateful to him for not displaying a single sign of warmth, for not uttering even one word which could give Fay cause to imagine the relationship might be redeemed. Settle, too, was sitting upright at the table, watching Fay and the image of her husband with an attentiveness which contrasted with his former apathy. His deep-set eyes looked feverish and, again, Lorimer found himself wishing that Fay was wearing a less revealing garment. As soon as the call had ended, and the screen had gone blank, he went to Fay and caught both her hands in his.

'This is it, sweetheart,' he said. 'Everything's falling into place for us.'

'Ah . . . I'm afraid not,' Settle put in unexpectedly .

Lorimer turned on him. 'What are you talking about?'

Settle's face was haggard, but when he spoke his voice was strangely resolute. 'I've been thinking the whole thing over while I was watching Mr. Willen on the screen, and I've realised I can't go through with it. In spite of all the things you say about merely displacing his personality, I could never make myself shoot another human being.

'I'm afraid there's no way you can talk me into it.'

Several times, as he waited in the near-darkness beyond the patio, Lorimer took out the cloud gun and checked it over. It was one of the most perfect killing machines ever devised, but so much was depending on it that he was unable to resist examining its settings again and again. Settle stood impassively beside him, unmoving, his black-cloaked figure like something carved in obsidian. Above their heads, a tiny greenish moon threaded its way among thickets of stars.

The hours had passed slowly, and it was close to midnight when the light from a window in the upper part of the house abruptly faded. Lorimer's heart began to beat faster and his gloved palms grew moist.

'Fay's gone to bed,' he whispered. 'We'll be able to move in soon.'

'Ready when you are.'

'I'm glad to hear it.' As the final minutes dragged by, Lorimer felt relieved that his period of dependence on the unstable and unpredictable Settle would soon be over. Settle's announcement, on the previous night, that he would be unable to shoot Willen had seemed like the end of everything. Lorimer had experienced a few unpleasant moments until it had been established that Settle was still prepared to fulfil most of his bargain. He was prepared to accept the blame for the shooting, and to yield his life for it, as long as somebody else actually pulled the trigger. Lorimer was far from happy with the modified plan, because it involved his being at the scene of the crime instead of establishing an alibi elsewhere, but he had learned that it was difficult to coerce a determined suicide. There was simply no leverage. Given time he might have been able to work something out, but an instinct was telling him it would be a bad thing to give Fay and the artist the chance to develop an association. It was better to press ahead, regardless of minor imperfections in the scheme.

'Come on – we've waited long enough,' Lorimer said. He moved on to the patio, walking as quietly as possible to avoid disturbing Willen prematurely. It was vital that the shooting should take place under cover of the darkness within the house so that Willen would not recognise his attacker and – after being restored to life in Settle's body – give evidence to the police. With Settle close behind him, Lorimer avoided the pool of mellow light

49

issuing from the window of Willen's study. He reached the french windows of the adjoining room, went inside and drew Settle in after him by the arm.

'You stand right here by the window,' Lorimer said. 'If Gerard sees anything when he opens the door, we want it to be you.'

He took a large ceramic vase from a shelf, then crouched down behind a chair, holding the vase in his left hand and the cloud gun in his right. It occurred to Lorimer that he should wait a few minutes to let his eyes grow accustomed to the near-blackness, but now that the time had come he was tense and impatient. He lobbed the vase into the air and it shattered against the opposite wall.

The suddenness of the sound was almost explosive. There was a moment of ringing silence, then a muffled exclamation filtered through from the next room.

Lorimer aimed the gun at the door and tightened his finger on the trigger. There were footsteps outside in the corridor. The door was flung open, and Lorimer – in the same instant – squeezed the trigger. Once, twice, three times.

Three clouds of immediate-acting toxin hissed through the clothing and skin of the vague figure silhouetted in the doorway, each a guarantee of instantaneous death, and a split-second later the room lights came on. Lorimer cowered back under the shock of the unexpected brilliance, his eyes staring.

Gerard Willen stood motionless in the doorway, hand on the light switch, gazing at Lorimer with a look of pure astonishment on his long face.

Lorimer leaped to his feet, terrified, instinctively levelling the gun. Gerard Willen lurched towards him, but there was no accompanying movement of his feet. He toppled forward, his face smashed into the corner of a low table with a pulpy sound, and he slumped sideways on to the floor. He had died so quickly that his body had been taken by surprise.

'Oh, Christ,' Lorimer quavered, 'that was awful!'

He found himself staring down at the gun in his hand, awed by its powers, then his sense of purpose and urgency returned. Every citizen of Oregania had to wear a biometer implanted under the skin of his left shoulder, and Willen's – reacting to the cessation of bodily functions – would be broadcasting an alarm signal. The fact that there had been no medical symptoms prior to the death would be regarded by the computer at Biometer Central as a circumstance worthy of investigation. Lorimer calculated that it would be less than five minutes until an ambulance and a police vessel floated down on to the lawns of the Willen house. He turned to Settle, who was staring fixedly at the body on the floor, and handed him the gun. Settle accepted the weapon with trembling hands.

'Don't let it throw you,' Lorimer said.

'I can't help it – look at his face.'

'It isn't worrying him. Concentrate on what you have to do next. As soon as Fay comes in that door and screams, you throw down the gun and get the hell out of here. Go out the front way and down Ocean Drive. The street lights are good out there, so somebody's bound to see you. With any luck the police could spot you from the air. Okay?'

'Okay.'

'When that happens, all your troubles will be over.'

Settle nodded. 'I know it.'

'Listen, Raymond ...' Something about the way the other man had spoken, about the way he was so ready to accept death, aroused Lorimer's compassion. He touched Settle awkwardly on the shoulder. '... I'm sorry about the way things worked out for you.'

'Don't worry about me, Mike.' Settle managed a brief, wistful smile.

Lorimer nodded and, aware that he had wasted enough time, turned and ran towards his skimmer. As he left the patio and sped across the grass, a woman's scream echoed behind him, and he knew the plan was being completed right on schedule. He located the skimmer, jumped in and slammed the canopy down. The vehicle lifted responsively and, without turning on his lights, Lorimer accelerated away from the house. He drove inland on full boost, flitting among the trees like a night-flying bird, invisible in the darkness, until he reached a secondary road several kilometres from the coast.

The road was free of traffic, as Lorimer had expected. He reduced power and brought the skimmer down to the regulation traffic height of one metre, then turned on his lights and flew towards the city at a moderate and unremarkable speed. As the distance markers slipped by in soothing progression, the tension which had been causing the gnawing sensation in his stomach began to abate.

There had been a certain amount of risk, but it had been worth taking. All he had to do now was remain discreetly in the background until Settle was convicted and Gerard Willen's identity was transferred into his body. Divorce under those circumstances was always rushed through by the Office of the Primate in a matter of days, and then Lorimer would be able to step forward and claim his prize. Or, rather, his multiplicity of prizes. There was Fay herself, the three houses, the money, the status ...

By the time Lorimer reached the apartment building where he lived he was almost drunk with happiness. He drove his skimmer up the ramp, grounded it with a flourish, and rode up to his apartment in the elevator tube. In the privacy of his own rooms, he stood for a moment savouring the sheer pleasure of being alive, then poured himself a tall drink. He was raising it to his lips when the door chimes sounded. Lorimer carried his drink to the door, sipping it as he walked. He opened the door, saw two grim-faced men standing on the threshold, and a stab of anxiety pierced his euphoria.

'Michael T. Lorimer?' one of the men said.

Lorimer nodded cautiously. 'What of it?'

'Police. You're under arrest. We're taking you to Police Central.'

'That's what you think,' Lorimer said, with automatic defiance, and began to back away.

The man who had spoken to him glanced at his companion and said, 'Don't take any chances with him.'

'Right.' The companion raised his hand, and Lorimer glimpsed the flared snout of a bolas gun. Without hesitaiton, the policeman fired the weapon and a weighted ribbon of metal wrapped itself around Lorimer's shins, solidifying into an unbreakable bond in less than a second. Another shot hit him in the chest, pinning his arms to his sides. Deprived of all power of movement, he over-balanced and would have gone down had the two men not caught him. They dragged him to the elevator tube, and took him down to a large skimmer and lifted him inside. One of them slipped into the driving seat, and Lorimer fought to control his panic as the vehicle surged towards the exit ramp.

'You're making one hell of a mistake,' he said, forcing his voice to sound both angry and confident. 'What am I supposed to have done?'

Neither of the men answered and Lorimer guessed they had no intention of speaking to him no matter what he said. He watched the route the vehicle was taking, until he was certain they really were heading for Police Central, then he turned his attention to the problem of what he ought to do next. Something had gone wrong – that much was only too obvious – but what? The only thing he could think of was that Settle had been picked up very quickly and, at the last minute, had funked making a confession. The obvious thing for him to do then would be to accuse Lorimer of the killing.

Lorimer forced himself to think calmly about the situation, and felt a growing conviction that he had hit on the truth. Settle's weakness and instability had been an adverse factor all along, and it would be in character for him to back away from the final decisive state which would lead to his death. It was just what one would expect from an ineffectual suicidal type, but – Lorimer felt an upsurge of optimism – Settle was backing a loser. His finger-prints, not Lorimer's, were on the murder weapon, and he had entered the house in a manner which was an indictment in itself. These two circumstances were damning enough, but the blackest mark against him was that Fay would not corroborate his story. It was the word of a shabby down-and-out against the combined testimonies of a rich and respected woman and a citizen who had never been in any previous trouble.

In a few minutes of ghosting through quiet streets the skimmer reached Police Central and came to rest in the entrance bay. One of the men snipped the coil away from Lorimer's legs, making it possible for him to get out of the vehicle with reasonable dignity, but they left his arms strapped to his sides. Inside the brightly lit building a number of people glanced curiously at Lorimer and, while he was being bundled into the elevator tube, he began re-hearsing his lines. An air of injured innocence would, he decided, be more effective than loud indignation. Perhaps, a tone of mild reproach and a hint of reluctance to consider suing for wrongful arrest . . .

When he was led into an office to face three officials in the blue collarettes of Inspectors, Lorimer was fully composed and almost looking forward to the contest of wits.

'Perhaps one of you gentlemen will explain what's going on here,' he said, meeting their eyes unflinchingly. 'I'm not accustomed to this sort of thing.'

'Michael Thoms Lorimer.' The senior Inspector of the three spoke in a careful voice while glancing at a compcard in his hand. 'I am charging you with the murder of Gerard Avon Willen.'

'Gerard Willen? *Dead?*' Lorimer looked shocked. 'I can't believe it.'

'Have you anything to say in reply to the charge?'

'Who would want to . . . ?' Lorimer paused for a moment as though he had just comprehended the Inspector's opening statement. 'Wait a minute – you can't charge me with murder. I didn't know anything about it. I haven't been near the Willen place for weeks.'

'We have a witness.'

Lorimer gave a comfortable laugh. 'I'd like to know who he is.'

'The principal witness is not a man. Mrs. Willen has testified that she saw you shoot her husband and run from the house.'

The floor seemed to heave beneath Lorimer's feet. 'I don't believe you,' he said.

One of the other Inspectors shrugged and held up a recorder. On its small screen there appeared an image of Fay, her cheeks glistening with tears, and Lorimer heard her say the words which condemned him. *I've been had,* he thought strickenly, as a dark flood of understanding welled in his mind. *The bitch has decided to drop ME!* Awareness of his peril jolted Lorimer's brain into desperate activity.

'This is a big shock for me,' he said urgently, 'but I think I can explain why Mrs. Willen told you a lie like that.'

'Proceed.' There was a flicker of interest in the senior Inspector's eyes.

'You see, I got to know Mrs. Willen when I was teaching her to fence. We got to talking quite a bit and she invited me up to her house a few times. I thought she was just being normally friendly – so you can imagine the way I felt when I realised she wanted me to have an affair with her.'

'How did you feel, Mr. Lorimer?'

'Disgusted, of course,' Lorimer said with maximum candour. 'She's an attractive woman and I'm only human, but I draw the line at adultery. When I turned her offer down she seemed to go insane for a few minutes – I've never seen anybody so angry. She said things I don't like to repeat.'

'Under the circumstances, I think you should put your scruples aside.'

Lorimer hesitated. 'Well, she said she would get out of her marriage to Gerard Willen somehow, no matter what it took. And she said she'd make me sorry for the way I'd treated her. I never thought anything like this would come out of it . . .' Lorimer gave a shaky laugh. '. . . but now I'm beginning to understand that old saying about a woman scorned.'

54

'You tell an interesting story, Mr. Lorimer.' The senior Inspector examined his fingernails for a moment. 'Have you ever met a man called Raymond Settle?'

'I don't think so.'

'That's odd. He was at the Willen house tonight, and he too says he saw you shoot Mr. Willen.'

'*What?* But why should I kill Gerard?'

'There's a sum of twenty thousand monits in cash missing from the wall safe in the room where Willen was killed. Money we recovered from your apartment tonight. Settle says he was in the study with Willen when they heard a sound in the next room. Settle says that Willen went to investigate and ... '

'That's ridiculous,' Lorimer shouted. 'Who *is* this man Settle, anyway? He must be in on it with Fay – they must have cooked this up between them. That's it, Inspector! He must be Fay Willen's latest boy friend. He must have sneaked into the house ...' Lorimer stopped speaking as he saw that the Inspector was shaking his head.

'It won't do, Mr. Lorimer.' The Inspector's voice was almost kind. 'Raymond Settle was a trusted business associate of Mr. Willen, and a friend of the family for many years. He had every right to visit Gerard Willen this evening.'

Lorimer opened his mouth to argue, then closed it without uttering a sound. Wordless – and helpless – he was just beginning to appreciate the full extent of what had been done to him.

Exactly a year later, three people attended a discreet celebration in the many-mirrored dining-room of the large house overlooking the sea.

Gerard Willen, clothed in the flesh which had once belonged to a young and ambitious fencing coach, poured three glasses of imported champagne. As he did so, he delighted in the easy strength and steadiness of the hand in which he held the dewed bottle. It was a pleasure which never seemed to fade.

'You know,' he remarked, 'this is a superb body I have ... inherited. It was a great pity that friend Lorimer didn't have mental equipment to match.'

Raymond Settle shook his head. He was as gaunt as ever, but when freshly groomed and expensively clad his tall frame appeared wiry rather than frail. His left arm was around Fay's waist, and she had nestled contentedly against his side.

'It was lucky for us that Lorimer wasn't too bright,' he said. 'I thought I was going to laugh and give the game away when I was feeding him that mush about a baby daughter in an orphanage.'

Fay smiled up at him. 'You were very good, Raymond. Very convincing.'

'Perhaps. Though sometimes I feel a bit guilty about the way we played him like a fish.'

'Forget it. Wasn't he a murderer?' Willen handed round the beaded glasses and raised his own. 'Here's to me!'

'Why not to all of us?' Fay said.

Willen smiled. 'Because I got the most out of it. You escaped from a marriage we both had grown tired of, and now you're happily married to Ray. But I wanted the divorce, too, and into the bargain I got a new physique which lets me work twenty hours a day if I feel like it.'

'You always did work too much,' Fay told him. 'That's why I think I did best. In one night I managed to lose both an in-attentive husband and a dull lover who didn't realise he was *passé*. And now I've got Raymond instead.'

Willen looked thoughtful. 'I suppose the old me must have been rather boring.'

'Not rather boring. *Very* boring.'

'I think I deserve that. Mind you . . .' Willen glanecd appreci-atively at Fay. '. . . the new me could be different. Now that I've got the hormone production of a young stallion, I've realised there are more enjoyable pastimes than work.'

'How interesting!' Fay detached herself from Settle, laughing, and moved closer to Willen with an exaggerated sway of her hips. 'Perhaps you'll come around and see me sometime – when Ray-mond's not here, of course.'

'Cut that out, you two,' Settle protested with a good-natured grin. 'You're beginning to worry me.'

'Don't be silly, darling.' Fay smiled at him over the rim of her champagne glass. 'We all know this is one planet where you can't get away with adultery. Or murder.'

'I'll drink to that.' Settle drained his glass, and then – when he noticed that Fay and Willen were gazing at him with amused expectancy – began to wonder if his drink had tasted exactly the way champagne should.

TRAVELLERS

by Robert P Holdstock

HOW MUCH courage does it take, we've asked before, to give up a secure professional career for the slightly more precarious life of a full-time freelance writer? In Rob Holdstock's case his training has been in the biological sciences but, he decided recently, writing is much more important.

That's why it gives me particular pleasure to report Rob's successes so far – he has had science fiction stories in a number of other collections and magazines, several historical novels and non-fiction books sold, and his first science fiction novel, Eye Among the Blind, *is due out from Faber during 1976.*

In 'Travellers' Rob Holdstock succeeds in achieving almost the impossible – in finding a fresh way of looking at one of the oldest and hoariest of SF themes. Yes, indeed, zoology's loss is our gain....

When we finally reached the outskirts of the city the time-node was well advanced. In a sense this meant I had lost valuable hours for searching, but as yet, we were told, the visiting forms from the past and future were tenuous and unstable, flitting into vision and out again as fast as they realised they could not find a positive hold in this alien era.

In all likelihood, if Margaretta *was* in the node I would find her again after all these years. But what a frightening number of obstacles stood in the path of that achievement! Had she been alive when this sequence of inconsistency in time reached the fourth millennium? Had she been able to find the node and penetrate it? Was she looking for me as I would be looking for her? And my conscious dreams of her – no, *our* – daughter ... were they just imaginative fantasy? Or had she indeed conceived a child, and thus, inexplicably, secured our brief contact across a thousand years?

Too many obstacles, too many uncertainties ...

'Wake up, Jaim.'

My travelling companion, Herok, was shaking my arm. I

snapped out of my drifting dream and followed him towards the first of the gate-checks. As we walked, burdened by our packs and the necessary implements of survival, he looked round at me and shook his head. 'Still thinking of her? You're going to lose us the chance of a smooth entry.'

'I'm sorry, Herok,' I said. 'I just feel very ... anxious.'

'I know.'

'And anxiety is a great distraction.'

'It's all right, Jaim. I'll keep an eye on you.'

Herok was a grand fellow. He was younger than me by ten years. We were both in middle grade, but in two years' time, when I reached forty, I would rise to the next level of the student ladder, the senior grade. My degree would follow within the decade; and a junior lectureship, with luck, within the decade following that. Now, however, we were travelling companions, bronzed and burned by the sun of Southern Asia, and hardened by our adventures in North Africa, where every day had been a test of our fitness to survive.

Over the years I had come to regard Herok as both peer and brother, and if we looked dissimilar – he being tall and thin, and covered with a fine blond down, myself being of shorter, stockier stature, with burnt-umber hair and a fashionable beard – this did not discourage us from pretending a family relationship when it suited us, or when it was convenient.

'I can see the gate up ahead,' said Herok suddenly; I craned to see above the heads of the travelling crowds, and saw it, a primitive barbed and armed barrier to progression, through which a trickle of visitors were being permitted.

We were watched from houses and offices on every side. Here, at the outskirts of the city, the streets were wide, and we joined the queue of travellers, finding ourselves buried in a mass of silken, silky bodies, all pushing and jostling as they waited, impatiently, to try and talk their ways into the time-node. They would fail, of course, but there were always the thousands who believed that persuasion was a powerful weapon.

We jostled, bustled, edged towards the barrier.

'You are approaching the zone of observation,' said a loud and indifferent voice, speaking apparently from mid air. 'Red and green passes only.'

We both had green passes, which would take us through to the node itself. The passes had arrived a few weeks before, shortly after the first signs of the impending node had been spotted. The allocation was based partly on the particular fields of research with which Herok and I were concerned, and partly upon the Psychoscan that had preceded our successful entry into a similar node, ten years before.

We were among the luckiest men on Earth, and I was thankful for the fact.

At the gate we were assigned to one of the many armed guards who took us aside and scrutinised our cards carefully; no doubt he was looking for evidence of forgery, but he found none, naturally, and passed us on.

We were now in the zone of observation and from here much of the node itself could be seen. The whole area appeared normal – if a trifle crowded – and the great mass of human beings that sprawled on walls and rooftops, staring and scanning down the mile or so to the edge of the node, seemed well content with their lot. Looking downhill towards the centre of the city (for the node had risen across most of the city centre and a fraction of the western sector) we saw the tenuous white ghosts of future travellers trying to break through into this time, and failing, although Herok stated positively that he could see the ludicrous garb of men from the next millennium, a time with which we were both well versed, naturally, having secured a great many friends in many future ages.

At the edge of the observation zone a force field of some considerable strength had been erected to prevent any unlawful penetration into the strange time flow beyond, and here we came to the final barrier through which we would have to pass. We were surrounded by men and women of all races and all ages, each and every one of them waving thick wadges of bank notes, or great clusters of sparkling jewellery. Why? The rich, the poor alike were begging us for our entrance passes, and in truth we could have made ourselves among the richest men on Earth that day, for the richest men on Earth were there, begging our favour. Money, wealth, possession, power ... these were not the ways to acquire the green passes into the time field. The unseen men who commanded such entry, who imposed the rules upon society during the duration of a node, were interested only in natural attributes, it seemed – perhaps imagination, perhaps intellectual honesty; most of us who found ourselves together beyond this final wall shared something in common – a desire for knowledge for its own sake.

The pitiful creatures who clustered around us during that last walk towards the final gate were wasting their efforts. Communication with other times could far too easily take the form of torment and torture, and the sick and bestial elements of humankind were kept at bay. Even if their bribing succeeded, the passes they would have so obtained would have been useless to them!

A glittering diamond was thrust into my hand by a man who smelled of hyacinth and grinned in his fatty face, plucked nervously at the spun silver cloth he wore. The jewel, I was sure, would have bought me a city, or taken me on an endless cruise of our solar system; a treasure indeed. But beyond the barrier, in the zone of inconsistent time, there was a greater treasure. Margaretta.

I pushed the jewel back and mumbled my apology, but the man followed me, weeping, clutching at my sleeve. I tried to shake him off but his grip moved to my arm, became almost desperate.

Herok was being pestered by two women, both well past their prime, but both splendidly dressed and devastatingly beautiful. They were – I could be certain – offering far more than themselves, and I sympathised with Herok for his predicament.

We were silent and depressed by the time we were facing the armoured guards who stood between the zone of Observation and the huge examination hall at the edge of the time node itself. My arms were bruised from the attentions of the beggars; there were tears in Herok's eyes, but I recognised the after-effects of SymPathyn, a drug no doubt worn by many of the women in this zone.

The guards were satisfied with our credentials and passed us on and we walked into the cool, white-walled building, and stood for a moment getting our bearings. There were two queues of people, shuffling slowly forwards. The largest queue was for those with one-day passes, and movement was slow because each person bearing such an entry permit was being fitted with a recall-stud, just below their skin. The other queue was shorter, but the Examiners looked far more intense.

Apprehensive, excited, we joined this queue and within ten minutes were being interrogated as to our purposes and aims for the next few months. As students we had ready answers to most of the questions; Herok, as a trained Security Man, could answer truthfully that he would become such during the stay in the node, and could fit in his study between-times.

Everybody during their stay in the time node was expected to contribute to the maintenance of the enclosed environment.

I, as a trained mental therapist, could truthfully answer that my assistance could be called upon to help badly disoriented travellers from times when security was less stringent than in our own, or in the next few hundred millennia.

The toughest question came last. 'Do you swear that you have no emotional involvement with travellers from any other age?'

'I so swear,' said Herok quietly, and I could almost feel his anxiety. Would the guards notice? They could hardly fail to detect our feelings of worry, but with luck by now their senses would be dulled by repetition.

I could not, I knew, get away with denying my involvement if the minds of the guards were fully tuned, and searching for the tell-tale signs of a lie. Margaretta's importance to me was too great, the love I felt too deep for me to have replied an outright affirmative. I knew this, and Herok knew this, but in the course of our journey across the world from Penang, to Africa, and then to Western Europe, we had rarely discussed either the girl from the next millennium, or the obstacle that she presented to us gaining entrance into this node, the second node we had visited and probably the last that would manifest during our lifetimes.

Now: the crunch.

'No emotional involvement,' I said quickly, and before there was time for any reaction, went on, 'As part of my project I hope to re-contact several people from the next millennium and gain an idea of their time's developments during the intervening years.'

Immediate suspicion. 'Male or female?'

'Both sexes,' I said quickly. I was feeling cooler, now, but the fixed stare from the nearest Examiner, a tall, sour-looking man, with piercing grey eyes, made my heart stutter and the electrical conductivity of my skin seemed to short-circuit all over my face.

'What's your project?' asked this emotionless figure.

'Social dynamism,' I replied obscurely. He frowned briefly, then glanced at his companion, an equally sour man, shorter, possibly an inferior. Behind them four guards stood rigidly to attention, eight eyes fixed upon my face.

'Sounds feasible,' said the shorter Examiner. 'You can hardly re-contact people without *some* anticipation . . .' He glanced at Herok, then back at me. There was a long tense moment. Then the Examiner nodded, 'Let them pass.'

Herok and I bowed low, and smiled at each other. We gathered up our packs and strode out into the daylight on the time node side of the Examination Hall.

'We've done it,' Herok murmured as we walked through the streets, getting faster with every pace. 'Jaim, we've *done* it! We're in again!'

He began to run, and I followed. He began to laugh, and his laughter was infectious. In the cover of a ramshackle red-brick building we stood, leaning heavily against each other, and yelled our delight, forgetting completely how near we had come to being refused entrance!

We walked through crowded streets and listened to the rising pitch of excitement, the laughing and shouting of men and women hardly able to restrain their enthusiasm for the days to come. Around us ghosts appeared for brief moments and vanished again, some so quickly that there was not even time to turn and look to see from what era of time they had come. I nudged Herok and pointed to where a semi-naked man stood in the shadow of an office block and stared up the glass facing and bulging transparent walls. 'Fifth millennium,' I said, and Herok gave it a moment's consideration before nodding. 'Possibly. Margaretta was from the fourth, wasn't she?'

'Late third, early fourth, yes. I wish you had known her, Herok.'

Although ten years ago we had been together in the previous time node we had led separate lives therein and separate adventures. Afterwards I had refused to talk about her for several months, and when I did talk of Margaretta I suppose it had been the ramblings of a lovelorn fool. I had wanted it to be that Herok knew her, had met her, and could therefore appreciate my love for her, but she was a stranger to him, an image created by my inadequate descriptions.

We found lodgings in a huge and draughty hostel and took bunks and meal seats in the wing devoted to men and women from all ages. The wing reserved for third and fourth millennia visitors was already full, and within a couple of weeks visitors would find themselves slotted into any available space, in very mixed company indeed!

The only man already in our wing was a fourth-millennium student-type, a middle-aged man with deep brown eyes who gazed at us nervously as we unpacked and unrolled, and discussed our plans.

'Are you from the third?' he asked abruptly, speaking with the nasal slant to his words that characterises fourth-millennium interLing. It was the same accent that Margaretta had, and it was instantly warming.

'Yes,' I replied, seating myself by him. I extended my hand after a moment and he gripped it happily, shaking my arm with great gusto. His clothes were sparse and not very warm; a neck and waist band, joined by thin strips of cloth; a pouch to contain and support his genitals, and thick leather bindings down his legs. I felt overdressed in my mock mid-second-millennium kaftan.

'Garri D'rath,' he said. 'My name. Last time I was in a node I found out that I was descended from a family line called Rathbone. Interesting. I'm fascinated by your era ... that's why I've come here. You probably think it's a bit unusual to stay in only one millennium ...' He was smiling, almost self-consciously. There was a splash of soup on his chin and I wiped it off for him; he tensed, but laughed when I held up my green-stained finger. Slightly embarrassed, he wiped his mouth and chin with a small red tissue.

'Not unusual at all,' I replied. 'I'm Jaim Barron, by the way. This is Herok Vuutgenstein. We're both social dynamism students.'

'There are enough of them about,' laughed Garri. 'But this co-incidence makes it a valuable field of study, I suppose.'

'You mean the two nodes so close together?'

He nodded. My insides tensed. It was estimated there were just fifty of the node sequences, each spanning the greater part of time and along each of which a lucky few could travel. And for two of these sequences to have stopping points within the space of a man's lifetime was coincidence and gift indeed!

I was worried, however. Just because there had been one thousand and ten years separating the nodes of that first sequence, when I had met Margaretta, didn't mean that in this second, un-related sequence the time between the nodes had to be the same. If eleven hundred years separated us, Margaretta would be long since dead.

'How long ago was the last node you visited?'

'How long?' He frowned, sought to remember. 'About twelve years. Yes, twelve years.'

She would have aged two years more than I, only two years!

63

It was ten years since we had met, ten years of wandering and remembering. For Margaretta, a twelve-year wait. But was she here? Had she gained entry? Had she even *heard* of this sequence of time nodes?

Garri was saying, 'Myself, I'm a time engineer. That's really all I can tell you at the moment. As you know, there are strict controls about the acquisition of information. Until something is actually discovered, or realised, or worked out, it doesn't become general information to people from earlier times.'

Herok nodded soberly. As a security junior whilst in the node he worked, part of the time, to ensure that that rule was enforced, without knowing what information he was himself restricting. He said, 'Is this node of some importance, then?'

Garri looked thoughtful for a moment, then glanced around, a grossly theatrical concession to secrecy. Looking at us both for a second he nodded slowly. 'You bet,' he said with a wink. 'You just wait and see.'

A loudspeaker blared through the dormitory, summoning all new arrivals to the nearest Control and Allocation Centre. Herok slapped his hands together and called to me. I shook Garri by the hand again. 'We'll see you later. This is where the hard work starts.'

He chuckled. 'Okay. I'll be here.'

As we walked swiftly along the broad streets, through people in amorphous throngs, through seated circles of contemporaries busily discussing what they would do with their three-month liberation in time, so we saw the first signs of more ambitious journeys. A figure, a woman, a beautifully robed woman, shimmered into existence before us, suspended fractionally above the ground; she couldn't see us, of course, as she tried to move into our time, but we watched her for the few seconds that she tried to break across the barrier of years. She was a sixth-millennium visitor and had obviously broken as far back as the fourth millennium, but couldn't summon the mental energy to push back here, to the third. Her limbs waved as she lost control of her body with the pressure of her mind-direction, and for a few seconds she was a silent image of frustrated beauty, threshing in an age a thousand years removed, before finally fading back into future reality, to wait for the node to advance further and facilitate the extra movement required.

64

Herok laughed as we walked through the space where her image had been, and then a thought struck him and he glanced at me; I caught the unvoiced suggestion and grinned and he shouted, 'Come on!' and gripped me by the hand. He dragged me into a breathtaking run. 'Now!' he yelled, and we directed our minds into the future, and felt the surge of blood as our bodies followed, and the swirling colours of scattering third-millennium denizens left us to be replaced by the sober movement of people a thousand years hence.

We were in a vast square, green and white pavement stones beneath our feet and tall, impossibly tall, sparkling buildings at each of four corners.

As we came into the present, so we turned. She was behind us, watching us (we had arrived still shrieking our excitement) and we stopped, staring at her face and at her body, full and exciting beneath the white translucent material of her robe. Then Herok took the initiative and ran across to her. She seemed startled, and her hands clutched at the folds of her gown as she regarded first the breathless form of Herok, then my own grinning features. Herok said, 'We witnessed your attempts to move into our time, my lady, and when you finally succeed I shall be delighted to act as escort.'

She smiled, then, and bowed to Herok. 'Thank you,' she said. 'I'd like that very much. Your era is my final destination, and if I can return the favour, I have a large apartment in this city – in the sixth millennium – of which you may avail yourself.'

Herok bowed again and behind his back his hand was waving excitedly, the fingers spread wide in a sign of success. She gave him her address on a small blue card, and turned to walk away. Herok and I ran across the square and vaulted back into the past, moving through two walls (strange sense of cold and dark) and returning to the open roadway.

Back in our own time Herok stopped and wiped his face, his hands shaking. 'What a magnificent body,' he said. 'And they say sixth-millennium women are animals ... animals!'

'Filthy dog!' I shouted, and he laughed. 'Remember your age, Herok. You're not a child any more.'

'Oh but I feel it, Jaim. I feel – rejuvenated! Excited!' He was grinning all over his face.

'Your exuberance is nauseating,' I pointed out, looking round to see if his noisiness was being observed.

And I saw her!

'Margaretta!' I shouted as she vanished behind a house. Herok grabbed my arm as I started to run. 'The signing on, Jaim. You have to sign on.'

He was right, I shouldn't delay registering but I had seen Margaretta, she was here. And even now was perhaps losing herself in the crowded streets closer to the centre of the city.

I thrust my green identity card into Herok's hand. 'Explain that an important part of my project began prematurely, and that I'll be sure to show my face later.'

I began to run towards the squat, ugly building, with it's sharply angular corners and gruesome air-vents behind which Margaretta had vanished. Herok called, 'You'll need this in case you're stopped.'

Running, I shouted back, 'I'll take that chance.' Then Herok was out of sight and I was facing a long, narrow street, and there was no sign of Margaretta.

As I ran I prayed to God that I hadn't been mistaken, that the slim girl in the trousers and red blouse who had flitted so briefly through my field of vision had indeed been my fourth-millennium lover.

At the end of the street I faced five ways to go, streets, alleys, entrances. There were people milling about, mostly contemporary with just a smattering of the multifarious types from the next millennium.

For a moment I panicked, and then, again seen from a distance and from behind, I spotted her; she was walking down a roadway beneath a sign that, in many different time languages, said 'City Centre'. As she was about to vanish from sight she looked round, seemed to look right at me . . .

Margaretta! Without any shadow of doubt, it was Margaretta. I became ecstatic, raced after her, my heart pounding with joy. But when I reached the end of the road there was no sign of her. I jumped to the next millennium, but she was not visible there either. For a moment I felt anxiety, and for a second moment despair, but if I knew Margaretta she would be moving towards the centre of the node, drawn by curiosity and the thought – I hoped – of perhaps finding me in the greater crowds who gathered there.

Back in my own time I pressed on, down side streets and across plazas, pushing through the drifting crowds, avoiding the white and grey forms that filled the air, some successfully breaking through into this time, others fading back into the future (or the past?) to wait a few hours longer.

At length I came to the centre of the node. There was, as I had expected, a huge crowd of sightseers, formed in a vast, excited ring several hundred feet deep. At the centre of the ring was the enigma, and though I had seen it before I felt an urge, a great temptation, to push through the ranks of visitors and natives and view it again . . .

A white shape shimmered momentarily before me, but faded quickly when it realised its mistake. Time travel was not permitted this close to the centre. It was too dangerous by far.

I began to push through the crowds; some, inspired by my positive motion, followed in my wake or began to stir up the motionless mob themselves, insinuating their bodies into every crack and gap in the circle of human forms. I kept an eye for Margaretta, and every woman with a babe in arms caused me to stop and stare, even though I had already seen Margaretta without a child, and even though that child, our mutual daughter, would be twelve . . . no, eleven years of age and certainly not in her mother's arms.

After a few moments, a smattering of minutes, I reached the innermost ring of the group of humans and found myself pressed against the unseen but impenetrable wall of force that would always protect the enigma from the curious touch of we mortals.

In a small clear space, perhaps eight feet across, surrounded by a wall of silent humanity, was the Traveller. He, she, it . . . what was appropriate?

It squatted on the ground and not a fibre, not a muscle moved. It was totally, absolutely black. Not black because of its skin or its clothes, but black because of the total absence of light or shade. The features of the Traveller were distinguishable only by the swelling and rippling of its surface and when one looked closely, when one focused carefully upon those unbroken black surfaces one could see eyes, a nose, organs and organelles upon the body that did not really relate to anything terrestrial. It appeared to be clad in armour plate, and clutched in its two broad hands an all-black machine, a box with black featureless buttons, and it never moved to switch a switch or press a knob, and it never seemed to breathe. Its closed eyes never opened to show us a moment of its black, depthless mind.

It squatted there, the absolute centre of the time node, pro-

67

tected by its force shield, oblivious to its curiosity value. And we stared and did not fully comprehend, except to realise that the figure was a Traveller through space-time moving across our frame of reference for a few brief months.

I pulled away from the enigma and bustled out through the crowds, into the clear plaza beyond. There I stood for a moment catching my breath and searching the environs. Margaretta had well and truly vanished.

Sadly I walked back to the hostel. If only ... if only my mind link had remained after the birth of the girl. And what strangeness was contained within that single moment of regret! A *mind link* ... across a thousand years ...

Sounds and sights vanished during those next few minutes, as I walked heavily through streets that could have been paved with burning coals and I'd not have noticed. I was experiencing a vivid reliving of the months following the decline of the previous node, the gathering place of ages when I had first met Margaretta. As the node had faded, as the people around me had faded over the days into ghost forms, as more and more of my contemporaries had arrived back, reluctantly, from far-flung millennia, unable to maintain their space-time distortion, so I had watched Margaretta fade from me, slip into the sea of time, her hand outstretched, her eyes filled with tears. It had been a matter of seconds between the kiss and the loss, and I carried the memory of that last touch for many hours before a biting wind had chafed my lips to numbness and the moisture in my eyes had begun to sparkle and crack.

Sank into depression.

Months. Three months.

Waking during a night, during a dream, during a kiss, a moment's excited touch of Margaretta's body. Awoke and felt heart beat, warm rush of blood, sonorous shift of muscle ...

Room swam. Lay back and stared at ...

Listened to ...

My daughter. My daughter. In fluid womb, floating in warm liquid, basking in Margaretta's awareness.

My daughter?

Our daughter, Jaim.

Margaretta I love you.

Always, Jaim, always. I visit your grave and love you more every moment ...

Shifting, blood runs faster, heart beats harder, across a thousand years.

Fully awake. Vision goes. Dream?

Oh Margaretta ... visiting my grave, cracked gravestone, crumbled bones, but loving me as I live, united through her womb, through the sparkling embryo, the squirming tadpole, the fusion of two ages in the bloody wall of future.

A touch across a thousand years; a vanished hand, holding me close.

Back in the dormitory I found Herok pulling the final piece of his new uniform on to his tall, spare frame. He looked very smart in the green and white outfit of the Security Force, for which he would have to work four hours every day. As I strolled into the long room he turned and smiled.

'When's your first shift?' I asked.

'Right now,' he said ruefully, picking up a sheet of names and jabbing his own name with a gloved finger. 'Right now. But fortunately there are a fair number of faces and figures to memorise ...' He picked up a sheaf of mug shots and flipped through them. 'So shift number one is memory work. Ugly bunch,' he went on. 'Most of them will be making the Big Run, which should mean some action.'

'The *big run*,' I repeated, chuckling. 'I wonder who first called it that?'

Herok shrugged, continued to study one of the faces in his file of illegal node-entrants.

There were two Big Runs: one was into the distant future, and one was into the distant past. The most usual avenue of attempted escape by those criminal types who managed to get into the node in the first place was to move to the distant future and hope to escape the time field that way. The future was more secure than the past, which was a difficult place to survive in and not only because of the flesh-eating Saurians that prevailed at that almost unreachable end of the node sequence. The atmosphere back then was stinkingly rich in toxic gases.

With Herok, the previous time we had ventured into a time node (our first and, so we had thought, our last) we had attempted to move back to the Age of Dinosaurs. We had almost made it, but it had been too difficult. The peak of that node had already passed and there were only a few seconds, a few moments, when the full range of travelling time, which always ended in the mid-Cretaceous, was available for the smallest of mental efforts; it was rumoured that only at that moment, at the peak of the node, could escape from the confines of the pocket of time be effected. Was there truth in such rumours? It was difficult to know, but enough denizens of future ages believed the rumour sufficiently to try and beach themselves at the ends of time, to escape whatever oppression they had been born to.

'Oh by the way,' said Herok suddenly, 'You have to report to Control and Allocation tomorrow, early.'

'Oh.'

Herok grinned and passed me back my identity card. 'Don't worry. I've spun a good yarn on your behalf. I think they fell for it.'

More visitors were arriving and taking bunks in the dormitory. We lingered for a while making their acquaintance and searching for people of specific interest, but found no-one whom we would have wanted to stick with. Most of the arrivals were early fourth millennium; a few were contemporary and there were a few from the second millennium who stood, nervously, watching their confident dormitory mates. Their clothes looked hideously uncomfortable, and their expressions quite moronic, but this was almost certainly due to Time Shock.

Part of my job, whilst in the node, would be to help 'earlier' visitors adjust to later eras, and so we – Herok and I – moved ourselves into conversation with the small band of seconds.

There were the usual questions, the usual anxieties, from those entering their first node, experiencing the strangeness for the first time. We explained, over and over, how it would become easier to move through time as the node advanced, and how they were in no danger of impacting with objects because of the sense of getting frozen and the ease with which one could move away to a safe spot. How time, *in all nodes*, was moving forward, and no-one could ever move to a moment before the moment they had left. Detailed accounts of how paradoxes were impossible because of the Security Force (Herok took a bow), the information embargo, which was imposed on the first four or five millennia after their own (stopping things being known before they were discovered) and the unseen Surveillance Corps, always watching the activities in the nodes. No-one knew who the Surveillance Corps were, but they had absolute authority: yet despite their vigilance the nodes had given rise to all manner of legend and myths, visitations and

70

strange phenomena in times before the second millennium.

Most of the questions concerned the Traveller, and here we had to be careful, remembering that only a certain amount of detail had been ascertained that thousand years past. We told them what we thought was safe to tell, and sent them to their own Control for any extra allowable information. Thus they learned more or less what we ourselves knew, that the enigma was a time traveller, from when to when we didn't know with certainty, or at least, whether travelling forwards or backwards we didn't know; the ends of its run, certainly, were in the middle Cretaceous and at a time in the future nearly five million years removed from the present. The view most often expressed by third-millennium people was that in the distant future, Earth – at that time deserted, we knew – was being used as a Way Station by aliens, exploring the Galaxy, perhaps just the Earth, of the Saurian Age. It was frustrating not knowing, when virtually everyone else in the node *did* know.

Garri arrived back looking thoughful. He was pleased to see us and we went out into the city for a drink together, Herok deciding to shirk his first shift. Garri's thoughtfulness developed into excitement; he was obviously burning to tell us something, but when we pressed for him to open up he shook his head, looked worried.

'I don't know if I dare, but . . .'

'What? Come on, Garri, tell us what you know!'

'The information restriction, though . . .'

We huddled closer together. Finally Garri said, 'This node represents a great step forward, anyway, and the information will be declassified before the end, so I suppose it doesn't matter if I tell you.'

We waited. Finally Garri said, 'One of your third-millennium mathematicians is – even now! – making observations that permit almost full understanding of the time nodes. What he works out, what he *is* working out, will lead directly to the establishment of the Surveillance Corps, and to many experiments with time. We are living at a turning point . . . history, which most of us have known for all our lives, is being made!'

'Without the sums . . . what's he discovered?'

Garri ordered more drinks. We'd drunk too much already and my head was swimming, but we sipped the bitter concoction that he favoured and listened.

'The cause of the nodes,' he said. 'The time traveller theory

71

is right, of course. In the distant future on this world there is an alien installation sending individuals back to the Cretaceous. If the Surveillance Corps know why, they're not telling. Each of the Travellers, though, travels through time in a series of jumps, stopping for infinitely small fractions of his subjective seconds in order to *pull power from the Earth's magnetic field*. They fuel themselves during transit.'

'Wonderful,' murmured Herok. Perhaps he had been expecting something a little more exciting. Myself, I felt quite emotionally moved by what Garri was telling us.

He went on, 'The jumps are very frequent to begin with, which is why there are only half-millennia separating the nodes up-time; they get more and more infrequent as the Traveller builds his time momentum, so that by the Cretaceous there are thousands of years between nodes.'

'Has he worked out – this mathematician – how the nodes get linked?' Herok asked.

'Yes he has, and it's sound maths, too. Practically speaking, each momentary stop by the Traveller distorts the time matrix, and during the few seconds of his time trip those distortions are accumulated and released at the moment of his landing, back in the past. The astronomically small time spans of these distortions and releases actually measure several months – on *our* time scale. The effect is that for several months at the time of each stop for power there is a narrow vein of captured time stretching from the past to the future, and this is what we are riding.'

'Mumbo jumbo,' commented Herok. 'I didn't understand a word.'

Garri laughed, 'I know how you feel. Social science is poles apart from time maths . . . but we don't have to let our professional differences spoil a good time, do we?'

Herok, happier, raised his glass and grinned. 'Certainly not, my good fellow.' He knocked the lot back, signalled for more.

For my part I declined a refill but pressed Garri for information about himself. I felt the tingle of static that said a member of the Surveillance Corps had, at some time during the last few minutes, tuned in on our conversation and decided we should be watched, and was now coming close enough to intervene.

Phrasing his words carefully, also aware of our observer, Garri said, 'I'm quite a junior researcher, really, at an Institute for Sub-Quantum Physics. 'I'm involved with time theory, and am involved with certain practical developments from the maths being turned out at this instant. In fact, there are several tests and experiments being carried out along this node sequence ...' he broke off, looking uncomfortable. After a moment the sense of being watched went away. He said, 'I think you'd better steer clear of me, for a while ...'

Over the days I searched for Margaretta, between my compulsory service and the necessary work for my project. She had vanished, however, utterly and completely, and I never saw any sign of her. Herok was no help. He had never seen the woman and my description was too sentimental for him to obtain a clear mind's view of her.

I began to feel panic. My excursions through time became thoughtless and reckless; twice in the far future I nearly drowned when I came into a time when the node had opened over the sea; once, in the distant past, when it had opened across the mouth of a volcano, I nearly crisped.

The node advanced, and time flowed easier into the future and the past; other ages arrived and departed, many in groups with a single interpreter; the first of the real aliens showed its face, and all at once a mood of festivity and total excitement burst upon the city, not just in my natural time but in all times. The peak was approaching.

I watched the ninth Roman Legion, bedraggled and muddy, pace across rain-logged, marshy European landscape; fifty or sixty men, weary from battle – clattering beneath their equipment, pacing north to join their garrison. They would never arrive. I searched the crowds who watched them, knowing that Margaretta had a fascination for that greatest of European empires, but there was no sign of her. She could not have failed to have heard the Site-watcher's announcement in every time that the legionaries were passing; she must have declined the temptation to stand, with the hundreds of others behind an Invisibility Seal, and watch their progress.

I went into the distant future and watched the building of huge ships; and further still to see the strange life forms that crawled across the Earth after man had deserted his home world. I talked with a Dhorr, from the Sirian empire that was still, in his time,

73

subservient to the Earth Empire in the Galaxy. He told me, through an interpreter (which itself had nearly as many air-holes as the Dhorr, but which could manifest Earth sound through each one of them rather than speaking different pitches with each set of lips) that he had talked with his own kind of the millennia beyond the extinction of the human race, and they had despatched and received unmanned vessels between the galaxies. There was a great race in Andromeda who were trying to cross the gulf between the star cities, and the Dhorri had a strong feeling that their intentions were not particularly friendly.

We stood, the tubular alien and I, and stared at the black and enigmatic structure of the Traveller, and we wondered . . .

'If they had conquered time,' said the Dhorr, 'and crossed the gulf in deep sleep, and thus travelled naturally many millions of years into their own futures, they might use a planet such as this to return, once their journey was finished, to their own time.'

'It's an intriguing thought,' I said.

'And a happy one,' said the Dhorr. 'If they want to conquer the Galaxy of three hundred million years ago, they are very welcome. Neither your race nor mine were around at that time.'

'And if they *did* spread throughout this Galaxy, their conquest has been forgotten. Their leavings dissolved in the natural span of centuries.'

A happy thought indeed!

I searched for Margaretta in her own millennium, stood in the middle of that vast plaza and felt the wind blowing cold against my flesh; shouted her name, searched the crowds.

The beautiful white-robed woman came towards me and remembered me, and asked wistfully after Herok. We talked, and she left.

The node was approaching its peak. Half-way done and I had not found Margaretta. Half-way wasted!

I went back to my own time and found it was night, and I walked through the streets towards the hostel, my soft bunk and a depressed period of sleep. I was nearly home when she called to me from the shadows, and when I stopped she moved into the light and stared at me.

'Jaim?'

'Margaretta!' I cried; ran to her; and for a long time I just hugged her to me and wept with joy.

'I thought I'd never find you, Margaretta.'

'I've been searching for you too,' she said, and stood back to examine me closely. She was still as I remembered her, and age had left little mark; a few more lines around her eyes, a slightly more tired expression; her hair was cut short and her clothes were styled more youthfully. But it was Margaretta in every way, and I thought my heart would burst!

We still had six weeks. Six weeks together until time separated us again, almost certainly for good.

'Where is . . .?'

'Jayameeka?'

Jayameeka! She had been called after me! (Well, almost).

'Yes. Our daughter.'

She looked sad. Her arms unwound from me. 'She's safe, Jaim. But I couldn't bring her. I'm sorry, Jaim, but they . . . they wouldn't let me bring her.'

Stunned!

'Who wouldn't let you?'

She shrugged. 'Whoever's in control. The Time Authorities.'

'But why? Why such a restriction?'

'Jaim . . . she was conceived in your time – this time; but born in mine, a thousand years hence. She belongs to two times, Jaim, and the authorities are terrified of her . . .' She was hiding something; in her voice, in her manner, in her words were the hints of a deception, advanced, perhaps, to protect my feelings.

'Margaretta,' I said, as we stood in the darkened city. 'Tell me.'

When Jayameeka had been born (Margaretta told me) the story, the facts, of our relationship had been made known. Jayameeka had been taken away from her, and brought up in an Institute devoted to obscure scientific studies; Margaretta had had full access to the child, and had spent much time with her, but she had become the object of study; a child of two times might – they had said – give a clue to the nature of time travel. She was too important to waste. And for all those years she had been the centre of interest for a small group of researchers, working in the field of temporal dynamics.

I would never see my daughter!

I had waited eleven years to see the offspring of our love, a desire that had been drowned, certainly, beneath my anxiety, my desire to see Margaretta herself; now that the truth was known, I felt a great emptiness, a substantial and painful sense of loss.

And anger! My daughter, an experimental animal! Why, if they had wanted such children for their studies they could easily have arranged such consummations!

A shiver down my spine; an uneasy glance at Margaretta as we walked through the night streets. Perhaps . . .

Had she too thought of the shocking possibility?

Surely, though, such an experiment would not have been undertaken without the awareness of the participating bodies?

Creeping into the dormitory we slipped silently into my bunk and vanished beneath the sheets. She was nervous at first, almost hesitant, a span of so many years causing her desire to be drowned by apprehension; at least, this is what I assumed, since it was happening to me as well.

But after a few minutes of hugging and warming, of gentle touching and featherlight kissing, we became bolder, more confident, and Margaretta returned with passion. If Herok heard, or felt, our joyous reunion he said nothing from the upper bunk.

Strangely the sensation of basking in each other's awarenesses, the slight empathy that had linked us through time (for however brief a span of time) never returned as it had those eleven years back. I didn't comment on it; it would come in a few days, no doubt.

In the morning . . .

I opened my eyes and found myself staring at the floor. During the night I had slipped out of the bunk, possibly pushed by Margaretta's sleeping form, and was now draped across the edge of the bed, my right cheek dented and sore from its contact with the rough wooden underfoot.

Margaretta was gone, and for a moment I just sat on the edge of the bunk and rubbed my eyes; then I felt a great panic! If she had left, perhaps too upset by the thought of eventually parting for ever . . . how would I ever find her again? It had taken so long, would take too long to repeat the search . . .

'Herok!' I shouted and stood up to rouse him out of bed. He too was gone, his night-shift folded neatly across the pillow, the bunk highly presentable. He had been gone some while, probably about his part-time duties as a Security man.

At that moment the door at the end of the dormitory burst

open and Herok arrived, running frantically, and breathing like he would burst.

'Where've you been?' I demanded. He waved me quiet.

'Where's that mug file? Ah . . .' he found his folder of criminal faces and was leafing through the pages rapidly, excitement in his face, nervousness in his fingers.

'Who are you looking for?'

'I'm sure I've just seen . . . ah, yes . . . it *was*! Can't stop, Jaim. I'm about to make my first arrest.' He uttered a little yell of pleasure and raced out of the dormitory, drawing his gun from its pouch on his hip.

I smiled and shook my head at his exuberance, and turned the open folder towards me to see whom he had seen.

Margaretta!

MARGARETTA!

I nearly collapsed, but somehow kept my suddenly useless legs in a straight position and I stared at the picture of Margaretta. He must have seen her as she left . . .

My eyes picked out the words below the picture. Wanted . . . Time criminal . . . illegal entry into node . . . Jayameeka Strahn . . . *Jayameeka.*

My world collapsed. I remember hitting the floor with a deafening crash and feeling all sensation leave me.

I came round to the sound of Herok's urgent voice. He was bending over me and looking very anxious. When I recovered consciousness he smiled and helped me up. 'What happened?' he asked. Garri was crouched beside me and holding out a glass of blue liquid; I suspected something very potent and decided that I needed it; sipping the drink I nearly choked, then looked at Herok.

Careful, I thought. Very careful.

'I got out of bed too fast,' I said. 'Fainted.' He grinned; he knew I'd been drinking fairly heavily for the previous few days, and no doubt was imagining pains and unco-ordinations in my head that were not, in fact, there. 'Did you get who you were after?' I asked.

They helped me up.

'No,' said Herok, disappointed. 'No, she gave me the slip. But I've alerted the Security forces up and down time. We'll get her.'

Garri said, 'I expect she'll be trying to make the Big Run. It's not long before that will be possible.'

Not long at all, I reflected. It couldn't be pin-pointed with total accuracy, but it would begin sometime this afternoon, the peak of the node, a mere twenty seconds!

If Jayameeka – Jayameeka! My daughter! Where had I miscalculated? – if she could locate that moment and avoid the gathering of Security men, she could slip away into the past or future and, if God was on her side, 'beach' herself on the real world at whichever extreme of the node sequence she was planning on heading for. When – if – time slipped away from her, she would be free of whatever oppression had driven her to such despair. And she would be free of me, lost to me for ever ...

Herok left.

'Don't go away,' said Garri, cryptically, and he made to follow Herok. I grabbed his arm.

'Garri ... what went wrong?'

He looked blank. 'I don't understand.'

'The nodes ... you told me twelve years ... twelve years since your last entry into a node sequence!'

He looked uncomfortable, glanced at the dormitory door, then back at me. 'I'm sorry, Jaim. I wasn't thinking at the time. Yes, I see the problem. I was never in the first node-sequence that you visited. My first entry was twelve years ago – a sequence that missed your own time, it arose earlier than you were born, and out over the ocean as well, which is why it was missed. It's thirty years since the first node sequence occurred ... thirty years.'

He walked to the door, checked to see if anyone was outside and then called back softly, 'I have a message for you, Jaim, so don't go away. I mean it. If you want to find her again, stay put for a few minutes.'

Before I could do or say a thing, he was gone. I stood slowly and stared after him. I was reluctant to remain in the dormitory, but something about Garri aroused my interest, and my suspicions. That he knew something was too apparent, but that he was more than he seemed to be was a subtle insinuation that I was only now beginning to notice. Who was our fourth-millennium friend, I wondered?

Things were happening just a little too fast for my constitution, I decided. I wanted to be out in the city, shirking my therapist's duties, searching for Jayameeka; but all I would do, I knew, would be to run around aimlessly, and possibly attract the sort of attention I could well do without.

Herok's attention, for example.

Oh Herok! I felt so bitter; not at him, not even at what he represented. He could not have known that my daughter would become one of his prey . . . and it would, I had to convince myself, be unfair and unwise to tell him so.

I was not bitter at him, no; but at fate . . . at fate I was angry, at the twist, the cruelty of the orderly universe, at that was I furious! They could have spared me the agony . . . it was for so few weeks, so insignificant a number of days in the span of the world . . . I could have been spared such grief.

I looked at Jayameeka's picture. She was truly beautiful, and looked so like Margaretta that it was almost difficult to believe they were two people. But the differences were there, and I should have seen them. The wider nose, the slightly darker green of her eyes. Her youthfulness. How blind I had been; how susceptible to my dreams, that I should have believed Margaretta would not have aged at all!

If I stood in that fourth-millennium plaza I would be standing in the same time as Margaretta, but she was outside of my grasp, beyond me. Perhaps dead. Perhaps herself locked away. Perhaps hiding behind that wall of twenty years, the difference between us now.

I wept, of course. If I was maudlin, I make no excuses, nor any apology. It was right to weep, and very necessary, and after a few minutes I was calm again.

A chill went through me, then, as I remembered the night. The reconsummation of our love, the virginal tightness of Margaretta/Jayameeka . . . the nervousness . . . the look in her eyes . . .

Oh God. It was not quite an unbearable thought. I dared not look inside the bed . . . dared not! The sight of her blood would have driven me to despair.

And yet – for all my worry – she had *permitted* our union – in the full knowledge of who I was, she had permitted it? Was that an act of despair? Or of true love? Or a kiss, passed from Mar-

79

garetta to me, and communicated through the body of our mutual child?

Where was Garri? I couldn't wait about all day. There were only four hours before the first possible moment of the peak!

He arrived as secretively as he had left. He was carrying a package, concealed half by some black fabric and half by his stooped body. He came up to me and placed the item on my bunk.

Without a word he took off the fabric covering. It was a small head-set and a copper-coloured belt attached to it by a single cord.

He looked at me. I said, 'Her message. What was her message?'

'She's going down time,' said Garri. 'The main concentration of Security men will be policing the up-time nodes.'

'How do you know all this?'

Garri smiled, said simply, 'She told me.'

'Yes, but why? Why you? Who are you, Garri?'

He stared at me for a long time, and gradually the façade of innocence and naïvete dropped away. His eyes grew dark, his mouth solemn. 'The trouble is,' he said, 'one never knows how much a third-millennium person knows. You're a difficult period in history, the only period, really, where there's any substantial editing of information in-put. You know she's your daughter, and you know why, although she doesn't know you know. Part of her message to you was to tell you of her true identity. It's a social custom in our era to lose one's virginity to one's father, but I imagine there was a deeper, more inexplicable motivation for her action, don't you?'

I said nothing. Garri was building up to something.

'We knew each other, of course. She was being studied by the Institute where I work. What she represents, a woman born between two times, a woman perhaps free of the full restrictions of space-mind-time, is what myself and many others have been studying, and trying to achieve. There are many like her, though she was unplanned for. She has great strength of mind, is the best subject we have. I say we,' he smiled self-consciously, 'I don't mean we. My own work has been on . . . this,' he patted the apparatus. 'I became very close to Jayameeka, very close. She was severely restricted in the Institute, and I began to feel it was cruel, heartless – I began to revolt against it. After all, I thought. I'm making more progress than my colleagues . . .' again he patted the belt. 'So I helped her escape. It's as simple as that. I got her access to this node, but regrettably her illegal presence was discovered, though not my own participation. Her only chance is to beach herself – if it's possible . . .' again his strange smile : he knew full well whether or not it was possible to escape the node-sequences; it was information denied to my own time. 'Once beached we hope she will demonstrate her ability to move freely through time; for her sake, for our sake . . . I hope she has developed that ability. If she ever returns, I shall marry her. But my interest is solely in seeing her out of the criminal clutches of my own Institute.'

He stopped, then, and picked up the strange apparatus. After a moment he said, 'I really love her, Jaim. I know how you felt, now, leaving Margaretta all that time ago, knowing the wall that would separate you.'

I reached out and gripped his shoulder. 'I love her too, Garri; more than father to daughter, but not as lover to lover. I just need to be with her for a while, need to talk, to know she is safe. Garri, I must stop her making that run. It's selfish, I know. But I must stop her. Or go with her.'

He nodded. 'You can't stop her, Jaim. But go with her? With luck. And this is what will get you back.'

He held the belt towards me. 'What is it?' I asked.

'I imagine something very similar in principle to what is powering the Traveller.'

'A time machine?'

'Mechanical. Effective. Well tested, but it takes some real effort of mind. It will never be released, of course; it is the tool of the authority that guards these nodes and prevents unwarranted passing of information. My era developed it from your era's maths. The fifth millennium will begin to apply it to the policing of these frequent nodes of time.

'I told you, Jaim, that yours is a critical time in history. Before now the nodes have been virtually unknown; after now they are a part of life. This era is at the junction . . . denied the results of its own inquisitiveness. But that inquisitiveness will lead to this belt, and to the decision to mate individuals from different times. Until everything was fully tested we ourselves, a millennium hence, didn't know if we *could* develop time travel.'

'And you're giving this to me? Out of *friendship*?'

'Out of a desire to see Jayameeka safe, wherever she is.'

I was incredulous. I took the belt and the headpiece and turned them over in my fingers. Such power! Such potential in so small a fragment of material. 'And no strings ... no catches ...?'

He laughed. 'The age of paranoia was in the second millennium. No strings, Jaim. If you like, you are a final test for the belt; a run through time from the age of the Saurians. Trust me, Jaim. There is a recall mechanism – not well tested, I confess – with which I shall return the belt to my own hands within six subjective months. I'm not making a *gift*, merely a convenience!'

He instructed me on its use, a remarkably facile system of safety buttons, and a great deal of brain power. It would, if my own mind failed, be a boost to my projected brain waves to carry me out of the node and into the prehistoric past ... to 'beach' me, hopefully with Jayameeka safely in my arms.

'You understand,' said Garri finally, 'that you are now no longer a part of your own millennium, that you know too much about the future to live your life without a guardian ...'

I accepted what he said, grimly, unhappily.

I obtained breathing apparatus from the depository on the ground floor of my barracks, and strapped the lightweight system over the head-piece of the time machine. As I ran through the streets towards the centre I saw only a few others who had, in this time at least, opted for the legal excursion down-time to the acrid swamps of an era nearly (not quite) at the end of the Traveller's run. Those going into futurity would not need any special equipment since the air, after man's decline, was rich and sweet.

A Security man halted me as I ran, and warned me about going too close to the centre. I acknowledged the warning and took a moment's respite before walking a few paces further and coming into sight of the central area of the node.

Here the crowds were thick and just as monotonous, most staring at the intergalactic enigma (if that were indeed its nature). I searched for Jayameeka but not surprisingly failed to see her.

I jumped through time.

My passage was swift and remarkably easy. The blur of colour and sensation of roaring were more pronounced. I stopped and found myself in stone ruins, with green and wet countryside all around, and just a few travellers like myself walking and exploring. It was a cold day in the dawn of civilised man; beyond the wall of the node I could see undomesticated sheep. The ruins, chiselled stone and traces of wattle, were long deserted.

Back further and a strong and biting wind howled across the shrub-covered highland; trees were scattered about, and distantly the land was forest covered and impenetrable.

Five travellers, seated, talking together. As I watched, a sixth, from a very distant future time, slipped into sight and out again.

Back further. Motion through time still very easy and natural.

Sun, baking mudflats, lizard life and prowling mammals. They ran from me as I appeared. The topography of the world was changed, and now I was in a valley, and jagged rock hills rose about me. A river had once passed this way.

A shape flickered in and out of vision, a woman, far older than Jayameeka. As I stood in the heat and watched the shimmering air around me I could see the passage of many travellers. Distantly, hidden almost completely by an overhang of rock, was the black shape of the Traveller himself, unaware of his brief stop at the beginning of the Quaternary.

Back. Water.

And further ... storm clouds and the discharge of lightning. Granitic monoliths rising high above me, shadowy, grey, dimly seen. The heavy movement of animal life, a distant thundering as of water pouring down slopes. White ghosts from the future fading in and out of sight ...

A voice, shouting. Lightning flashes. Thunder, the crumble of rock, the roaring of a great beast, white teeth highlit in the electrically tense atmosphere.

Back. Calm, evening, vegetation of many colours. Moisture dripping from broad leaves.

A figure watching me from the jungle.

'Jayameeka!' I cried.

'Go back, Jaim,' she shrieked, and the tears were in her voice as well as her eyes. I ran towards her. 'You can't follow me,' she sobbed.

'Wait ...'

But she was gone, and I jumped after her, feeling the passage of the centuries measured against the stuttering of my heart. She had seemed surprised, shocked to see me. Had Garri lied to me after all?

Travel became difficult, the passing of the millennia slowed, and I froze, in a time of dinosaurian peak, breathing through my mask and staring into the thick, swampy landscape. The peak of the node had not yet arrived ... Jayameeka was struggling half in and half out of this time, a ghost form split between now and this location as it had been over a million years ago.

I waded through slush towards her, terrified that I might at any moment sink, or be consumed by some huge reptilian swamp dweller, but nothing occurred, save that the peak approached nearer and suddenly we both slipped a million years back in time.

A huge silver platform stood before me, rising out of the swamp, cutting brilliantly through the hazy, leafy air. All around me, half concealed, looking somehow very dead, were the ruins of a gigantic building, perhaps a station, perhaps a city. It was half submerged, but had lost no fragment of glitter, no ounce of sparkle.

Domes and towers, some of them twisted and bent by time and the impact of weather – great glass panels and the remnants of machines. Jayameeka was running along a buckled metal road-way, her feet leaving slimy imprints on the almost flawless ground beneath her. I waded through the mire and heaved myself up on to a ledge of metal, and dragged my soaking body up the steeply sloping surface until I reached level ground. I raced into a large room, where golden snakes hung coiled around tubular rafters, and climbed through the broken window that looked out upon the roadway. I followed Jayameeka as fast as I could, noticing as I ran the dark shape of the Traveller secure and settled in a pit in the middle of the building (idle thought: what was so special about this Traveller that he had his point of arrival marked by such a monument?). Protected against all ravaging agents, this was his last stop, perhaps, before he returned to his own kind, a single jump further into the past, to a moment that no human could reach, a moment beyond us all.

The seconds were racing past. I called for Jayameeka and saw her struggling against the unseen edge of the node. So close, but this far back the confinement of the node was smaller, tighter. There was dry ground above the swamp, and she was struggling to jump towards it from the overhanging metal roadway, but she seemed unable to pass through ...

A figure came into view off to my right. I heard a voice shout, 'Stop! Stop or I shoot!'

I could hardly believe what I heard. It was Herok, uniformed and protected, and he was levelling his handgun at the struggling shape of Jayameeka. I could see the tension in his form; the sure sign of a man about to kill . . .

'NO, HEROK!'

He faltered, glanced at me and realised who I was. 'Jaim! What the hell are you . . . STOP!' Still shouting at Jayameeka, about to kill at any moment.

'Don't shoot her, Herok,' I begged, and without realising it my own weapon was in my hands.

'Stay away, Jaim. Stay out of this . . .'

And without thinking, without bothering to argue any more, I levelled my gun and squeezed the trigger. At the last moment Herok realised what was happening and his mouth opened, his head turned, the gun in his hand fell limply to the roadway and he stared at me . . .

Too late.

My calm, unhurried shot took his head off at the lower jaw. I shot him as dead as the ruins into which his body tumbled, lost in the darkness of an alien structure and the swamp that was consuming it.

When I looked at Jayameeka she was watching me.

'Come on, Jaim . . .'

Distantly, all around, other shapes were materialising, some not fading in, some actually coming to rest in this era, anonymous, faceless travellers, each a potential threat.

As I ran towards my daughter she had turned again and was pushing through the wall. There was a tug at my body and my mind, the sensation of being drawn back up time, but I fought it . . . came closer to Jayameeka when . . . without a flash, without a scream, she was through the node . . . she had escaped the confines of distorted time and was free in the age of the giant reptiles.

Twenty seconds!

If the helmet failed, I had just twenty seconds to try and force my way out of the node. If any thoughts of *why* I should want to beach myself in the Cretaceous period occurred to me, I pushed them aside. To be with Jayameeka was the only thing of importance now—

Less than twenty seconds—

(as I ran three, four strides to the second)

—to achieve that which few man had ever succeeded in achieving.

The edge of the node held me back and I began to push, think-ing, mentally urging myself through the wall as hard as I could. And behind me—

'Hold it right there! Stop or we shoot!'

The air became filled with fire, and from each corner of my eye I saw the shapes of Security men bursting through from the future to try and stop my illegal breakout.

Jayameeka appeared before me, shooting calmly and care-fully through the edge of the node. The buzz and roar of blaster charges declined ...

Two seconds!

I was not going to make it ...

One second!

The pressure in front of me vanished and I sprawled upon the dry hard ground, felt the stillness of the air. Jayameeka stopped shooting and crouched beside me, stroking the hair from my face. She was smiling, but shaking her head. We looked into the node and saw the great wall of red and yellow fire spreading in front of us as the frustrated Security men shot towards us, hoping that a solitary charge might escape the confines of time.

Even through the filters the air was acrid. The ground shook with the passage of some beast. Its bass vocality was frightening.

The node faded, and with it the fire and the frustrated men of future ages. Just the swamp and the great metal ruin remained, and the threat of creatures of this time.

'You shouldn't have followed me,' said Jayameeka. But she was smiling.

'Garri told me you wanted me to ...'

'Garri? *He* told you?'

'He said you were friends ...'

Jayameeka laughed. 'Friends! He helped me escape for his own rotten ends. He's trapped us both in the past, got rid of me and if I can't travel through time as my ... experimenters, to call them kindly ... would hope I can do, having tuned my mind in ... well, you and me both are doomed to a very early grave, Jaim.'

I couldn't help smiling at her unintentional pun. I hugged her to me and then showed the belt, and explained its principle.

She gasped, looked incredulous, then stared at me. 'You've *really* been suckered, Jaim. That belt has never been tested, not prop-erly.' She laughed, then, almost hysterically. 'Used to the last. Me, you, used to the last. I'll bet, you know, that my whole escape was intricately planned, that every twist and turn I made trying to survive in the node was monitored and planned for.'

The ground shook again, but we took no notice. I fingered the belt controls, feeling dry-mouthed and apprehensive. A test pilot of sorts, I tried to think us three or four days into the future, holding tightly to Jayameeka as I went.

A tingle of electricity on the skin, an abrupt transition from dry day to wet night!

'It works!' I shouted. 'Garri *hasn't* let us down!'

Drenched, we hugged. Frozen, we jaunted through the Cretaceous. Laughing, we began the slow journey back to the third millennium after Christ.

We would take our time getting there.

VALLEY OF THE BUSHES

by Naomi Mitchison

WHO CAN forget Memoirs of a Spacewoman, *Naomi Mitchison's utterly delightful novel of sex and communication among the diverse races of our cosmos? And yet not for some years did I realise Lady Mitchison is the daughter of the late J B Haldane and, far from an unusually talented newcomer to writing, has in fact had something like eighty books published on an incredibly wide range of subjects.*

Now a sprightly seventy-eight, she is a member of the Highlands and Islands Advisory Council, Scotland, and also Mmarona (Mother) to the Bakgatla of Botswana. In the last year or two she seems to be returning to science fiction as this tight little piece is evidence. 'Valley of the Bushes' is the story of a remote community, in South America, perhaps, or Africa; who knows? One wonders what Lady Mitchison has seen on her travels that the rest of the world does not yet suspect....

Three times during the late summer the old woman made the hearths for the fires, carefully smoothing the special clay over them. The girls brought in the bushes, pulling them with great attention, root and all. Then on a calm day came the burning and at last the sifting of the ash. This was hand work and special songs went with it, always curiously muffled by the fine, beautifully coloured material of the masks which all wore on these occasions. The light ash was tossed and scattered and then came the sieving of the darker, heavier part and on the sieves, made and used for this alone, appeared the nodules of metal which had run together in the heat of the fire.

The girls and younger women learned the songs, some praising the cleverness of the plant which had gathered the precious and dangerous stuff out of the soil, some telling of their great-great-grandmother – but how very far back was she? – who, taking the shape of an enormous butterfly, first whispered to the plant and learned what it was doing. Sometimes these huge blue and bronze butterflies still came and all gathered round and watched and praised and were glad, speaking with low laughter to one another over what secrets might be being passed. There were many other butterflies that came and it was always possible that one of them might also one day pass on some simple and enormously important fact. A special butterfly: something or someone else disguised as a butterfly.

Yet for the moment all went well. The sifted nodules, praised and handled and washed like small infants, were taken downstream to the men, weighed and beaten together into such shapes as were considered luckiest. All the handlers, men and women, wore gloves, beautifully made of tenderest kid skin; these were stripped and left in running water, downstream of the village. Nor did anyone eat or drink during the hours of burning, sifting and packing. These rare metals which occur here and there through Earth's surface layers are often poisonous when their natural scatter is gathered into visible form. So it was in the valley. Fortunately, the effect on the lungs was minimal, though the masks were always worn.

After their shaping, the heavy pieces were packed into leaves and then into kid-skin cases; after that into baskets ready for their journey over the mountains. The traders at the far side were equally careful. What happened at a further stage of the trade was not their affair. On the journey back came presents for everyone. There were guns and silk and medicines, including spectacles for the elderly, tools of many kinds, down pillows and brandy and finer woollens and furs than any from their own valley; instamatic cameras and small expensive bottles of scent and torches with spare batteries and hand mirrors, watches, salt and sets of chessmen, for there was much chess played in the evenings; cases of such fruit as they did not grow and beautiful, sparkling, drinking glasses and fine Chinese washing bowls, jars of honey and ginger and new kinds of musical instruments, though they did not care for transistor radios since the sounds that came from them were uncouth and in jarring rhythms. Not seldom the men brought back plants which might prove useful: as the coffee plantation, the better bananas and nuts, the opium poppy to be used in moderation during the winter months and many roses. But never, never to encroach on the preferred ground of their own bushes.

Often they heard stories of wars and religions in the outer world and felt happy and cosy not to be part of it. They also heard about aeroplanes and helicopters and had seen many pictures of these both in war and peace. It was clear to them all that such things were not welcome. It was clear also that they might all the same come to the valley and that plans must be made accordingly. There was no surprise then when the speck in the sky was sighted and watched as it grew and came lower.

'This it? You're sure?'

'Yes, we're going to find out what we can. Then back. While the weather holds. These mountains—'

'Yes, next time. With the money raised. In force. But we have to have samples. There's a man coming!'

'Yes. Apparently unarmed. And several women. Looks all right.'

They tried several languages – both were good at this. The third man followed but said nothing – languages were not his thing. In fact he was a botanist or had been, but there had been an unfortunate incident involving a misclassification. So now he was doing a bit of trading, a bit of painting, making notes for a book that never got written, reading old copies of learned journals and trying to make up his mind whether or not to stay on. He kept wondering what truth there was in the story about the bushes and if so which they were. Certainly some plants, especially perhaps marine ones, but also a few in singularly unpleasing parts of Australia, have unsuspected powers of collecting minerals. But this particular one! The chelating agent must be most peculiar. Well, they must see. There were in any case some interesting botanical specimens around in the valley, quite apart from their particular interest.

The two crew men stayed by the 'copter, occupying themselves with the engine. All that had been arranged and paid for. The others went ahead. Quite soon communication was established. After all, those who came down to trade were bound to have a large vocabulary so the trading language served insofar as it could be stretched. It was not known what kind of government there was in the valley, but probably a chief and council in some form. Naturally gifts had been brought.

The man took them down to the main village; it was attractively built with well-smoothed timber and nicely trimmed thatch. There were even glass windows – trade, no doubt. More people, both men and women, the latter mostly elderly but handsome and well dressed with silk showing at neck and wrists of their heavy coats. They were brought into a large house where food and drink were offered and accepted, the gifts laid out and inspected with interest but not so far taken up by anyone. There did not appear to be a ruler of any kind.

The third man had hoped for a tour of inspection and yet it might be unwise to raise the question of the bushes so soon. As evening came on more food was brought and now the possibility of the visit to places of interest was raised. And what did they want to see? Ah, now, this was it. Although samples had not specifically been mentioned there seemed to be some embarrassment. All three were aware that the elderly women were listening – had they in fact understood? Did they know the trading language? Had they ever left the village? The men appeared to be quite pleased. 'What have they said?' the botanist asked. Suddenly he was thinking that if this expedition turned out as they all hoped, if above all he could get a specimen of the fabled bush, if he could isolate the chelating agents, he would make up his mind, he would go back, he would have a place again in the scientific world.

'Tomorrow, they say.'

'To see – everything? They admit that it is true?'

'Oh, they were quite open. Seems we shall have a conducted tour.'

'These old women—'

'Might be some younger ones tomorrow!'

The evening meal was delicious. Local herbs must have been extensively used in preparation of the game stew; the botanist tried to identify them by the smell, sniffing at the excellent gravy in his carved horn spoon. Beside him one of the elderly women patted his shoulder and smiled. There were comfortable rugs to sleep on and indeed it had been a somewhat anxious and tiring day. Now one could relax. They slept. The next morning they did not wake.

The men of the valley went back to the 'copter, this time with guns which they trained suddenly on the crewmen. 'Go!' they said.

'Where are the others?' one of the crew asked in the trading language but backing away towards the 'copter.

'They are staying here,' said one of the men. 'You go!'

The crewmen had wisely insisted on payment in advance so they got off as quickly as they could. It was a near thing getting over the mountains but they made it and in time reported to the police, not that anything was likely to be done.

The expedition was suitably and quietly interred. Several of the elderly women, appropriately veiled, went through the wailing as was only proper for guests. As the earth was being shovelled on it was noticed by one of the old ladies that a very large blue and bronze butterfly, that rare beautiful visitor, flitted out from the trees and dipped for a moment towards the moist loam before taking its way on.

'She has come once more to greet and say goodbye,' said the old lady, deeply satisfied.

AN INFINITE SUMMER

by Christopher Priest

'*I would have made a terrible accountant,*' *Chris Priest confessed. Back when we first met, in 1963, we were both studying for professions we didn't much care for, and subsequently neither of us stuck it for very long. But Chris took a bold decision; he had the urge to write science fiction and he was going to support himself by writing, even though at the time he had sold comparatively little.*

Against all advice he became a full-time freelance, without the cushions of royalty cheques from previous work to carry him through the hard times; against all odds (and they are high, if you like to eat occasionally), he succeeded.

Now Chris Priest is one of Britain's foremost writers of science fiction. His first novel, Indoctrinaire, *was nominated for the John W Campbell Award, and subsequent books have received an excellent critical response.* Inverted World *was a runner-up for the coveted Hugo Award in 1975. This current story is, I think, one of his very best to date.*

August, 1940.

There was a war on, but it made no difference to Thomas James Lloyd. The war was an inconvenience, and it restricted his freedom, but on the whole it was the least of his preoccupations. Misfortune had brought him to this violent age, and he wanted none of its crises. He was apart from it, shadowed by it.

He stood now on the bridge over the Thames at Richmond, resting his hands on the parapet and staring south along the river. The sun reflected up from it, and he took his sunglasses from a metal case in his pocket and put them on.

Night was the only relief from the tableaux of frozen time; dark glasses approximated the relief.

It seemed to Thomas Lloyd that it was not long since he had last stood untroubled on this bridge, although by deduction he knew that this was not so. The memory of the day was clear, itself a moment of frozen time, undiminished. He remembered

95

how he had stood here with his cousin, watching four young men from the town as they manhandled a punt upstream.

Richmond itself had changed from that time, but here by the river the view was much as he remembered it. Although there were more buildings along the banks, the meadows below Richmond Hill were untouched, and he could see the riverside walk disappearing around the bend in the river towards Twickenham.

For the moment the town was quiet. An air-raid alert had been sounded a few minutes before, and although there were still some vehicles moving through the streets, most pedestrians had taken temporary shelter inside shops and offices.

Lloyd had left them to walk again through the past.

He was a tall, well-built man, apparently young in years. He had been taken for twenty-five several times by strangers and Lloyd, a withdrawn, uncommunicative man, had allowed such errors to go uncorrected. Behind the dark glasses his eyes were still bright with the hopes of youth, but many tiny lines at the corners of his eyes, and a general sallowness to his skin, indicated that he was older. Even this, though, lent no clue to the truth. Thomas Lloyd had been born in 1881, and was now approaching sixty.

He took his watch from his waistcoat pocket, and saw that the time was a little after twelve. He turned to walk towards the pub on the Isleworth road, but then noticed a man standing by himself on the path beside the river. Even wearing the sunglasses, which filtered away the more intrusive reminders of past and future, Lloyd could see that it was one of the men he called freezers. This was a young man, rather plump and with prematurely balding hair. He had seen Lloyd, for as Lloyd looked down at him the young man turned ostentatiously away. Lloyd had nothing now to fear from the freezers, but they were always about and their presence never failed to make him uneasy.

Far away, in the direction of Barnes, Lloyd could hear another air-raid siren droning out its warning.

June, 1903.
The world was at peace, and the weather was warm. Thomas James Lloyd, recently down from Cambridge, twenty-one years of age, moustachioed, light of tread, walked gaily through the trees that grew across the side of Richmond Hill.

It was a Sunday and there were many people about. Earlier in the day Thomas had attended church with his father and mother and sister, sitting in the pew that was reserved traditionally for the Lloyds of Richmond. The house on the Hill had belonged to the family for more than two hundred years, and William Lloyd, the present head of the family, owned most of the houses on the Sheen side of town as well as administering one of the largest businesses in the whole of Surrey. A family of substance indeed, and Thomas James Lloyd lived in the knowledge that one day the substance would be his by inheritance.

Worldly matters thus assured, Thomas felt free to divert his attention to activities of a more important nature; namely, Charlotte Carrington and her sister Sarah.

That one day he would marry one of the two sisters had been an inevitability long acknowledged by both families, although precisely which of the two it would be had been occupying his thoughts for many weeks.

There was much to choose between the two – or so Thomas himself considered – but if his choice had been free then his mind would have been at rest. Unfortunately for him it had been made plain by the girls' parents that it would be Charlotte who would make the better wife for a future industrialist and landowner, and in many ways this was so. The difficulty arose because Thomas had fallen impetuously for her younger sister Sarah, a state of affairs of absolutely no moment to Mrs. Carrington.

Charlotte, twenty years of age, was an undeniably handsome girl, and Thomas much enjoyed her company. She appeared to be prepared to accept a proposal of marriage from him, and to be fair she was endowed with much grace and intelligence, but whenever they had been together neither had had much of interest to say to the other. Charlotte was an ambitious and emancipated girl – for so she styled herself – and was constantly reading historical tracts. Her one consuming interest was in touring the various churches of Surrey to take brass-rubbings from the plates there. Thomas, a liberal and understanding young man, was pleased she had found a hobby, but could not own to any mutual interest.

Sarah Carrington was an altogether different proposition. Two years younger than her sister, and thus, by her mother's estimation, not yet eligible for marriage (or not, at least, until a husband had been found for Charlotte), Sarah was at once a person to be coveted by virtue of her unavailability, and yet also a delightful personality in her own right. When Thomas had first paid visits to Charlotte, Sarah was still being finished at school, but by astute questioning of Charlotte and his own sister, Thomas had discovered that Sarah liked to play tennis and croquet, was a keen bicyclist, and was acquainted with all the latest dance-steps. A surreptitious glance into the family's photographic album had established that she was also astoundingly beautiful. This last aspect of her he had confirmed for himself at their first meeting, and he had promptly fallen in love with her. Since then he had contrived to transfer his attentions, and with no small measure of success. Twice already he had spoken to her alone . . . no minor achievement when one considered the enthusiasm with which Mrs. Carrington encouraged Thomas always to be with Charlotte. Once he had been left alone with Sarah for a few minutes in the Carringtons' drawing-room, and on the second occasion he had managed a few words with her during a family picnic. Even on this brief acquaintance, Thomas had become convinced that he would settle for no less a wife than Sarah.

So it was that on this Sunday Thomas's mood was full of light, for by a most agreeable contrivance he had ensured himself at least an hour alone with Sarah.

The instrument of this contrivance was one Waring Lloyd, a cousin of his. Waring had always seemed to Thomas a most unconscionable oaf, but remembering that Charlotte had once remarked on him (and feeling that each would be eminently suited to the other), Thomas had proposed a riverside stroll for the afternoon. Waring, suitably confided in, would delay Charlotte while they walked, so allowing Thomas and Sarah to go on ahead.

Thomas was several minutes early for the rendezvous, and paced to and fro good-naturedly while waiting for his cousin. It was cooler by the river, for the trees grew right down to the water's edge, and several of the ladies walking along the path behind the boathouse had folded their parasols and were clutching shawls about their shoulders.

When at last Waring appeared, the two cousins greeted each other amiably – more so than at any time in the recent past – and debated whether they should cross by the ferry, or walk the long way round by the bridge. There was still plenty of time in hand, so they opted for the latter course.

Thomas once again reminded Waring of what was to happen during the stroll, and Waring confirmed that he understood. The arrangement was no sacrifice to him, for he found Charlotte no less delightful than Sarah, and would doubtless find much to say to the older girl.

Later, as they crossed Richmond Bridge to the Middlesex side of the river, Thomas paused, resting his hands on the stone parapet of the bridge. He was watching four young men struggling ineptly with a punt, trying to manoeuvre it against the stream towards the side, while on the bank two older men shouted conflicting instructions.

August, 1940.
'You'd better take cover, sir. Just in case.'

Thomas Lloyd was startled by the voice at his side, and he turned. It was an air-raid warden, an elderly man in a dark uniform. On his shoulder, and stencilled on his metal helmet, were the letters A.R.P. In spite of his polite tone of voice he was looking suspiciously at Lloyd. The part-time work Lloyd had been doing in Richmond paid barely enough for food and lodgings, and what little spare there was usually went on drink; he was still wearing substantially the same clothes as he had five years ago, and they were the worse for wear.

'Is there going to be a raid?' Lloyd said.

'Never can tell. Jerry's still bombing the ports, but he'll start on the towns any day now.'

They both glanced towards the sky in the south-east. There, high in the blue, were several white vapour-trails curling, but no other evidence of the German bombers everyone so feared.

'I'll be safe,' Lloyd said. 'I'm going for a walk. I'll be away from the houses if a raid starts.'

'Thats all right, sir. If you meet anyone else out there, remind them there's an alert on.'

'I'll do that.'

The warden nodded to him, then walked slowly towards the town. Lloyd raised his sunglasses for a moment and watched him.

A few yards from where they had been standing was one of the freezers' tableaux: two men and a woman. When he had first noticed this tableau Lloyd had inspected the people carefully, and had judged by their clothes that they must have been frozen at some time in the mid-19th century. This tableau was the oldest he had so far discovered, and as such was of especial interest to him. He had learned that the moment of a tableau's erosion was unpredictable. Some tableaux lasted for several years, others only a day or two. The fact that this one had survived for at least ninety years indicated just how erratic the erosions were.

The three frozen people were halted in their walk directly in front of the warden, who hobbled along the pavement towards them. As he reached them he showed no sign of awareness, and in a moment had passed right through them.

Lloyd lowered his sunglasses, and the image of the three people became vague and ill-defined.

June, 1903.
When Waring's prospects were compared with those of Thomas they seemed unremarkable, but by normal standards they were nonetheless considerable. Accordingly, Mrs. Carrington (who knew more about the distribution of the Lloyd wealth than anyone outside immediate family circles) greeted Waring with civility.

The two young men were offered a glass of cold lemon tea, and then asked for their opinion on some matter concerning an herbaceous border. Thomas, by now well used to Mrs. Carrington's small talk, couched his reply in a few words, but Waring, anxious to please, set forth into a detailed response. He was still speaking knowledgeably of replanting and bedding when the girls appeared. They walked out through the french window and came across the lawn towards them.

Seen together it was obvious that the two were sisters, but to Thomas's eager eye one girl's beauty easily outshone the other's. Charlotte's expression was more earnest, and her bearing more practical. Sarah affected a modesty and timorousness (although Thomas knew it to be just an affectation), and her smile when she saw the young men was enough to convince Thomas that from this moment his life would be an eternity of summer.

Twenty minutes passed while the four young people and the girls' mother walked about the garden. Thomas, at first impatient to put his scheme to the test, managed after a few minutes to control himself. He had noticed that both Mrs. Carrington and Charlotte were amused by Waring's conversation, and this was an unexpected bonus. After all, the whole afternoon lay ahead, and these minutes were being well spent!

At last they were released from their courtesies, and the four set off for their planned stroll.

The girls each carried a sunshade: Charlotte's was white, Sarah's was pink. As they went through the grounds towards the riverside walk the girls' dresses rustled on the long grass, although

Charlotte raised her skirt a little, for she said that grass so stained cotton.

Approaching the river they heard the sounds of other people: children calling, a girl and a man from the town laughing together, and a rowing-eight striking in unison to the cox's instructions. As they came to the riverside path, and the two young men helped the girls over a stile, a mongrel dog leaped out of the water some twenty yards away and shook itself with great gusto.

The path was not wide enough for them to walk abreast, and so Thomas and Sarah took the lead. Just once he was able to catch Waring's eye, and the other gave the slightest of nods.

A few minutes later, Waring delayed Charlotte to show her a swan and some cygnets swimming by the reeds, and Thomas and Sarah walked slowly on ahead.

By now they were some distance from the town, and meadows lay on either side of the river.

August, 1940.

The pub was set back a short distance from the road, with an area in front of it laid with paving-stones. On these, before the war, there had been five circular metal tables where one could drink in the open air, but they had been removed for scrap-iron during the last winter. Apart from this, and the fact that the windows had been criss-crossed with tape in Home Office approved fashion, to prevent glass splinters flying, there was no outward sign that business was not normal.

Inside Lloyd ordered a pint of bitter, and took it with him to one of the tables.

He sipped the drink, then regarded the other occupants of the bar.

Apart from himself and the barmaid there were four other people present. Two men sat morosely together at one table, half-empty glasses of stout before them. Another man sat alone at a table by the door. He had a newspaper on the table before him, and was staring at the crossword.

The fourth person, who stood against one of the walls, was a freezer. This one, Lloyd noted, was a woman. She, like the men freezers, wore a drab grey overall, and held one of the freeze instruments. This was shaped rather like a modern portable camera, and was carried on a lanyard strung around the neck, but it was much larger than a camera and was approximately cubical in shape. At the front, where on a camera would be a viewfinder and lens, there was a rectangular strip of white glass, apparently opaque or translucent, and it was through this that the freezing-beam was projected.

Lloyd, still wearing his dark glasses, could only just see the woman. She did not seem to be looking in his direction, but after a few seconds she stepped back through the wall and disappeared from his sight.

He noticed that the barmaid was watching him, and as soon as she had caught his eye she spoke to him.

'D'you think they're coming this time?'

'I shouldn't care to speculate,' Lloyd said, not wishing to be drawn into conversation. He took several mouthfuls of the beer, wanting to finish it and be on his way.

'These sirens have ruined the trade,' the barmaid said. 'One after the other, all day and sometimes in the evenings too. And it's always a false alarm.'

'Yes,' Lloyd said.

She continued with her complaints for a few more seconds, but then someone called her from the other bar and she went to serve him. Lloyd was greatly relieved, for he disliked speaking to people here. He had felt isolated for too long, and had never mastered the modern way of conversation. Quite often he was misunderstood, for it was his way to speak in the more formal manner of his own contemporaries.

He was regretting having delayed. This would have been a good time to go to the meadows, for while the air-raid alert was on there would be only a few people about. He disliked not being alone when he walked by the river.

He drank the rest of his beer, then stood up and walked towards the door.

As he did so he noticed for the first time that there was a recent tableau by the door. He did not seek out the tableaux, for he found their presence disturbing, but new ones were nevertheless of interest.

There were two men and a woman seeming to sit at a table; the image of them was indistinct, and so Lloyd took off his sunglasses. At once the brilliance of the tableau surprised him, seeming to overshadow the man who still sat regarding his crossword at the far end of the table.

One of the two frozen men was younger than the other two people, and he sat slightly apart. He was smoking, for a cigarette lay on the edge of the table, the end overhanging the wooden surface by a few millimetres. The older man and the woman were together, for the woman's hand was held in the man's, and he was bending forward to kiss her wrist. His lips rested on her arm, and his eyes were closed. The woman, still slim and attractive although apparently well into her forties, seemed amused by this for she was smiling, but she was not watching her friend. Instead, she was looking across the table at the younger man, who, beer-glass raised to his mouth, was watching the kiss with interest. On the table between them was the man's untouched glass of bitter, and the woman's glass of port. They had been eating potato crisps, for a crumpled paper bag and the blue salt-packet lay in the ash-tray. The smoke from the young man's cigarette, grey and curling, was motionless in the air, and a piece of ash, falling towards the ground, hovered a few inches above the carpet.

'You want something, mate?' It was the man with the cross-word.

Lloyd put on his sunglasses again with unseemly haste, realising that for the last few seconds he had been seeming to stare at the man.

'I beg your pardon,' he said, and fell back on the excuse he gave when such embarrassments occurred. 'I thought for a moment I recognised you.'

The man peered myopically up at him. 'Never seen you before in my life.'

Lloyd affected a vacant nod, and passed on towards the door. For a moment he caught a glimpse again of the three frozen victims. The young man with the beer-glass, watching coolly; the man kissing, bent over so that his upper body was almost horizontal; the woman smiling, watching the young man and enjoying the attention she was being paid; the cigarette smoke static.

Lloyd went through the door, and into the sunshine.

June, 1903.
'Your mama wishes me to marry your sister,' Thomas said.
  'I know. It is not what Charlotte desires.'
'Nor I. May I enquire as to your feelings on the matter?'
'I am in accord, Thomas.'
They were walking along slowly, about three feet apart from

each other. Both stared at the gravel of the path as they walked, not meeting the other's eyes. Sarah was turning her parasol through her fingers, causing the tassels to swirl and tangle. Now they were in the riverside meadows they were almost alone, although Waring and Charlotte were following about two hundred yards behind.

'Would you say that we were strangers, Sarah?'

'By what standards do you mean?' She had paused a little before responding.

'Well, for instance this is the first occasion on which we have been allowed any degree of intimacy together.'

'And that by a contrivance,' Sarah said.

'What do you mean?'

'I saw you signal to your cousin.'

Thomas felt himself go a little red, but he considered that in the brightness and warmth of the afternoon a flush would go unnoticed. On the river the rowing-eight had turned, and were now passing them again.

After a few moments, Sarah said: 'I am not avoiding your question, Thomas. I am considering whether or not we are strangers.'

'Then what do you say?'

'I think we know each other a little.'

'I should be glad to see you again, Sarah. Without the need for contrivance, that is.'

'Charlotte and I will speak to Mama. You have already been much discussed, Thomas, although not as yet with Mama. You need not fear for hurting my sister's feelings, for although she likes you she does not yet feel ready for marriage.'

Thomas, his pulse racing, felt a rush of confidence within him.

'And you, Sarah?' he said. 'May I continue to court you?'

She turned away from him then, and stepped through the long grass beside the edge of the path. He saw the long sweep of her skirt, and the shining pink circle of her parasol. Her left hand dangled at her side, brushing lightly against her skirt.

She said: 'I find your advances most welcome, Thomas.'

Her voice was faint, but the words reached his ears as if she had pronounced them clearly in a silent room.

Thomas's response was immediate. He swept his boater from his head, and opened his arms wide.

'My dearest Sarah,' he cried. 'Will you marry me?'

She turned to face him and for a moment she was still, regarding him seriously. Her parasol rested on her shoulder, no longer turning. Then, seeing that he was in earnest, she smiled a little, and Thomas saw that she too had allowed a blush of pink to colour her cheeks.

'Yes, of course I will,' Sarah said.

She stepped towards him extending her left hand, and Thomas, his straw hat still held high, reached forward with his right hand to take hers.

Neither Thomas nor Sarah could have seen that in that moment a man had stepped forward from beside the water's edge, and was levelling at them a small black instrument.

August, 1940.

The all-clear had not sounded, but the town seemed to be returning to life. Traffic was crossing Richmond Bridge, and a short distance down the road towards Isleworth a queue was forming outside a grocer's shop while a delivery-van was parked alongside the kerb. Now that he was at last setting off on his daily walk, Thomas Lloyd felt more at ease with the tableaux, and he took off his dark glasses for the last time and returned them to their case.

In the centre of the bridge was the overturning carriage. The driver, a gaunt middle-aged man wearing a green coat and shiny black top hat, had his left arm raised. In his hand he was holding the whip, and the lash snaked up over the bridge in a graceful curve. His right hand was already releasing the reins, and was reaching forward towards the hard road-surface in a desperate attempt to soften the impact of his fall. In the open compartment at the rear was an elderly lady, much powdered and veiled, wearing a black velvet coat. She had been thrown sideways from her seat as the wheel-axle broke, and was holding up her hands in fright. Of the two horses in harness, one was apparently unaware of the accident, and had been frozen in mid-stride. The other, though, had tossed back its head and raised both its forelegs. Its nostrils were flaring, and behind the blinkers its eyes were rolled back.

As Lloyd crossed the road a red G.P.O. van drove through the tableau, the driver quite unaware of its presence.

Two of the freezers were waiting at the top of the shallow

ramp which led down to the riverside walk, and as Lloyd turned to follow the path towards the distant meadows, the two men walked a short distance behind him.

June, 1903, to January, 1935.
The summer's day, with its two young lovers imprisoned, became a moment extended.

Thomas James Lloyd, straw hat raised in his left hand, his other hand reaching out. His right knee was slightly bent, as if he were about to kneel, and his face was full of happiness and expectation. A breeze seemed to be ruffling his hair, for three strands stood on end, but these had been dislodged when he removed his hat. A tiny winged insect, which had settled on his lapel, was frozen in its moment of flight, an instinct to escape too late.

A short distance away stood Sarah Carrington. The sun fell across her face, highlighting the locks of auburn hair that fell from beneath her bonnet. One foot, stepping towards Thomas, showed itself beneath the hem of her skirt, shod in a buttoned boot. Her right hand was lifting a pink parasol away from her shoulder, as if she were about to wave it in joy. She was laughing, and her eyes, soft and brown, gazed with affection at the young man before her.

Their hands were extended towards each other's. Sarah's left hand was an inch from his right, her fingers already curling in anticipation of holding his.

Thomas's fingers, reaching out, revealed by irregular white patches that until an instant before his fists had been clenched in anxious tension.

The whole: the long grass moist after a shower a few hours before, the pale brown gravel of the path, the wild flowers that grew in the meadow, the adder that basked not four feet from the couple, the clothes, their skin ... all were rendered in colours bleached and saturated with preternatural luminosity.

August, 1940.
There was a sound of aircraft in the air.

Although aircraft were unknown in his time, Thomas Lloyd had now grown accustomed to them. He understood that before the war there had been civilian aircraft, but he had never seen any of these, and since then the only ones he had seen were warplanes.

Like everyone else of the time he was familiar with the sight of the high black shapes, and with the curious droning, throbbing sound of the enemy bombers. Each day air-battles were being fought over south-east England; sometimes the bombers evaded the fighters, sometimes not.

He glanced up at the sky. While he had been inside the pub, the vapour-trails he had seen earlier had disappeared; a new pattern of white had appeared, however, more recently made, further to the north.

Lloyd walked down the Middlesex side of the river. Looking directly across the river he saw how the town had been extended since his day: on the Surrey side of the river the trees which had once concealed the houses were mostly gone, and in their place were shops and offices. On this side, where houses had been set back from the river, more had been built close to the bank. As far as he could see, only the wooden boathouse had survived intact from his time, and that was badly in need of a coat of paint.

He was at the focus of past, present and future: only the boathouse and the river itself were as clearly defined as he. The freezers, from some unknown period of the future, as ethereal to ordinary men as their wishful dreams, moved like shadows through light, stealing sudden moments with their incomprehensible devices. The tableaux themselves, frozen, isolated, insubstantial, waiting in an eternity of silence for those people of the future generation to see them.

Encompassing all was a turbulent present, obsessed with war.

Thomas Lloyd, of neither past nor present, saw himself as a product of both, and a victim of the future.

Then, from high above the town, there came the sound of an explosion and a roar of engines, and the present impinged on Lloyd's consciousness. A British fighter-plane banked away towards the south, and a German bomber fell burning towards the ground. After a few seconds two men escaped from the aircraft, and their parachutes opened.

January, 1935.
As if waking from a dream, Thomas experienced a moment of recall and recognition, but in an instant it was gone.

He saw Sarah before him, reaching towards him; he saw the

bright garishness of the heightened colours; he saw the stillness of the frozen summer's day.

It faded as he looked, and he cried out Sarah's name. She made no move or reply, stayed immobile, and the light around her darkened.

Thomas pitched forward, a great weakness overcoming his limbs, and he fell to the ground.

It was night, and snow lay thickly on the meadows beside the Thames.

August, 1940.

Until the moment of its final impact, the bomber fell in virtual silence. Both engines had stopped, although only one was on fire, and flame and smoke poured from the fuselage, leaving behind a thick black trail across the sky. The 'plane crashed by the bend in the river, and there was a huge explosion. Meanwhile, the two Germans who had escaped from the aircraft drifted down across Richmond Hill, swaying beneath their parachutes.

Lloyd shaded his eyes with his hands, and watched to see where they would land. One had been carried further by the aircraft before jumping and was much nearer, falling slowly towards the river.

The Civil Defence authorities in the town were evidently alert, for within a few moments of the parachutes appearing, Lloyd heard the sound of police- and fire-bells.

There was a movement a short distance from Lloyd, and he turned. The two freezers who had been following him had been joined by two others, one of whom was the woman he had seen inside the pub. The freezer who seemed to be the youngest had already raised his device, and was pointing it across the river, but the other three were saying something to him. (Lloyd could see their lips moving, and the expressions on their faces, but, as always, he could not hear them.) The young man shrugged away the restraining hand of one of the others, and walked down the bank to the edge of the water.

One of the Germans came down near the edge of Richmond Park, and was lost to sight as he fell beyond the houses built near the crest of the Hill; the other, buoyed up temporarily by a sudden updraught, drifted out across the river itself, and was now only some fifty feet in the air. Lloyd could see the German aviator pulling on the cords of his parachute, trying desperately to steer himself towards the bank. As air spilled from the white shroud, he fell more quickly.

The young freezer by the edge of the river was levelling his device, apparently aiming it with the aid of a reflex sight built into the instrument. A moment later the German's efforts to save himself from falling into the water were rewarded in a way he could never have anticipated: ten feet above the surface of the water, his knees raised to take the brunt of the impact, one arm waving, the German was frozen in flight.

The freezer lowered his instrument, and Lloyd stared across the water at the hapless man suspended in the air.

January, 1935.

The transformation of a summer's day into a winter's night was the least of the changes that Thomas Lloyd discovered on regaining consciousness. In what had been for him a few seconds he had moved from a world of stability, peace and prosperity to one where dynamic and violent situations obtained. In that same short moment of time, he himself had lost the security of his assured future, and become a pauper. Most traumatically of all, he had never been allowed to take to its fruition the surge of love he had felt for Sarah.

Night was the only relief from the tableaux, and Sarah was still held in frozen time.

He recovered consciousness shortly before dawn, and, not understanding what had happened to him, walked slowly back towards Richmond town. The sun had risen shortly after, and as light struck the tableaux that littered the paths and roads, and as it struck the freezers who constantly moved in their half-world of intrusive futurity, Lloyd realised neither that in these lay the cause of his own predicament, nor that his perception of the images was itself a product of his experience.

In Richmond he was found by a policeman, and was taken to hospital. Here, treated for the pneumonia he had contracted as he lay in the snow, and later for the amnesia that seemed the only explanation for his condition, Thomas Lloyd saw the freezers moving through the wards and corridors. The tableaux were here too: a dying man falling from his bed; a young nurse – dressed in the uniform of fifty years before – frozen as she walked from a ward, a deep frown creasing her brow; a child throwing a ball in the garden by the convalescent wing.

As he was nursed back to physical health, Lloyd became obsessed with a need to return to the meadows by the river, and before he was fully recovered he discharged himself and went directly there.

By then the snow had melted, but the weather was still cold and a white frost lay on the ground. Out by the river, where a bank of grass grew thickly beside the path, was a frozen moment of summer, and in its midst was Sarah.

He could see her, but she could not see him; he could take the hand that was rightly his to take, but his fingers would pass through the illusion; he could walk around her, seeming to step through the green summer grasses, and feel the cold of the frozen soil penetrating the thin soles of his shoes.

And as night fell so the moment of the past became invisible, and Thomas was relieved of the agony of the vision.

Time passed, but there was never a day when he did not walk along the riverside path, and stand again before the image of Sarah, and reach out to take her hand.

August, 1940.

The German parachutist hung above the river, and Lloyd looked again at the freezers. They were apparently still criticising the youngest of them for his action, and yet seemed fascinated with his result. It was certainly one of the most dramatic tableaux Lloyd himself had seen.

Now that the man had been frozen it was possible to see that his eyes were tightly closed, and that he was holding his nose with his fingers in anticipation of his plunge. In addition, it now became clear that he had been wounded in the aircraft, because blood was staining his flying-jacket. The tableau was at once amusing and poignant, a reminder to Lloyd that, however unreal this present might be to him, it was no illusion to the people of the time.

In a moment Lloyd understood the particular interest of the freezers in this unfortunate airman, for without warning the pocket of frozen time eroded and the young German plunged into the river. The parachute billowed and folded in on top of him. As he surfaced he thrashed his arms wildly, trying to free himself of the constraining cords.

It was not the first time Lloyd had seen a tableau erode, but he had never before seen it happen so soon after freezing. It had always seemed to him a matter of chance, but having seen the distance from which the beam had been released – the airman had been at least fifty yards away – he surmised that the time a tableau survived was probably dependent on how close the subject was to the freezer. (He himself had escaped from his own tableau; had Sarah been nearer the freezer when the beam was released?)

In the centre of the river the German had succeeded in freeing himself of the parachute, and was swimming slowly towards the opposite bank. His descent must have been observed by the authorities, because even before he reached the sloping landing-stage of the boathouse, four policemen had appeared from the direction of the road, and helped him out of the water. He made no attempt to resist capture but lay weakly on the ground, awaiting the arrival of an ambulance.

Lloyd remembered the only other time he had seen a tableau erode quickly. A freezer had acted to prevent a traffic-accident: a man stepping carelessly into the path of a car had been frozen in mid-step. Although the driver of the car had stopped abruptly, and had looked around in amazement for the man he thought he had been about to kill, he had evidently assumed that he had imagined the incident, for he eventually drove off again. Only Lloyd, with his ability to see the tableaux, could still see the man: stepping back, arms flailing in terror, still seeing too late the oncoming vehicle. Three days later, when Lloyd returned to the place, the tableau had eroded and the man was gone. He, like Lloyd – and now the German aviator – would be moving through a half-world, one where past, present and future co-existed uneasily.

Lloyd watched the shroud of the parachute drift along the river until at last it sank, and then turned away to continue his walk to the meadows. As he did so he realised that even more of the freezers had appeared on this side of the river, and were walking behind him, following him.

As he reached the bend in the river, from which point he always gained his first sight of Sarah, he saw that the bomber had crashed in the meadows. The explosion of its impact had set fire to the grass, and the smoke from this, together with that from the burning wreckage, obscured his view.

January, 1935, to August, 1940.
Thomas Lloyd never again left Richmond. He lived inexpensively, found occasional work, tried not to be outstanding in any way.

What of the past? He discovered that on 22nd June, 1903, his apparent disappearance with Sarah had led to the conclusion that he had absconded with her. His father, William Lloyd, head of the noted Richmond family, had disowned him. Colonel and Mrs. Carrington had announced a reward for his arrest, but in 1910 they had moved away from the area. Thomas also discovered that his cousin Waring had never married Charlotte, and that he had emigrated to Australia. His own parents were both dead, there was no means of tracing his sister, and the family home had been sold and demolished.

(On the day he read the files of the local newspaper, he stood with Sarah, overcome with grief.)

What of the future? It was pervasive, intrusive. It existed on a plane where only those who were frozen and released could sense it. It existed in the form of men who came to freeze the images of the present.

(On the day he first understood what the shadowy men he called freezers might be, he stood beside Sarah, staring around protectively. That day, as if sensing Lloyd's realisation, one of the freezers had walked along the river-bank, watching the young man and his time-locked sweetheart.)

What of the present? Lloyd neither cared for the present nor shared it with its occupants. It was violent, alien, frightening. The machines and men were threatening. It was, to him, as vague a presence as the other two dimensions. Only the past and its frozen images were real.

(On the day he first saw a tableau erode he ran all the way to the meadows, and stood long into the evening, trying ceaselessly for the first sign of substance in Sarah's outstretched hand.)

August, 1940.
Only in the riverside meadows, where the town was distant and the houses were concealed by trees, did Thomas ever feel at one with the present. Here past and present fused, for little had changed since his day. Here he could stand before the image of Sarah and fancy himself still on that summer's day in 1903, still the young man with raised straw hat and slightly bended knee. Here too he rarely saw any of the freezers, and the few tableaux visible (further along the walk an elderly fisherman had been time-locked

as he pulled a trout from the stream; towards the distant houses of Twickenham, a little boy in a sailor-suit walked sulkily with his nanny) could be accepted as a natural part of the world he had known.

Today, though, the present had intruded violently. The exploding bomber had scattered fragments of itself across the meadows. Black smoke from the wreckage spread in an oily cloud across the river, and the smouldering grass poured white smoke to drift beside it. Much of the ground had already been blackened by fire.

Sarah was invisible to him, lost somewhere in the smoke.

Thomas paused, and took a kerchief from his pocket. He stooped by the river's edge and soaked it in the water, then, after wringing it out, he held it over his nose and mouth.

He glanced behind him and saw that there were now eight of the freezers with him. They were paying no attention to him, and walked on while he prepared himself, insensible to the smoke. They passed through the burning grass, and walked towards the main concentration of wreckage. One of the freezers was already making some kind of adjustment to his device.

A breeze had sprung up in the last few minutes, and it caused the smoke to move away smartly from the fires, staying lower on the ground. As this happened, Thomas saw the image of Sarah above the smoke. He hurried towards her, alarmed by the proximity of the burning aircraft, even as he knew that neither fire, explosion nor smoke could harm her.

His feet threw up smouldering grasses as he went towards her, and at times the variable wind caused the smoke to swirl about his head. His eyes were watering, and although his wetted kerchief acted as a partial filter against the grass-smoke, when the oily fumes from the aircraft gusted around him he choked and gagged on the acrid vapours.

At length he decided to wait; Sarah was safe inside her cocoon of frozen time, and there was no conceivable point to his suffocating simply to be with her, when in a few minutes the fire would burn itself out.

He retreated to the edge of the burning area, rinsed out his kerchief in the river, and sat down to wait.

The freezers were exploring the wreckage with the greatest interest, apparently drifting through the flames and smoke to enter the deepest parts of the conflagration.

There came the sound of a bell away to Thomas's right, and in a moment a fire-tender halted in the narrow lane that ran along the distant edge of the meadows. Several firemen climbed down, and stood looking across the field at the wreckage. At this Thomas's heart sank, for he realised what was to follow. He had sometimes seen photographs in the newspapers of crashed German aircraft; they were invariably placed under military guard until the pieces could be taken away for examination. If this were to happen here it would deny him access to Sarah for several days.

For the moment, though, he would still have a chance to be with her. He was too far away to hear what the firemen were saying, but it looked as if no attempt was going to be made to put out the fire. Smoke still poured from the fuselage, but the flames had died down, and most of the smoke was coming from the grass. With no houses in the vicinity, and with the wind blowing towards the river, there was little likelihood the fire would spread.

He stood up again, and walked quickly towards Sarah.

In a few moments he had reached her, and she stood before him: eyes shining in the sunlight, parasol lifting, arm extending. She was in a sphere of safety; although smoke blew through her, the grasses on which she stood were green and moist and cool. As he had done every day for more than five years, Thomas stood facing her and waited for a sign of the erosion of her tableau. He stepped, as he had frequently done before, into the area of the time-freeze. Here, although his foot appeared to press on the grasses of 1903, a flame curled around his leg and he was forced to step back quickly.

Thomas saw some of the freezers coming towards him. They had apparently inspected the wreckage to their satisfaction, and judged none of it worth preserving in a time-freeze. Thomas tried to disregard them, but their sinister silence could not be forgotten easily.

The smoke poured about him, rich and heady with the smells of burning grass, and he looked again at Sarah. Just as time had frozen about her in that moment, so it had frozen about his love for her. Time had not diminished, it had preserved.

The freezers were watching him. Thomas saw that the eight vague figures, standing not ten feet away from him, were looking at him with interest. Then, on the far side of the meadow, one of the firemen shouted something at him. He would seem to be standing here alone; no one could see the tableaux, no one knew of the freezers. The fireman walked towards him, waving an arm, telling him to move away. It would take him a minute or more to reach them, and that was time enough for Thomas.

One of the freezers stepped forward, and in the heart of the smoke Thomas saw the captured summer begin to dim. Smoke curled up around Sarah's feet, and flame licked through the moist, time-frozen grasses around her ankles. He saw the fabric at the bottom of her skirt begin to scorch.

And her hand, extended towards him, lowered.

The parasol fell to the ground.

Sarah's head drooped forward, but immediately she was conscious . . . and the step towards him, commenced thirty-seven years before, was concluded.

'Thomas?' Her voice was clear, untouched.

He rushed towards her.

'Thomas! The smoke! What is happening?'

'Sarah . . . my love!'

As she went into his arms he realised that her skirt had taken fire, but he placed his arms around her shoulders and hugged her intimately and tenderly. He could feel her cheek, still warm from the blush of so long ago, nestling against his. Her hair, falling loose beneath her bonnet, lay across his face, and the pressure of her arms around his waist was no less than that of his own.

Dimly, he saw a grey movement beyond them, and in a moment the noises were stilled and the smoke ceased to swirl. The flame which had taken purchase on the hem of her skirt now died, and the summer sun which warmed them shone lightly in the tableau. Past and future became one, the present faded, life stilled, life for ever.

DOLL

by Terry Greenhough

*'DOLL' is short yet it succeeds in showing one of the most
thoroughly alien worlds I've seen depicted in science fiction. Is it
our world, in some future yet to be? Or somewhere else? In fact, I
don't think it matters. Here is a vision of a strange symbiosis between man and something else, something small, sluglike, vaguely
telepathic, in fact almost a perfect reversal of Heinlein's classic*
The Puppet Masters.

Terry Greenhough is the author of several novels, Time and
Timothy Grenville, *and* Friends of Pharaoh, *a novel of ancient
Egypt, as well as many short stories. Once again he is young,
British (from North Derbyshire), and obviously destined To Go
Far.*

Carefully, Jolan selected a Doll. It must be just right for the approaching child, flesh that could reflect its flesh. The task was
difficult because Jolan had no experience.

Next door, his mate sobbed at the pangs of their first baby.

Jolan wondered what it would be: male, female, neuter? Not
that it really mattered. Cyric the Doll-Moulder would soon shape
the Doll correctly for gender, before tuning it. Jolan blinked that
part of the burden away and went back to studying the Dolls.

There were thousands of them in the building adjoining the
birthing-hut. Shelves of thick wood lined each wall. On the
shelves rested Dolls and Dolls and Dolls: immobile, dimly alive,
featureless, waiting. At the moment they were quiescent, untuned.

Jolan chose a Doll.

The birthing-hut was large and full. Jolan's mate lay with her
legs spread, bearing down. Helpers surrounded her. There were
mumurs of advice, encouragement. Nobody mentioned danger.

Cyric the Doll-Moulder stood by a wall, not needed yet.

It struck him as odd that they should tolerate his presence. Of course, Doll-Moulders had attended every birth since time before time, out of simple necessity. What good was a child without its Doll? And what good was a Doll without a Moulder?

(Cyric thought: *Where would the Dolls be without us?*)

Even so, strict rules existed for the conduct at a birthing and for the permitted attendants: no sniffing of the hallucination-herb, no known adulterers, no women with fewer than six labours behind them.

In Cyric's opinion, some of the rules were sensible and some weren't.

There must be no males present except the father and the necessary Doll-Moulder, if the Doll-Moulder happened to be a male. Several villages nearby had female Moulders. One even had a neuter. There was no telling where the gods would choose to drop the ability to Mould.

(Cyric thought: *Where would we be without the Dolls?*)

It struck him as odd that they should tolerate his presence. This was a village currently swept up in the winds of changing opinions, opinions swayed not at all by the traditions adhered to since time before time. Many of the women radicals insisted that the Doll could be taken to the Moulder outside, afterwards, if the village's Moulder were a male.

Why should he see what only the straining woman's mate should see? Why shouldn't he wait outside and Mould the Doll, then enter the birthing-hut to tune it when the not-to-be-seen had been decently covered?

Hard glances flashed Cyric's way, resentful.

They didn't upset him. Jolan was his friend. Jolan's mate was unmoved by the change-winds. Cyric didn't even find her attractive. Her nakedness disgusted him a little. He felt safe, confident the radicals wouldn't prevail for three or four generations, if then.

(Not needed yet, he repeated his previous questions to himself, this time together: *Where would the Dolls be without us? Where would we be without the Dolls?*)

(Both questions had the same answer: *Extinct.*)

A sharp wind bit Jolan's face as he left the building. The Doll, soft and motionless but alive, he held tucked under one arm gently. He wondered why he was holding the thing so tenderly, as though it were as fragile as a—

Baby!

The thought put a briskness into his steps and he turned towards the door of the birthing-hut, clutching the soft Doll. Soft it might be, but fragile it certainly wasn't. The springy flesh had a toughness Jolan envied, a toughness a dozen times more reliable that that possessed by the flesh of a man or a woman or a neuter.

Out in the rock-deserts where the Dolls lived naturally, dying, that which wasn't strong didn't survive. Wild cyclones sucked up rocks of every size, to drop them impartially and fiercely in a crashing stone-rain. Oddly, the rocks caused less harm to the Dolls than the slugs did. The Dolls had withstood the rains for a million years. They might withstand them for a million more. But they couldn't long survive the simplest of diseases transmitted by people. They soon succumbed.

And in that fact lies our salvation, Jolan thought, reaching for the door. *That, and the peculiar sympathy we have.*

He entered the birthing-hut. Between his mate's legs he noticed a head emerging. She was too busy to turn to him, but he crossed her vision and her pain-filled gaze rested on him for a moment. She seemed to recognise him.

'The Doll,' he said, handing it to Cyric. 'Do your best.'

'I will, Jolan.' The Doll-Moulder felt stares of bitterness on him from the radicals around Jolan's mate. They were at their most intense now, because this was the instant in which, without saying a word, he asserted himself and vindicated hs presence. He held the Doll, and the child was almost born. Now, a Doll-Moulder's work was about to begin.

He sensed clouds of hate in the empty air of the hut.

'There! A boy,' one of the women said in a satisfied voice, and Cyric's hands blurred into action. A Moulder had to work quickly, set about Moulding as soon as the sex of the child became known.

Until the Doll was tuned, the child hung vulnerable in the face of danger. Invisibly, viruses leapt to attack. Invisibly, disease tried to pounce into the newborn, unprotected, non-Dolled body. The signs, written in a hostile atmosphere poisoned by some incomprehensible conflict way back, were all in favour of death until the child owned a tuned Doll.

So a Moulder had to work quickly.

Dextrously, Cyric fashioned the pliable flesh of the amoeboid animal into a boy-semblance. Wherever he set the flesh, there it stayed. His fingers prodded, drew out appendages. He twisted a fingernail twice in the front of the head: eyes. A pinch of flesh and there was a tiny nose. Again using his fingernail, he scratched a mouth, then drew lines to represent hair.

The resentful glares were tinged slightly with respect.

Holding the completed boy-Doll, Cyric approached the relaxing woman. Somebody muttered as his eyes fell inadvertantly on the not-to-be-seen. He ignored her. She was as mindless as a desert-slug!

He reached for the child, clasped in its mother's arms. Cyric's left hand clutched the Doll while his right lay tenderly on the tiny head. As always, it seemed like an explosion in his brain. There were stars and stray baby-thoughts and spinning flashes. He felt the infant's inchoate brain-pattern race up his right arm, tingling, then flicker into his head and through it.

The tingle ran down his left arm and the Doll jerked just a little. It was tuned. The Doll had become an extension of the child, at least in a limited manner. The first few moments of most extreme danger had passed and Jolan's son had protection.

Cyric sighed.

The operation looked easy. For a Moulder, it was easy; for a person without the talent, impossible. *They need us*, Cyric mused, *inside the birthing-hut or out.*

He gave the Doll back to Jolan. Suddenly it twitched. Cyric's hand was still in contact and he gasped at the abrupt agony that leapt up his arm from the Doll from the child. His brow creased with anguish. Thankfully, he let go and the pain vanished.

He whirled, knowing what he'd see. He saw it: continued pain in the baby. It writhed in the arms that held it. The face had turned yellow and breathing appeared difficult, slowing, threatening to stop.

In tuned sympathy, the Doll jerked in Jolan's hands.

'Out!' snapped an old woman, a mother twelve times. She had two surviving children, both sickly. More Dolls had been incinerated behind her house, dead and useless, than she could remember. 'Everybody out!'

Cyric knew it was natural and sensible. The old woman snatched the ailing child and was the first outside. The other helpers followed, then Jolan left after a quick word with his mate. The Moulder went last, hurrying, and the new mother remained – as was proper – alone.

Cyric saw the sense of it. When her baby was ill, perhaps dying, a mother didn't want the distress of watching *its* distress. She needed solitude, secure in the knowledge that her child would be tended by fit women not weakened from childbirth. A mother didn't want the burden of her baby with her while it choked for breath. Therefore the baby must be taken away and she must be left by herself, to rest.

Anything else would be cruel and unnatural.

'How is he?' Jolan asked worriedly. 'Tell me truthfully, Cyric!'

'Would I do otherwise? You know I wouldn't. The child is – Jolan, my friend, he may not live.' Cyric glanced over his shoulder at a closed door. Behind it, the women were trying to hold off death.

Jolan looked longingly at the Doll in the Moulder's hands. 'If only I had it with me, to watch its progress – some indication—'

'It would be, yes,' Cyric agreed quietly. 'Yet you know it cannot be.'

Though why not? Cyric wondered. Because the Doll had to be in the room with the child. Very well, but what was to prevent poor Jolan's being in the room, too?

The laws again, Cyric knew. The father couldn't be present; no males, unless the Moulder were a male. The Moulder had to be there, with the child, with the helpers, with the Doll – and with a spare Doll, untuned, in case it became necessary.

'Please try and be patient,' Cyric urged, and returned to the attempted death-prevention.

The baby had deteriorated. His breaths were snatched gasps, his face a small picture of enormous torture. The women flocked around, doing what they could. It wasn't much.

The Doll jumped feebly in Cyric's grasp, dying. The agony in it, focused through it from the infant, screamed in his head. He wasn't sure how he'd hidden it from Jolan just now.

Unquestionably the Doll wouldn't last long. As Cyric's tolerance was far greater than the child's, so was the child's far greater than the Doll's. It had to die. Did the child have to die also?

Cyric threw a swift look at the untuned spare Doll. He thought in sudden helpless anger: *Why can't a single brain be tuned to two Dolls at once?* He didn't know. That was one of Nature's laws, for which She kept the reason a close secret, as She did with the uncanny Safe Zone.

He wished he could Mould the spare immediately, to save time later. If the baby's Doll died – and it definitely would die, soon – the other would have to be Moulded and tuned with feverish speed. During the interval between Dolls, the child would be unprotected again.

Cyric's was an idle wish. He simply couldn't Mould the spare Doll now. He required both hands to do so, but one hand had to hold the dying Doll. It was the only way – and a very painful way – in which he could keep the women informed of what was happening in the child's suffering brain : where the pain hit worst, where it lifted momentarily when it clamoured, when it merely murmured.

Acting on what came to him from the small head, he snapped orders. The women obeyed promptly enough, though sullenly in some cases – the radicals, angry at Cyric's being there. He wondered what illogic they'd use to back up their resentment. This was hopefully a death-prevention, not a birth. There was nothing here he didn't ought to see. Surely even *their* strange new opinions couldn't dream up a plausible reason for his exclusion !

He decided the bitterness must be a carry-over from the birthing-hut. The women had been too rushed to filter it out of their minds yet. He took no notice of the radicals.

The Doll died.

He flung it aside – later, Jolan would burn it – and grabbed the other. The crucial time had arrived. The perils pressing on the baby were even more severe now than directly after birth. Then, it had been presumably healthy yet threatened by ubiquitous disease. Now, it was less than healthy and the same diseases swirled in the unclean air.

Quickly, quickly, quickly, he made a boy-Doll.

He always hated a second tuning. It meant a tormented brain had to be transferred. Torment always made the brain sluggish, or so it seemed to Cyric. He laid his right hand on the sweating head and the blurred brain-pattern crawled up his arm, instead of racing.

It crept into his head. The usual explosion followed : sunbursts, vague thoughts, spinning flashes – but so terribly slowly, hanging on inside his head so long he felt he must faint. Then mercifully the pattern left his skull, to travel down his left arm and into the Doll.

It was tuned, reflecting the baby's distress in amoeboid leaps.

(*Where would we be without the Dolls?* Cyric asked himself again — *without their singular inexplicable capacity to drink in some of the suffering from our ailments, thus reducing the load we have to bear?*)

And it truly was a load, a hazard and a death-in-air lying over every individual permanently throughout all the years of life. Some people insisted that the poisons would clear one day, yet no one would go so far as to predict exactly when. In Cyric's view, they'd stay for ever, killing and killing and killing.

He pictured his own Doll at home, his twentieth. Whilst he was enduring the baby's pains shot at him through the Doll he held, his own Doll would be moving in quiet anguish in sympathy with his own lesser pain, shot at him from the baby through the Doll he held.

It was rather a mind-twisting idea.

They die for us in their thousands, he mused, knowing it for truth. A minor malady and they died after a lengthy period. A serious illness and they expired swiftly. Owing to the poisoned atmosphere, serious illnesses were frequent, minor maladies uncountable. Yes, the people were definitely dependent on the Dolls to no small degree.

The little animals could survive through the rock-hails of the turbulent deserts, but face them with a simple germ and—

We all have our strengths and weaknesses, Cyric told himself philosophically. He considered it fortunate that the Dolls had been discovered out in their desolate fastnesses, long ago. The two species helped each other – not a natural symbiosis, but a mutually beneficial co-operation brought about by intelligence to combat the swirling poison.

He wondered if the Dolls had sufficient intelligence to realise they were being helped.

The second Doll twisted across Cyric's hand with the reflection of agony from Jolan's son. Then fractionally the pain in the Moulder's mind lessened. Could the baby be improving? It was possible. Also it could ultimately prove a good thing that the child had been infected straight at the outset of its life. Certain diseases, once contracted and outlived, never attacked the same individual again. The first bout, though it might confront a person with the grinning skull-face of death, left a kind legacy of immunity.

Cyric glanced at the old woman who'd brought the baby from the birthing-hut. His sympathies squirmed with the effort to flick out and touch her with tenderness. Of her twelve children, ten had in youth been struck down by awful illnessess – ten *different* illnesses, each one of a variety in which survival ensured immunity.

All ten children had died.

She must surely have offended the gods in some way!

Suddenly Cyric's legs bowed. Lightning crashed across his brain. Fires blazed black charred patches on the inside of his skull. He bit his lip to keep from crying out. Glancing down, he saw the Doll jerking in desperate frenzy.

Pain must have showed on his face acutely and unmistakably. He caught a look of quick horror and sympathy from one of the radicals. It gladdened him, but he couldn't say so. His tongue wouldn't work and he couldn't give orders.

He didn't need to.

The women crowded over the baby, trying to soothe it, rubbing on analgesic herb preparations. They didn't ask Cyric where the pain was or how bad it was. They knew from his expression. It was everywhere and unbearable.

Somebody – another radical – ran out to fetch a fresh Doll.

Cyric had never seen three Dolls used in a successful operation. He managed to think: *Not much chance now, Jolan. I'm sorry. If I can feel it as wickedly as this, I daren't imagine how it is for the child!*

The woman returned with the third Doll. Like the second, it wasn't Jolan's choice. A father always selected the first, pretending he could distinguish between one Doll and another – pure sentiment, sanctioned by tradition. Oddly, even the radicals didn't object.

In Cyric's head roared pain more exquisite than any in previous experience. Somehow, he felt sure his own Doll at home had died. He was alone, without an ally to drain off some of the pain.

The second Doll perished. He threw it away, hating himself for the relief that sang in him at the cessation of agony. He worked on the third Doll with desperate haste, mostly by touch, watching the baby. It threshed and screamed, a tiny defenceless bundle of terror. Cyric wondered if he could finish the third Doll in time.

He finished it and Jolan's son was still alive; quiet now, barely conscious, hardly breathing, but alive. Cyric's hand met a cold head. The brain-pattern fluttered like an arrowed bird spiralling down the sky towards a grateful hunter. The agony had subsided into the mental depths, so deep that Cyric could scarcely feel it.

An echo slithered ticklingly up his arm, through his head in a slow flurry of dull sparks, then down his other arm with what seemed to be reluctance. The Doll squirmed.

Silently, Cyric cursed the necessity for Moulding. Oh, the Dolls were malleable enough, no doubt about it — but why did they absolutely *have* to be Moulded? Why couldn't a normal, un-changed Doll-amoeba manifest the same saving sympathy as a changed, Moulded one? Why did similarity of shape matter so much?

Another of Nature's inscrutable laws, he supposed. Shape *did* matter, so why wonder why? A boy-Doll was useless with a girl-child, a neuter-Doll useless with a male or a female. The sym-pathy simply didn't exist. They wouldn't tune unless the shape more or less matched. Hence the Moulders.

Cyric glanced at the third Doll. It moved slowly, its tough flesh rippling. Obviously it was still alive, but he could tell from its behaviour the condition of the baby: dead.

These few moments following a death never failed to frighten him. He looked at the infant: pale, quiet, immobile — dead. Then he looked at the Doll: rippling, moving, twitching — alive. He was glad when the Doll finally died.

Always, those several heartbeats of moving afterdeath almost made him believe in an afterlife. Undeniably the child's body was dead, yet some unguessable discharge from its brain continued for a short while to activate the Doll. Inside his head, he could feel the fading brain-pattern as a terrifying blackness touched by grey splashes of dimming consciousness – *after death*!

He shuddered. The women gazed at him with silent feeling, even the radicals who despised him. He thought: *A moment such as that one transcends mere mundane emotions*, then watched, recovering, as the women filed out. The oldest, the ten-times-bereaved, carried a tiny corpse.

Cyric was alone with three dead Dolls.

You three died, he thought sadly, *but still we're saving you as a race. As you're saving us. I wonder if you realise?*

He remembered his trip to the lethal rock-deserts, just after puberty – a journey undertaken by all males, though it shortened their lives shockingly. The deserts swam hideously in his memory:

shifting sands, small rocks, large rocks, colossal rocks, savage winds howling around sombre mountains; the cheerless land-wreckage left over from the same cataclysmic conflict which had poisoned the air of the civilised world.

Legends spoke of vast villages there once, peopled by a fabled species now gone, with a thousand times more inhabitants to each village than there were stars in the sky. Cyric didn't believe the legends.

In the deserts lived the Doll-amoebae and very little else. He could still see them clinging to mountainsides, surviving despite the stupendous down-crashing of the atrocious stone-rains which claimed dozens of youngsters every year. But no Doll-animal ever died from the hammering rains of rock.

Strange, Cyric mused, *how you die from the touch of a grain of sand.* He shuddered again, remembering the slugs: ugly, fat, black, slimy, as big as a man's arm – a further distortion of Nature caused by the conflict, according to myth.

Cyric hated the slugs and marvelled at their peculiar ability to kill the Dolls, albeit indirectly. He knew of the trails the slugs left, the rippling oceans of slime that coated the deserts, but he didn't fully understand the manner of their slaughtering the Dolls: a violent wind whipping sticky sand on to the mountain-clinging Dolls, grains which stuck and clung immoveably – and then slowly, somehow, in some weird conflict-engendered fashion, ate into the Dolls with hard hot poison and destroyed them black and shrivelled.

Yes, we're saving you, he thought, *preserving you out in the Safe Zone in your thousands.* It disturbed his sensitive mind to think of the Dolls being brought away from their accustomed environment each year, yet surely there could be no cruelty involved if it kept the species alive.

And anyway, the Safe Zone, though safe, couldn't be in-habited by people. It was a narrow valley, high mountains edging a plain of stone. Nothing could grow on the stone, but it seemed to suit the Dolls well enough.

No poisoned air in the Safe Zone, he mused, wondering why. The radicals babbled of regular gales slashing down the canyon, scouring it clean of filthy air. Cyric found a chuckle. One could hardly accept everything the foolish radicals said.

The chuckle died as seriousness returned with a jolt.

Jolan's first son was dead. He'd know by now. Perhaps he was even now burying the child, possibly planning further attempts at a family. Cyric prayed for his success, because families were never gained easily. Then he gathered up the three Dolls to take them to poor Jolan, for the grief-filled necessity of a burning.

A BEAST FOR NORN

by George R R Martin

COINCIDENCES: one of the other contributors to this volume advised me, without prompting, 'Try and get a story from George R R Martin. I think that man is superb.*'*

The very next day my copy of the latest Analog *arrived, and it had a cover story by that very same George Martin. And the day after that, this story arrived, 'A Beast For Norn'.*

Did I get an accidental glimpse of the wheels-within-wheels mechanism that secretly orders the cosmos? Or is there a simpler explanation, something to the effect that 'Good news travels fast'? Whatever the answer the World Convention was obviously in on the secret, for in the following month they voted a Hugo Award for his novella, 'A Song For Lya'.

I know almost nothing about George R R Martin except that he lives in Chicago and is another writer rapidly making a name for himself in science fiction. With the allies he has, how can he lose?

Haviland Tuf was relaxing in an alehouse on Tamber when the thin man found him. He sat by himself in the darkest corner of the dimly-lit tavern, his elbows resting on the table and the top of his bald head almost brushing the low wooden beam above. Four empty mugs sat before him, their insides streaked by rings of foam, while a fifth, half-full, was cradled in huge calloused hands.

If Tuf was aware of the curious glances the other patrons gave him from time to time, he showed no sign of it; he quaffed his ale methodically, and his face – bone-white and completely hairless, as was the rest of him – was without expression. He was a man of heroic dimensions, Haviland Tuf, a giant with an equally gigantic paunch, and he made a singular solitary figure drinking alone in his booth.

Although he was not *quite* alone, in truth; his black tomcat Dax lay asleep on the table before him, a ball of dark fur, and Tuf would occasionally set down his mug of ale and idly stroke his quiet companion. Dax would not stir from his comfortable position among the empty mugs. The cat was fully as large, compared to other cats, as Haviland Tuf was compared to other men.

When the thin man came walking up to Tuf's booth, Tuf said nothing at all. He merely looked up, and blinked, and waited for the other to begin.

'You are Haviland Tuf, the animal-seller,' the thin man said. He was indeed painfully thin. His garments, all black leather and grey fur, hung loose on him, bagging here and there. Yet he was plainly a man of some means, since he wore a thin brass coronet around his brow, under a mop of black hair, and his fingers were all adorned with rings.

Tuf stroked Dax, and – looking down at the cat – began to speak. 'Did you hear that, Dax?' he said. He spoke very slowly, his voice a deep bass with only a hint of inflection. 'I am Haviland Tuf, the animal-seller. Or so I am taken to be.' Then he looked up at the thin man who stood there impatiently. 'Sir,' he said. 'I am indeed Haviland Tuf. And I do indeed trade in animals. Yet perhaps I do not consider myself an animal-seller. Perhaps I consider myself an ecological engineer.'

The thin man waved his hand in an infuriated gesture, and slid uninvited into the booth opposite Tuf. 'I understand that you own a seedship of the ancient Ecological Corps, but that does not make you an ecological engineer, Tuf. They are all dead, and have been for centuries. But if you would prefer to be called an ecological engineer, then well and good. I require your services. I want to buy a monster from you, a great fierce beast.'

'Ah,' said Tuf, speaking to the cat again. 'He wants to buy a monster, this stranger who seats himself at my table.'

'My name is Herold Norn, if that is what's bothering you,' the thin man said. 'I am the Senior Beast-Master of my House, one of the Twelve Great Houses of Lyronica.'

'Lyronica,' Tuf stated. 'I have heard of Lyronica. The next world out from here towards the Fringe, is it not? Esteemed for its gaming pits?'

Norn smiled. 'Yesyes,' he said.

Haviland Tuf scratched Dax behind the ear, a peculiar rhythmic scratch, and the tomcat slowly uncurled, yawning, and glanced up at the thin man. A wave of reassurance came flooding into Tuf; the visitor was well intentioned and truthful, it seemed. According to Dax. All cats have a touch of psi. Dax had more than a touch; the genetic wizards of the vanished Ecological Corps had seen to that. He was Tuf's mindreader.

'The affair becomes clearer,' Tuf said. 'Perhaps you would care to elaborate, Herold Norn?'

Norn nodded. 'Certainly, certainly. What do you know of Lyronica, Tuf? Particularly of the gaming pits?'

Tuf's heavy and stark white face remained emotionless. 'Some small things. Perhaps not enough, if I am to deal with you. Tell me what you will, and Dax and I will consider the matter.'

Herold Norn rubbed thin hands together, and nodded again. 'Dax?' he said. 'Oh, of course. Your cat. A handsome animal, although personally I have never been fond of beasts who cannot fight. Real beauty lies in killing-strength, I always say.'

'A peculiar attitude,' Tuf commented.

'Nono,' said Norn, 'not at all. I hope that your work here has not infected you with Tamberkin squeamishness.'

Tuf drained his mug in silence, then signalled for two more. The barkeep brought them promptly.

'Thank you, thank you,' Norn said, when the mug was set golden and foaming in front of him.

'Proceed.'

'Yes. Well, the Twelve Great Houses of Lyronica compete in the gaming pits, you know. It began – oh, centuries ago. Before that, the Houses warred. This way is much better. Family honour is upheld, fortunes are made, and no one is injured. You see, each House controls great tracts, scattered widely over the planet, and since the land is very thinly settled, animal life teems. The lords of the Great Houses, many years ago during a time of peace, started to have animal-fights. It was a pleasant diversion, rooted deep in history – you are aware, maybe, of the ancient custom of cock-fighting and the Old Earth folk called Romans who would set all manner of strange beasts against each other in their great arena?'

Norn paused and drank some ale, waiting for an answer, but Tuf merely stroked a quietly alert Dax and said nothing.

'No matter,' the thin Lyronican finally said, wiping foam from his mouth with the back of his hand. 'That was the beginning of the sport, you see. Each House had its own particular land, its own particular animals. The House of Varcour, for example, sprawls in the hot, swampy south, and they are fond of sending huge lizard-lions to the gaming pits. Feridian, a mountainous realm, has bred and championed its fortunes with a species of rock-ape which we call, naturally, *feridians*. My own house, Norn, stands on the grassy plains of the large northern continent. We have sent a hundred different beasts into combat in the pits, but we are most famed for our ironfangs.'

'Ironfangs,' Tuf said.

Norn gave a sly smile. 'Yes,' he said proudly. 'As Senior Beast-Master, I have trained thousands. Oh, but they are lovely animals! Tall as you are, with fur of the most marvellous blue-black colour, fierce and relentless.'

'Canine?'

'But *such* canines,' Norn said.

'Yet you require from me a monster.'

Norn drank more of his ale. 'In truth, in truth. Folks from a dozen near worlds voyage to Lyronica, to watch the beasts fight in the gaming pits and gamble on the outcome. Particularly they flock to the Bronze Arena that has stood for six hundred years in the City of All Houses. That's where the greatest fights are fought. The wealth of our Houses and our world has come to depend on this. Without it, rich Lyronica would be as poor as the farmers of Tamber.'

'Yes,' said Tuf.

'But you understand, this wealth, it goes to the Houses according to their honour, according to their victories. The House of Arneth has grown greatest and most powerful because of the many deadly beasts in their varied lands; the others rank according to their scores in the Bronze Arena. The income from each match – all the monies paid by those who watch and bet – goes to the victor.'

Haviland Tuf scratched Dax behind the ear again. 'The House of Norn ranks last and least among the Twelve Great Houses of Lyronica,' he said, and the twinge that Dax relayed to him told him he was correct.

'You know,' Norn said.

'Sir. It was obvious. But is it ethical to buy an offworld monster, under the rules of your Bronze Arena?'

'There are precedents. Some seventy-odd standard years ago, a gambler came from Old Earth itself, with a creature called a timber wolf that he had trained. The House of Colin backed him, in a fit of madness. His poor beast was matched against a Norn ironfang, and proved far from equal to its task. There are other cases as well.

'In recent years, unfortunately, our ironfangs have not bred well. The wild species has all but died out on the plains, and the few who remain become swift and elusive, difficult for our housemen to capture. In the breeding kennels, the strain seems to have softened, despite my efforts and those of the Beast-Masters before me. Norn has won few victories of late, and I will not remain Senior for long unless something is done. We grow poor. When I heard that a seedship had come to Tamber, then, I determined to seek you out. I will begin a new era of glory for Norn, with your help.'

Haviland Tuf sat very still. 'I comprehend. Yet I am not in the habit of selling monsters. *The Ark* is an ancient seedship, designed by the Earth Imperials thousands of years ago, to decimate the Hrangans through ecowar. I can unleash a thousand diseases, and in the cell-banks I have cloning material for beasts from more worlds than you can count. You misunderstand the nature of ecowar, however. The deadliest enemies are not large predators, but tiny insects that lay waste to a world's crops, or hoppers that breed and breed and crowd out all other life.'

Herold Norn looked crestfallen. 'You have nothing, then?'

Tuf stroked Dax. 'Little. A million types of insects, a hundred thousand kinds of small birds, full as many fish. But monsters, monsters – only a few – a thousand perhaps. They were used from time to time, for psychological reasons as often as not.'

'A thousand monsters!' Norn was excited again. 'That is more than enough selection! Surely, among the thousand, we can find a beast for Norn!'

'Perhaps,' Tuf said. 'Do you think so, Dax?' he said to his cat. 'Do you? So!' He looked at Norn again. 'This matter does interest me, Herold Norn. And my work here is done, as I have given the Tamberkin a bird that will check their rootworm plague, and the bird does well. So Dax and I will take the *Ark* to Lyronica, and see your gaming pits, and we will decide what is to be done with them.'

Norn smiled. 'Excellent,' he said. 'Then I will buy this round of ale.' And Dax told Haviland Tuf in silence that the thin man was flush with the feel of victory.

The Bronze Arena stood square in the centre of the City of All Houses, at the point where sectors dominated by the Twelve Great Houses met like slices in a vast pie. Each section of the rambling stone city was walled off, each flew a flag with its distinctive colours, each had its own ambience and style; but all met in the Bronze Arena.

The Arena was not bronze after all, but mostly black stone and polished wood. It bulked upwards, taller than all but a few of the city's scattered towers and minarets, and topped by a shining bronze dome that gleamed with the orange rays of the sunset. Gargoyles peered from the various narrow windows, carved of stone and hammered from bronze and wrought iron. The great doors in the black stone walls were fashioned of metal as well, and there were twelve of them, each facing a different sector of the City of All Houses. The colours and the etching on each gateway were distinctive to its House.

Lyronica's sun was a fist of red flame smearing the western horizon when Herold Norn led Haviland Tuf to the games. The housemen had just fired gas torches, metal obelisks that stood like dark teeth in a ring about the Bronze Arena, and the hulking ancient building was surrounded by flickering pillars of blue-and-orange flame. In a crowd of gamblers and gamesters, Tuf followed Herold Norn from the half-deserted streets of the Nornic slums down a path of crushed rock, passing between twelve bronze ironfangs who snarled and spit in timeless poses on either side of the street, and then through the wide Norn Gate whose doors were intricate ebony and brass. The uniformed guards, clad in the same black leather and grey fur as Herold Norn himself, recognised the Beast-Master and admitted them; others stopped to pay with coins of gold and iron.

The Arena was the greatest gaming pit of all; it *was* a pit, the sandy combat-floor sunk deep below ground level, with stone walls four metres high surrounding it. Then the seats began, just atop the walls, circling and circling in ascending tiers until they reached the doors. Enough seating for thirty thousand, although those towards the back had a poor view at best, and other seats were blocked off by iron pillars. Betting stalls were scattered throughout the building, windows in the outer walls.

Herold Norn took Tuf to the best seats in the Arena, in the front of the Norn section, with only a stone parapet separating them from the four-metre drop to the combat sands. The seats here were not rickety wood-and-iron, like those in the rear, but thrones of leather, huge enough to accommodate even Tuf's vast bulk without difficulty, and opulently comfortable. 'Every seat is bound in the skin of a beast that has died nobly below,' Herold Norn told Tuf, as they seated themselves. Beneath them, a work crew of men in one-piece blue coveralls was dragging the carcass of some gaunt feathered animal towards one of the entryways. 'A fighting-bird of the House of Wrai Hill,' Norn explained. 'The Wrai Beast-Master sent it up against a Varcour lizard-lion. Not the most felicitious choice.'

Haviland Tuf said nothing. He sat stiff and erect, dressed in a grey vinyl greatcoat that fell to his ankles, with flaring shoulderboards and a visored green-and-brown cap emblazoned with the golden theta of the Ecological Engineers. His large, rough hands interlocked atop his bulging stomach while Herold Norn kept up a steady stream of conversation.

Then the Arena announcer spoke, and the thunder of his magnified voice boomed all around them. 'Fifth match,' he said. 'From the House of Norn, a male ironfang, aged two years, weight 2.6 quintals, trained by Junior Beast-Master Kers Norn. New to the Bronze Arena.' Immediately below them, metal grated harshly on metal, and a nightmare creature came bounding into the pit. The ironfang was a shaggy giant, with sunken red eyes and a double row of curving teeth that dripped slaver; a wolf grown out of proportion and crossed with a sabre-toothed tiger, its legs as thick as young trees, its speed and killing grace only partially disguised by the blue-black fur that hid the play of muscles. The ironfang snarled and the arena echoed to the noise; scattered cheering began all around them.

Herold Norn smiled. 'Kers is a cousin, and one of our most promising juniors. He tells me that this beast will do us proud. Yes, yes. I like its looks, don't you?'

'Being new to Lyronica and your Bronze Arena, I have no standard of comparison,' Tuf said in a flat voice.

The announcer began again. 'From the House of Arneth-in-the-Gilded-Wood, a strangling-ape, aged six years, weight 3.1 quintals, trained by Senior Beast-Master Danel Leigh Arneth. Three times a veteran of the Bronze Arena, three times surviving.'

Across the combat pit, another of the entryways – the one wrought in gold and crimson – slid open, and the second beast lumbered out on two squat legs and looked around. The strangling-ape was short but immensely broad, with a triangular torso and a bullet-shaped head, eyes sunk deep under a heavy ridge of bone. Its arms, double-jointed and muscular, dragged in the arena sand. From head to toe the beast was hairless, but for patches of dark red fur under its arms; its skin was a dirty white. And it smelled. Across the arena, Haviland Tuf still caught the musky odour.

'It sweats,' Norn explained. 'Danel Leigh has driven it to kill-ing frenzy before sending it forth. His beast has the edge in ex-perience, you understand, and the strangling-ape is a savage creature as well. Unlike its cousin, the mountain feridian, it is naturally a carnivore and needs little training. But Kers' ironfang is younger. The match should be of interest. The Norn Beast-Master leaned forward while Tuf sat calm and still.

The ape turned, growling deep in its throat, and already the ironfang was streaking towards it, snarling, a blue-black blur that scattered arena sand as it ran. The strangling-ape waited for it, spreading its huge gangling arms, and Tuf had a blurred im-pression of the great Norn killer leaving the ground in one tremendous bound. Then the two animals were locked together, rolling over and over in a tangle of ferocity, and the arena be-came a symphony of screams. 'The throat,' Norn was shouting. 'Tear out its throat! Tear out its throat!'

Then, as sudden as they had met, the two beasts parted. The ironfang spun away and began to move in slow circles, and Tuf saw that one of its forelegs was bent and broken, so that it limped on the three remaining. Yet still it circled. The strangling-ape gave it no opening, but turned constantly to face it as it prowled. Long gashes drooled blood on the ape's wide chest, where the ironfang's sabres had slashed, but the beast of Arneth seemed little weakened. Herold Norn had begun to mutter softly at Tuf's side.

Impatient with the lull, the watchers in the Bronze Arena began a rhythmic chant, a low wordless noise that swelled louder and louder as new voices heard and joined. Tuf saw at once that the sound affected the animals below. Now they began to snarl and hiss, calling battlecries in savage voices, and the strangling-ape moved from one leg to the other, back and forth, in a macabre dance, while slaver ran in dripping rivers from the gaping jaws of the ironfang. The chant grew and grew – Herold Norn joined in, his thin body swaying slightly as he moaned – and Tuf recognised the bloody killing-chant for what it was. The beasts below went into frenzy. Suddenly the ironfang was charging again, and the ape's long arms reached to meet it in its wild lunge. The impact of the leap threw the strangler backwards, but Tuf saw that the ironfang's teeth had closed on air while the ape wrapped its hands around the blue-black throat. The ironfang thrashed wildly, but briefly, as they rolled in the sand. Then came

136

a sharp, horribly loud snap, and the wolf-creature was nothing but a rag of fur, its head lolling grotesquely to one side.

The watchers ceased their moaning chant, and began to applaud and whistle. Afterwards, the gold and crimson door slid open once again and the strangling-ape returned to where it had come. Four men in Norn House black and grey came out to carry off the corpse.

Herold Norn was sullen. 'Another loss. I will speak to Kers. His beast did not find the throat.'

Haviland Tuf stood up. 'I have seen your Bronze Arena.'

'Are you going?' Norn asked anxiously. 'Surely not so soon! There are five more matches. In the next, a giant feridian fights a water-scorpion from Amar Island!'

'I need see no more. It is feeding time for Dax, so I must return to the *Ark*.'

Norn scrambled to his feet, and put an anxious hand to Tuf's shoulder to restrain him. 'Will you sell us a monster, then?'

Tuf shook off the Beast-Master's grip. 'Sir. I do not like to be touched. Restrain yourself.' When Norn's hand had fallen, Tuf looked down into his eyes. 'I must consult my records, my computers. The *Ark* is in orbit. Shuttle up the day after next. A problem exists, and I shall address myself to its correction.' Then, without further word, Haviland Tuf turned and walked from the Bronze Arena, back to spaceport of the City of All Houses, where his shuttlecraft sat waiting.

Herold Norn had obviously not been prepared for the *Ark*. After his black-and-grey shuttle had docked and Tuf had cycled him through, the Beast-Master made no effort to disguise his reaction. 'I should have known,' he kept repeating. 'The size of this ship, the *size*. But of course I should have known.'

Haviland Tuf stood unmoved, cradling Dax in one arm and stroking the cat slowly. 'Old Earth built larger ships than modern worlds,' he said impassively. 'The *Ark*, as a seedship, had to be large. It once had two hundred crewmen. Now it has one.'

'You are the *only* crewman?' Norn said.

Dax suddenly warned Tuf to be alert. The Beast-Master had begun to think hostile thoughts. 'Yes,' Tuf said. 'The only crewman. But there is Dax, of course. And defences programmed in, lest control be wrested from me.'

Norn's plans suddenly withered, according to Dax. 'I see,' he said. Then, eagerly, 'Well, what have you come up with?'

'Come,' said Tuf, turning.

He led Norn out of the reception room down a small corridor that led into a larger. There they boarded a three-wheeled vehicle and drove through a long tunnel lined by glass vats of all sizes and shapes, filled with gently-bubbling liquid. One bank of vats was divided into units as small as a man's fingernail; on the other extreme, there was a single unit large enough to contain the interior of the Bronze Arena. It was empty, but in some of the medium-sized tanks, dark shapes hung in translucent bags, and stirred fitfully. Tuf, with Dax curled in his lap, stared straight ahead as he drove, while Norn looked wonderingly from side to side.

They departed the tunnel at last, and entered a small room that was all computer consoles. Four large chairs sat in the four corners of the square chamber, with control panels on their arms; a circular plate of blue metal was built into the floor amidst them. Haviland Tuf dropped Dax into one of the chairs before seating himself in a second. Norn looked around, then took the chair diagonally opposite Tuf.

'I must inform you of several things,' Tuf began.

'Yesyes,' said Norn.

'Monsters are expensive,' Tuf said. 'I will require one hundred thousand standards.'

'*What!* That's an outrage! We would need a hundred victories in the Bronze Arena to amass that sum. I told you, Norn is a poor House.'

'So. Perhaps then a richer House would meet the required price. The Ecological Engineering Corps has been defunct for centuries, sir. No ship of theirs remains in working order, save the *Ark* alone. Their science is largely forgotten. Techniques of cloning and genetic engineering such as they practised exist now only on Prometheus and Old Earth itself, where such secrets are closely guarded. And the Prometheans no longer have the stasis field, thus their clones must grow to natural maturity.' Tuf looked across, to where Dax sat in a chair before the gently-winking lights of the computer consoles. 'And yet, Dax, Herold Norn feels my price to be excessive.'

'Fifty thousand standards,' Norn said. 'We can barely meet that price.'

Haviland Tuf said nothing.

'Eighty thousand standards, then! I can go no higher. The

House of Norn will be bankrupt! They will tear down our bronze ironfangs, and seal the Norn Gate!'

Haviland Tuf said nothing.

'Curse you! A hundred thousand, yesyes. But only if your monster meets our requirements.'

'You will pay the full sum on delivery.'

'Impossible!'

Tuf was silent again.

'Oh, very well.'

'As to the monster itself, I have studied your requirements closely, and have consulted my computers. Here upon the *Ark*, in my frozen cell-banks, thousands upon thousands of predators exist, including many now extinct on their original homeworlds. Yet few, I would think, would satisfy the demands of the Bronze Arena. And of those that might, many are unsuitable for other reasons. For example, I have considered the selection to be limited to beasts that might with luck be bred on the lands of the House of Norn. A creature who could not replicate himself would be a poor investment. No matter how invincible he might be, in time the animal would age and die, and Norn victories would be at an end.'

'An excellent point,' Herold Norn said. 'We have, from time to time, attempted to raise lizard-lions and feridians and other beasts of the Twelve Houses, with ill success. The climate, the vegetation . . .' He made a disgusted gesture.

'Precisely. Therefore, I have eliminated silicon-based lifeforms, which would surely die on your carbon-based world. Also, animals of planets whose atmosphere varies too greatly from Lyronica's. Also, beasts of dissimilar climes. You will comprehend the various and sundry difficulties incumbent in my search.'

'Yesyes, but get to the point. What have you found? What is this hundred-thousand-standard monster?'

'I offer you a selection,' Tuf said. 'From among some thirty animals. Attend!'

He touched a glowing button on the arm of his chair, and suddenly a beast was squatting on the blue-metal plate between them. Two metres tall with rubbery pink-grey skin and thin white hair, the creature had a low forehead and a swinish snout, plus a set of nasty curving horns and dagger-like claws on its hands.

'I will not trouble you with species names, since I observe that informality was the rule of the Bronze Arena,' Haviland Tuf said. 'This is the so-called stalking-swine of Heydey, native to both forests and plain. Chiefly a carrion-eater, but it has been known to relish fresh meat, and it fights viciously when attacked. Said to be quite intelligent, yet impossible to domesticate. The stalking-swine is an excellent breeder. The colonists from Gulliver eventually abandoned their Heydey settlement because of this animal. That was some two hundred years past.'

Herold Norn scratched his scalp between dark hair and brass coronet. 'No. It is too thin, too light. Look at the neck! Think what a feridian would do to it.' He shook his head violently. 'Besides, it is *ugly*. And I resent the offer of a scavenger, no matter how ill-tempered. The House of Norn breeds proud fighters, beasts who kill their own game!'

'So,' said Tuf. He touched the button, and the stalking-swine vanished. In its place, bulking large enough to touch the plates above and fade into them, was a massive ball of armoured grey flesh as featureless as battle plate.

'This creature's homeworld has never been named, nor settled. A team from Old Poseidon once explored it, however, and cell samples were taken. Zoo specimens existed briefly, but did not thrive. The beast was nicknamed the rolleram. Adults weigh approximately six metric tons. On the plains of their homeworld, the rollerams achieve speed in excess of fifty kilometres per standard hour, crushing prey beneath them. The beast is all mouth. Thusly, as any portion of its skin can be made to exude digestive enzymes, it simply rests atop its meal until the meat has been absorbed.'

Herold Norn, himself half-immersed in the looming holograph, sounded impressed. 'Ah, yes. Better, much better. An awesome creature. Perhaps ... but no.' His tone changed suddenly. 'Nono, this will never do. A creature weighing six tons and rolling that fast might smash its way out of the Bronze Arena, and kill hundreds of our patrons. Besides, who would pay hard coin to watch this *thing* crush a lizard-lion or a strangler? No. No sport. Your rolleram is too monsterous, Tuf.'

Tuf, unmoved, hit the button once again. The vast grey bulk gave way to a sleek, snarling cat, fully as large as an ironfang, with slitted yellow eyes and powerful muscles bunched beneath a coat of dark blue fur. The fur was striped, here and there; long thin lines of bright silver running lengthwise down the creature's flanks.

'Ahhhhhhhh,' Norn said. 'A beauty, in truth, in truth.'

'The cobalt panther of Celia's World,' Tuf said, 'often called the cobalcat. One of the largest and deadliest of the great cats, or their analogues. The beast is a truly superlative hunter, its senses miracles of biological engineering. It can see into the infrared for night prowling, and the ears – note the size and the spread, Beast-Master – the ears are extremely sensitive. Being of felinoid stock, the cobalcat has psionic ability, but in its case this ability is far more developed than the usual. Fear, hunger, and bloodlust all act as triggers; then the cobalcat becomes a mindreader.'

Norn looked up, startled. 'What?'

'Psionics, sir. I said psionics. The cobalcat is very deadly, simply because it knows what moves an antagonist will make before those moves are made. It anticipates. Do you comprehend?'

'Yes.' Norn's voice was excited. Haviland Tuf looked over at Dax, and the big tomcat – who'd been not the least disturbed by the parade of scentless phantoms flashing on and off – confirmed the thin man's enthusiasm as genuine. 'Perfect, perfect! Why, I'll venture to say that we can even train these beasts as we'd train ironfangs, eh? Eh? And *mindreaders*! Perfect. Even the colours are right, dark blue, you know, and our ironfangs were blue-black, so the cats will be most Nornic, yesyes!'

Tuf touched his chair arm, and the cobalcat vanished. 'So then, no need to proceed further. Delivery will be in three weeks standard, if that pleases you. For the agreed-upon sum, I will provide three pair, two set of younglings who should be released as breeding stock, and one mated set full-grown, who might be immediately sent into the Bronze Arena.'

'So soon,' Norn began. 'Fine, but . . .'

'I use the stasis field, sir. Reversed it produces chronic distortion, a time acceleration if you will. Standard procedure. Promethean techniques would require that you wait until the clones aged to maturity naturally, which sometimes is considered inconvenient. It would perhaps be prudent to add that, although I provide Norn House with six animals, only three actual individuals are represented. The *Ark* carries a triple cobalcat cell. I will clone each specimen twice, male and female, and hope for a viable genetic mix when they crossbreed on Lyronica.'

Dax filled Tuf's head with a curious flood of triumph and confusion and impatience; Herold Norn, then, had understood nothing of what Tuf had said, or at any rate that was one interpretation. 'Fine, whatever you say,' Norn said. 'I will send the ships for the animals promptly, with proper cages. Then we will pay you.'

Dax radiated deceit, distrust, alarm.

141

'Sir. You will pay the full fee before any beasts are handed over.'

'But you said on delivery.'

'Admitted. Yet I am given to impulsive whims, and impulse now tells me to collect first, rather than simultaneously.'

'Oh, very well,' Norn said. 'Though your demands are arbitrary and excessive. With these cobalcats, we shall soon recoup our fee.' He started to rise.

Haviland Tuf raised a single finger. 'One moment. You have not seen fit to inform me overmuch of the ecology of Lyronica, nor the particular realms of Norn House. Perhaps prey exists. I must caution you, however, that your cobalcats will not breed unless hunting is good. They need suitable game species.'

'Yesyes, of course.'

'Let me add this, then. For an additional five thousand standards, I might clone you a breeding stock of Celian hoppers, delightful furred herbivores renowned on a dozen worlds for their succulent flesh.'

Herold Norn frowned. 'Bah. You ought to give them to us without charge. You have extorted enough money, trader, and . . .'

Tuf rose, and gave a ponderous shrug. 'The man berates me, Dax,' he said to his cat. 'What am I to do? I seek only an honest living.' He looked at Norn. 'Another of my impulses comes to me. I feel, somehow, that you will not relent, not even were I to offer you an excellent discount. Therefore I shall yield. The hoppers are yours without charge.'

'Good. Excellent.' Norn turned towards the door. 'We shall take them at the same time as the cobalcats, and release them about the estates.'

Haviland Tuf and Dax followed him from the chamber, and they rode in silence back to Norn's ship.

The fee was sent up by the House of Norn the day before delivery was due. The following afternoon, a dozen men in black-and-grey ascended to the *Ark*, and carried six tranquillised cobalcats from Haviland Tuf's nutrient vats to the waiting cages in their ships. Tuf bid them a passive farewell, and heard no more from Herold Norn. But he kept the *Ark* in orbit about Lyronica.

Less than three of Lyronica's shortened days passed before Tuf observed that his clients had slated a cobalcat for a bout in the Bronze Arena. On the appointed evening, he disguised himself as best a man like he could disguise himself – with a false beard and a shoulder-length wig of red hair, plus a gaudy puff-sleeved suit of canary yellow complete with a furred turban – and shuttled down to the City of All Houses with the hope of escaping attention. When the match was called (it was the third on the schedule), Tuf was sitting in the back of the Arena, a rough stone wall against his shoulders and a narrow wooden seat attempting to support his weight. He had paid a few irons for admission, but had scrupulously bypassed the betting booths.

'Third match,' the announcer cried, even as workers pulled off the scattered meaty chunks of the loser in the second match. 'From the House of Varcour, a female lizard-lion, aged nine months, weight 1.4 quintals, trained by Junior Beast-Master Ammari y Varcour Otheni. Once a veteran of the Bronze Arena, once surviving.' Those customers close to Tuf began to cheer and wave their hands wildly – he had chosen to enter by the Varcour Gate this time, walking down a green concrete road and through the gaping maw of a monstrous golden lizard – and, far away and below, a green-and-gold enamelled door slid up. Tuf had worn binoculars. He lifted them to his eyes, and saw the lizard-lion scrabble forward; two metres of scaled green reptile with a whip-like tail thrice its own length and the long snout of an Old Earth alligator. Its jaws opened and closed soundlessly, displaying an array of impressive teeth.

'From the House of Norn, imported from offworld for your amusement, a female cobalcat. Aged – aged three weeks.' The announcer paused. 'Aged three years,' he said at last, 'weight 2.3 quintals, trained by Senior Beast-Master Herold Norn. New to the Bronze Arena.' The metallic dome overhead rang to the cacophonous cheering of the Norn sector; Herold Norn had packed the Bronze Arena with his housemen and tourists betting the grey-and-black standard.

The cobalcat came from the darkness slowly, with cautious fluid grace, and its great golden eyes swept the arena. It was every bit the beast that Tuf had promised; a bundle of deadly muscle and frozen motion, all blue with but a single silvery streak. Its growl could scarcely be heard, so far was Tuf from the action, but he saw its mouth gape through his glasses.

The lizard-lion saw it too, and came waddling forward, its short scaled legs kicking in the sand while the long impossible tail arched above it like the sting of some reptilian scorpion. Then, when the cobalcat turned its liquid eyes on the enemy, the lizard-

143

lion brought the tail forward and down. Hard. With a bone-breaking crack the whip made contact, but the cobalcat had smoothly slipped to one side, and nothing shattered but air and sand.

The cat circled, yawning. The lizard-lion, implacable, turned and raised its tail again, opened its jaws, lunged forward. The cobalcat avoided both teeth and whip. Again the tail cracked, and again; the cat was too quick. Someone in the audience began to moan the killing chant, others picked it up; Tuf turned his binoculars, and saw swaying in the Norn seats. The lizard-lion gnashed its long jaws in frenzy, smashed its whip across the nearest entry door, and began to thrash.

The cobalcat, sensing an opening, moved behind its enemy with a graceful leap, pinned the struggling lizard with one great blue paw, and clawed the soft greenish flanks and belly to ribbons. After a time and a few futile snaps of its whip that only distracted the cat, the lizard-lion lay still.

The Norns were cheering very loudly. Haviland Tuf – huge and full-bearded and gaudily dressed – rose and left.

Weeks passed; the *Ark* remained in orbit around Lyronica. Haviland Tuf listened to results from the Bronze Arena on his ship's comm, and noted that the Norn cobalcats were winning match after match after match. Herold Norn still lost a contest on occasion – usually when he used an ironfang to fill up his Arena obligations – but those defeats were easily outweighed by his victories.

Tuf sat with Dax curled in his lap, drank tankards of brown ale from the *Ark* brewery, and waited.

About a month after the debut of the cobalcats, a ship rose to meet him; a slim, needle-browed shuttlecraft of green and gold. It docked, after comm contact, and Tuf met the visitors in the reception room with Dax in his arms. The cat read them as friendly enough, so he activated no defences.

There were four, all dressed in metallic armour of scaled gold metal and green enamel. Three stood stiffly at attention. The fourth, a florid and corpulent man who wore a golden helmet with a bright green plume to conceal his baldness, stepped forward and offered a meaty hand.

'Your intent is appreciated,' Tuf told him, keeping both of his own hands firmly on Dax, 'but I do not care to touch. I do require your name and business, sir.'

'Morho y Varcour Otheni,' the leader began.

Tuf raised one palm. 'So. And you are the Senior Beast-Master of the House of Varcour, come to buy a monster. Enough. I knew it all the while, I must confess. I merely wished – on impulse, as it were – to determine if you would tell the truth.'

The fat Beast-Master's mouth puckered in an 'o'.

'Your housemen should remain here,' Tuf said, turning. 'Follow me.'

Haviland Tuf let Morho y Varcour Otheni utter scarcely a word until they were alone in the computer room, sitting diagonally opposite. 'You heard of me from the Norns,' Tuf said then. 'Is that not correct?'

Morho smiled toothily. 'Indeed we did. A Norn houseman was persuaded to reveal the source of their cobalcats. To our delight, your *Ark* was still in orbit. You seem to have found Lyronica diverting?'

'Problems exist. I hope to help. Your problem, for example. Varcour is, in all probability, now the last and least of the Twelve Great Houses. Your lizard-lions fail to awe me, and I understand your realms are chiefly swampland. Choice of combatants being therefore limited. Have I divined the essence of your complaint?'

'Hmpf. Yes, indeed. You do anticipate me, sir. But you do it well. We were holding our own well enough until you interfered; then, well, we have not taken a match from Norn since, and they were previously our chiefest victims. A few paltry wins over Wrai Hill and Amar Island, a lucky score against Feridian, a pair of death-draws with Arneth and Sin Doon – that has been our lot this past month. Pfui. We cannot survive. They will make me a Brood-Tender and ship me back to the estates unless I act.'

Tuf quieted Morho with an upraised hand. 'No need to speak further. Your distress is noted. In the time since I have helped Herold Norn, I have been fortunate enough to be gifted with a great deal of leisure. Accordingly, as an exercise of the mind, I have been able to devote myself to the problems of the Great Houses, each in its turn. We need not waste time. I can solve your present difficulties. There will be cost, however.'

Morho grinned. 'I come prepared. I heard about your price. It's high, there is no arguing, but we are prepared to pay, if you can . . .'

'Sir,' Tuf said. 'I am a man of charity. Norn was a poor House, Herold almost a beggar. In mercy, I gave him a low price. The domains of Varcour are richer, its standards brighter, its victories more wildly sung. For you, I must charge three hundred thousand standards, to make up for the losses I suffered in dealing with Norn.'

Morho made a shocked blubbering sound, and his scales gave metallic clinks as he shifted in his seat. 'Too much, too much,' he protested. 'I implore you. Truly, we are more glorious than Norn, but not so great as you suppose. To pay this price of yours, we must need starve. Lizard-lions would run over our battlements. Our towns would sink on their stilts, until the swamp mud covered them over and the children drowned.'

Tuf was looking at Dax. 'Quite so,' he said, when his glance went back to Morho. 'You touch me deeply. Two hundred thousand standards.'

Morho y Varcour Otheni began to protest and implore again, but this time Tuf merely sat silently, arms on their armrests, until the Beast-Master, red-faced and sweating, finally ran down and agreed to pay his price.

Tuf punched his control arm. The image of a great lizard materialised between him and Morho; it stood three metres tall, covered in grey-green plate scales and standing on two thick clawed legs. Its head, atop a short neck, was disproportionately large, with jaws great enough to take off a man's head and shoulders in a single chomp. But the creature's most remarkable features were its forelegs; short thick ropes of muscle ornamented by metre-long spurs of discoloured bone.

'The *tris neryei* of Cable's Landing,' Tuf said, 'or so it was named by the Fyndii, whose colonists preceded men on that world by a millennium. The term translates, literally, as 'living knife'. Also called the bladed tyrant, a name of human origin referring to the beast's resemblance to the tyrannosaur, or tyrant lizard, a long-extinct reptile of Old Earth. A superficial resemblance only, to be sure. The *tris neryei* is a far more efficient carnivore than the tyrannosaur ever was, due to its terrible forelegs, swords of bone that it uses with a frightful instinctive ferocity.'

Morho was leaning forward until his seat creaked beneath him, and Dax filled Tuf's head with hot enthusiasm. 'Excellent!' the Beast-Master said, 'though the names are a bit long-winded. We shall call them tyrannoswords, eh?'

'Call them what you will, it matters not to me. The animals

146

have many obvious advantages for the House of Varcour,' Tuf said. 'Should you take them, I will throw in – without any additional charge – a breeding stock of Cathadayn tree-slugs. You will find that . . .'

When he could, Tuf followed the news from the Bronze Arena, although he never again ventured forth to the soil of Lyronica. The cobalcats continued to sweep all before them; in the latest featured encounter, one of the Norn beasts had destroyed a prime Arneth strangling-ape and an Amar Island fleshfrog during a special triple match.

But Varcour fortunes were also on the upswing; the newly-introduced tyrannoswords had proved a Bronze Arena sensation, with their booming cries and their heavy tread, and the relentless death of their bone-swords. In three matches so far, a huge feridian, a water-scorpion, and a Gnethin spidercat had all proved impossibly unequal to the Varcour lizards. Morho y Varcour Otheni was reported ecstatic. Next week, tyrannosword would face cobalcat in a struggle for supremacy, and a packed arena was being predicted.

Herold Norn called up once, shortly after the tyrannoswords had scored their first victory. 'Tuf!' he said sternly, 'you were not to sell to the other Houses.'

Haviland Tuf sat calmly, regarding Norn's twisted frown, petting Dax. 'No such matter was ever included in the discussion. Your own monsters perform as expected. Do you complain because another now shares your good fortune?'

'Yes. No. That is – well, never mind. I suppose I can't stop you. If the other Houses get animals that can beat our cats, however, you will be expected to provide us with something that can beat whatever you sell *them*. You understand?'

'Sir. Of course.' He looked down at Dax. 'Herold Norn now questions my comprehension.' Then up again. 'I will always sell, if you have the price.'

Norn scowled on the comm screen. 'Yesyes. Well, by then our victories should have mounted high enough to afford whatever outlandish price you intend to charge.'

'I trust that all goes well otherwise?' Tuf said.

'Well, yes and no. In the Arena, yesyes, definitely. But otherwise, well, that was what I called about. The four young cats don't seem interested in breeding, for some reason. And our Brood-

Tender keeps complaining that they are getting thin. He doesn't think they're healthy. Now, I can't say personally, as I'm here in the City and the animals are back on the plains around Norn House. But some worry does exist. The cats run free, of course, but we have tracers on them, so we can . . .'

Tuf raised a hand. 'It is no doubt not mating season for the cobalcats. Did you not consider this?'

'Ah. No, no, don't suppose so. That makes sense. Just a question of time then, I suppose. The other question I wanted to go over concerned these hoppers of yours. We set them loose, you know, and they have demonstrated no difficulty whatever in breeding. The ancestral Norn grasslands have been chewed bare. It is very annoying. They hop about everywhere. What are we to do?'

'Breed the cobalcats,' Tuf suggested. 'They are excellent predators, and will check the hopper plague.'

Herold Norn looked puzzled, and mildly distressed. 'Yesyes,' he said.

He started to say something else, but Tuf rose. 'I fear I must end our conversation,' he said. 'A shuttleship has entered into docking orbit with the *Ark*. Perhaps you would recognise it. It is blue-steel, with large triangular grey wings.'

'The House of Wrai Hill!' Norn said.

'Fascinating,' said Tuf. 'Good day.'

Beast-Master Denis Lon Wrai paid three hundred thousand standards for his monster, an immensely powerful red-furred ursoid from the hills of Vagabond. Haviland Tuf sealed the transaction with a brace of scampersloth eggs.

The week following, four men in orange silk and flame-red capes visited the *Ark*. They returned to the House of Feridian four hundred and fifty thousand standards poorer, with a contract for the delivery of six great armoured poison-elk, plus a gift herd of Hrangan grass pigs.

The Beast-Master of Sin Doon received a giant serpent; the emissary from Amar Island was pleased by his godzilla. A committee of a dozen Dant seniors in milk-white robes and silver buckles delighted in the slavering garghoul that Haviland Tuf offered them, with a trifling gift. And so, one by one, each of the Twelve Great Houses of Lyronica sought him out, each received its monster, each paid the ever-increasing price.

By that time, both of Norn's fighting cobalcats were dead, the first sliced easily in two by the bone-sword of a Varcour tyranno-sword, the second crushed between the massive clawed paws of a Wrai Hill ursoid (though in the latter case, the ursoid too had died) – if the great cats had espied their fate, they nonetheless had proved unable to avoid it. Herold Norn had been calling the *Ark* daily, but Tuf had instructed his computer to refuse the calls.

Finally, with eleven Houses as past customers, Haviland Tuf sat across the computer room from Danel Leigh Arneth, Senior Beast-Master of Arneth-in-the-Gilded-Wood, once the greatest and proudest of the Twelve Great Houses of Lyronica, now the last and least. Arneth was an immensely tall man, standing even with Tuf himself, but he had none of Tuf's fat; his skin was hard ebony, all muscle, his face a hawk-nosed axe, his hair short and iron grey. The Beast-Master came to the conference in cloth-of-gold, with crimson belt and boots and a tiny crimson beret aslant upon his head. He carried a trainer's pain-prod like a walking stick.

Dax read immense hostility in the man, and treachery, and a barely-suppressed rage. Accordingly, Haviland Tuf carried a small laser strapped to his stomach just beneath his greatcoat.

'The strength of Arneth-in-the-Gilded-Wood has always been in variety,' Danel Leigh Arneth said early on. 'When the other Houses of Lyronica threw all their fortunes on the backs of a single beast, our fathers and grandfathers worked with dozens. Against any animal of theirs, we had an optimal choice, a strategy. That has been our greatness and our pride. But we can have no strategy against these demon-beasts of yours, trader. No matter which of our hundred fighters we sent on to the sand, it comes back dead. We are forced to deal with you.'

'Not so,' said Haviland Tuf. 'I force no one. Still, look at my stock. Perhaps fortune will see fit to give you back your strategic options.' He touched the buttons on his chair, and a parade of monsters came and went before the eyes of the Arneth Beast-Master; creatures furred and scaled and feathered and covered by armour plate, beasts of hill and forest and lake and plain, predators and scavengers and deadly herbivores of sizes great and small. And Danel Leigh Arneth, his lips pressed tightly together, finally ordered four each of the dozen largest and deadliest species, at a cost of some two million standards.

The conclusion of the transaction – complete, as with all the other Houses, with a gift of some small harmless animal – did nothing to soothe Arneth's foul temper. 'Tuf,' he said when the dealing was over, 'you are a clever and devious man, but you do not fool me.'

Haviland Tuf said nothing.

'You have made yourself immensely wealthy, and you have cheated all who bought from you and thought to profit. The Norns, for example – their cobalcats are worthless.

'They were a poor House; your price brought them to the edge of bankruptcy, just as you have done to all of us. They thought to recoup through victories. Bah! There will be no Norn victories now! Each House that you have sold to gained the edge on those who purchased previously. Thus Arneth, the last to purchase, remains the greatest House of all. Our monsters will wreak devastation. The sands of the Bronze Arena will darken with the blood of the lesser beasts.'

Tuf's hands locked on the bulge of his stomach. His face was placid.

'You have changed nothing! The Great Houses remain, Arneth the greatest and Norn the least. All you have done is bleed us, like the profiteer you are, until every lord must struggle and scrape to get by. The Houses now wait for victory, pray for victory, depend on victory, but all the victories will be Arneth's. We alone have not been cheated, because I thought to buy last and thus best.'

'So,' said Haviland Tuf. 'You are then a wise and sagacious Beast-Master, if this indeed is the case. Yet I deny that I have cheated anyone.'

'Don't play with words!' Arneth roared. 'Henceforth you will deal no longer with the Great Houses. Norn has no money to buy from you again, but if they did, you would not sell to them. *Do you understand?* We will not go round and round for ever.'

'Of course,' Tuf said. He looked at Dax. 'Now Danel Leigh Arneth imputes my understanding. I am always misunderstood.' His calm gaze returned to the angry Beast-Master in red-and-gold. 'Your point, sir, is well taken. Perhaps it is time for me to leave Lyronica. In any event, I shall not deal with Norn again, nor with any of the Great Houses. This is a foolish impulse – by thus acting I forswear great profits – but I am a gentle man, much given to following my whim. Obedient to the esteemed Danel Leigh Arneth, I bow to your demand.'

Dax reported wordlessly that Arneth was pleased and pacified; he had cowed Tuf, and won the day for his House. His rivals would get no new champions. Once again, the Bronze Arena would be predictable. He left satisfied.

Three weeks later, a fleet of twelve glittering gold-flecked shuttles and a dozen work squads of men in gold-and-crimson armour arrived to remove the purchases of Danel Leigh Arneth. Haviland Tuf, stroking a limp lazy Dax, saw them off, then returned down the long corridors of the *Ark* to his control room, to take a call from Herold Norn.

The thin Beast-Master looked positively skeletal. 'Tuf!' he exclaimed. 'Everything is going wrong. You must help.'

'Wrong? I solved your problem.'

Norn pressed his features together in a grimace, and scratched beneath his brass coronet. 'Nono, listen. The cobalcats are all dead, or sick. Four of them dead in the Bronze Arena – we knew the second pair were too young, you understand, but when the first couple lost, there was nothing else to do. It was that or go back to ironfangs. Now we have only two left. They don't eat much – catch a few hoppers, but nothing else. And we can't train them, either. A trainer comes into the pen with a pain-prod, and the damn cats know what he intends. They're always a move ahead, you understand? In the arena, they won't respond to the killing chant at all. It's *terrible*. The worst thing is they don't even breed. We need *more* of them. What are we supposed to enter in the gaming pits?'

'It is not cobalcat breeding season,' Tuf said.

'Yesyes. When *is* their breeding season?'

'A fascinating question. A pity you did not ask sooner. As I understand the matter, the female cobalt panther goes into heat each spring, when the snowtufts blossom on Celia's World. Some type of biological trigger is involved.'

'I – Tuf. You *planned* this. Lyronica has no snowthings, whatever. Now I suppose you intend charging us a fortune for these flowers.'

'Sir. Of course not. Were the option mine, I would gladly give them to you. Your plight wounds me. I am concerned. However, as it happens, I have given my word to Danel Leigh Arneth to deal no more with the Great Houses of Lyronica.' He shrugged hopelessly.

'We won victories with your cats,' Norn said, with an edge of desperation in his voice. 'Our treasury has been growing – we have something like forty thousand standards now. It is yours. Sell us these flowers. Or better, a new animal. Bigger. Fiercer. I saw the Dant garghouls. Sell us something like that. We have nothing to enter in the Bronze Arena!'

'No? What of your ironfangs? The pride of Norn, I was told.'

Herold Norn waved impatiently. 'Problems, you understand, we have been having problems. These hoppers of yours, they eat anything, everything. They've gotten out of control. Millions of them, all over, eating all the grass, and all the crops. The things they've done to farmland – the cobalcats love them, yes, but we don't have enough cobalcats. And the wild ironfangs won't touch the hoppers. They don't like the taste, I suppose. I don't know, not really. But, you understand, all the other grass-eaters left, driven out by these hoppers of yours, and the ironfangs went with them. Where, I don't know that either. Gone, though. Into the unclaimed lands, beyond the realms of Norn. There are some villages out there, a few farmers, but they hate the Great Houses. Tamberkin, all of them, don't even have dog fights. They'll probably try to *tame* the ironfangs, if they see them.'

'So,' said Tuf. 'But then you have your kennels, do you not?'

'Not any more,' Norn said. He sounded very harried. 'I ordered them shut. The ironfangs were losing every match, especially after you began to sell to the other Houses. It seemed a foolish waste to maintain dead weight. Besides, the expense – we needed every standard. You bled us dry. We had Arena fees to pay, and of course we had to wager, and lately we've had to buy some food from Tamber just to feed all our housemen and trainers. I mean, you would never *believe* the things the hoppers have done to our crops.'

'Sir,' said Tuf. 'You insult me. I am an ecologist. I know a great deal of hoppers and their ways. Am I to understand that you shut your Ironfang kennels?'

'Yesyes. We turned the useless things loose, and now they're gone with the rest. What are we going to do? The hoppers are overrunning the plains, the cats won't mate, and our money will run out soon if we must continue to import food and pay Arena fees without any hope of victory.'

Tuf folded his hands together. 'You do indeed face a series of delicate problems. And I am the very man to help you to their solution. Unfortunately, I have pledged my bond to Danel Leigh Arenth.'

'Is it hopeless, then? Tuf, I am a man begging, I a Senior Beast-Master of Norn. Soon we will drop from the games entirely. We will have no funds for Arena fees or betting, no animals to enter.

We are cursed by ill fortune. No Great House has ever failed to provide its allotment of fighters, not even Feridian during its Twelve Year Drought. We will be shamed. The House of Norn will sully its proud history by sending dogs and cats on to the sand, to be shredded ignominiously by the huge monsters that you have sold the other Houses.'

'Sir,' Tuf said. 'If you will permit me an impertinent remark, and one perhaps without foundation – if you will permit this to me – well, then, I will tell you my opinion. I have a hunch – mmm, *hunch*, yes, that is the proper word, and a curious word it is too – a hunch, as I was saying, that the monsters you fear may be in short supply in the weeks and months to come. For example, the adolescent ursoids of Vagabond may very shortly go into hibernation. They are less than a year old, you understand. I hope the lords of Wrai Hill are not unduly disconcerted by this, yet I fear that they may be. Vagabond, as I'm sure you are aware, has an extremely irregular orbit about its primary, so that its Long Winters last approximately twenty standard years. The ursoids are attuned to this cycle. Soon their body processes will slow to almost nothing – some have mistaken a sleeping ursoid for a dead one, you know – and I don't think they will be easily awakened. Perhaps, as the trainers of Wrai Hill are men of high good character and keen intellect, they might find a way. But I would be strongly inclined to further suspect that most of their energies and their funds will be devoted to feeding their populace, in the light of the voracious appetites of scampersloths. In quite a like manner, the men of the House of Varcour will be forced to deal with an explosion of Cathadayn tree-slugs. The tree-slugs are particularly fascinating creatures. At one point in their life cycle, they become veritable sponges, and double in size. A large enough grouping is fully capable of drying up even an extensive swampland.' Tuf paused, and his thick fingers beat in drumming rhythms across his stomach. 'I ramble unconscionably. Sir. Do you grasp my point, though? My thrust?'

Herold Norn looked like a dead man. 'You are mad. You have destroyed us. Our economy, our ecology . . . but *why*? We paid you fairly. The Houses, the Houses . . . no beasts, no funds. How can the games go on? *No one* will send fighters to the Bronze Arena!'

Haviland Tuf raised his hands in shock. 'Really?,' he said.

Then he turned off the communicator and rose. Smiling a tiny tight-lipped smile, he began to talk to Dax.

THE GIANT KILLERS

by Andrew M Stephenson

IS THERE anyone else who can complain he doesn't get enough time to concentrate on writing because he is too busy painting Galaxy *covers?*

Andrew Stephenson is a telecommunication designer by trade, but leads a double and a triple life as a writer and as a highly-talented artist. His sketches accompanying Larry Niven's article, 'Alternatives for Worlds' appeared first in my own Speculation *and then, revised, in* Analog *– his first artistic sale to the SF magazines. Then, or so the story goes, the editor of another publication got Larry Niven out of bed at 3.00 am to ask, 'Who is Andrew Stephenson? How can I get in touch?' Subsequently Andrew has illustrated Niven and Pournelle's novel* Inferno, *and various other commissions.*

'But my main interest is writing,' he says. His is a highly techno-logical brand of science fiction, as 'Giant Killers' will demonstrate. Remember the deadly life-forms of Deathworld, *the roboticised warfare of Dick's* The Defenders? *There's a little of both here, but above all the story is about people; the little man, caught in the cogs of something which long ago got out of control.*

Something scurried across the ceiling of the tunnel. Tolbein spun round, reflexes bringing his gun to his shoulder, his finger to the trigger. For a heartbeat he paused, then he lowered the gun.

It was a simple, harmless Scarab. It hung on to the rough concrete upside-down by its eight legs and examined him with its miniature sensors. Snow-white, sterile, brilliant with glittering patches of polished metal, the robot seemed to be waiting for him. Tolbein waved a hand at it and immediately it stepped daintily across to the central guide rail on the ceiling and glided away, down the corridor and into the hazy distance. Tolbein shouldered his gun and went his own way.

He met the other two by the exit. Leader Granton and the tech, Hughes, were sitting on a metal bench beside the grey blast door.

By their expressions Tolbein guessed they had been waiting some time.

Granton looked up, his heavy face creasing as he gathered himself to demand an explanation. Forestalling him, Tolbein said,

'I saw a Scarab.'

Granton relaxed. He stood, saying matter-of-factly, 'So? What else do you expect to see during a plague?' He stopped and scrutinised Tolbein. 'Did it . . .' He licked his lips, evidently unsure what to ask. 'Did it take an interest in you?'

'I'm clean,' said Tolbein sourly. Scarabs only bothered with the dead and the dying; there were other robots for mere illness.

'Okay,' said Granton. 'You know Lin Hughes? Good, then let's get going.'

While Hughes was struggling to settle the bulky instrument pack on his back, Tolbein murmured to Granton: 'Is he up to it?'

Granton glanced at Hughes, then at Tolbein. 'I think so.'

'The Voyo's something new. Could be we ought to insist on having an experienced tech.'

'With the plague cutting back the available manpower?' Granton shook his head and started tapping out numbers on the keyboard set into the wall by the door. Lights flickered as the security system checked them. Cameras sank on articulated arms for a better view.

'We can't afford to wait, Kolak. As you say, the Voyo's new. Dangerously new. It's gotten Security and Intelligence sections in a panic. Now,' and he met Tolbein's eye with his level gaze, 'what would you do in their place: a damaged survivor is sighted moving west, alone, and in country we control; would you let it slip through your fingers, or would you take a chance and send three men after it?'

'I . . .' Tolbein watched Hughes tightening his straps. 'I guess I'd take the risk.' Then he laughed. 'What the hell, I *am* taking the risk!'

Smiling, Granton turned to Hughes. 'Ready, Hughes?'

The youngster nodded, his ungainly helmet bobbing ponderously on his narrow shoulders. Tolbein wondered how such a frail body could carry the weight of the complete Heimdall system, microminiaturised though the computer and its weapons might be.

Suddenly a klaxon blared. The security system was satisfied.

The three soldiers stood clear as the warning lights changed from red to yellow, from yellow to green; and then the massive door eased up and over until it snuggled flat against the tunnel ceiling.

Beyond the grey steel frame lay the red-lit cave of the airlock.

'Move,' said Granton, and they filed into the echoing space. Clammy air, redolent of damp earth, made Tolbein's nostrils tingle. 'Now check everything,' Granton added, '—thoroughly.'

Tolbein needed no more than a minute to run through his own checklist, and he watched abstractedly as Granton began inspecting Hughes.

'This strap's loose.' Granton tugged at one of the back pack cross-straps. 'If it slips at the wrong moment, in action say . . .'

'But Mult,' Hughes protested, 'it's thirty-five in shade out there! I'll get blisters with the sweat and the chafing.'

'Ever been Outside?'

'In the States, sure . . .'

'Well, son, you can copy the rest of us and forget the States and everything you learned there. This is Africa. Here at noon in October you sweat, along with the rest of whatever wildlife is left Outside, whether you're ventilated or not . . .' With a sharp tug Granton tightened the offending strap. 'And you stop the chafing by keeping everything secure. Besides, the air circulation system in your uniform will keep you dry. Now, what about your gun?'

'It's loaded, like you said.'

'Let me see it.'

'But I told you . . .'

'Dammit kid, give me that gun!'

Hughes unshouldered his GP and passed it butt first to his superior who began methodically opening and closing its various ports, loading points, power and control inspection hatches, until he paused.

'Thought so.'

'What's wrong?'

'I'm tempted to let you find out for yourself, except we'd probably all suffer.' Handing the gun back, Granton said, 'What kind of bullets did you load with?'

'Uh, HESH I think.' Hughes bent to look. 'Yeah, high-explosive squash head.'

'And in the rocket magazine?'

'Standard ground-air-ground.'

'And has nobody warned you against mixing GAG with HESH?'

Hughes' expression sagged into dismay. Granton said it for him:

'Wasted effort, Technician Hughes, is a capital crime in this war. Sure, you smear your target all over the landscape. But the object of a fight isn't to show off; it's to make the best of what

157

you've got. So lock in: use all *you*'ve got – including your intelligence.' Granton left Hughes to reload the bullet magazine with simple rounds, and approached Tolbein.

'Ready, Kolak?'

'Sir!' Tolbein's attention had been elsewhere, lost in a reverie. Now he reacted instinctively, but with a forcefulness that made Granton step back.

'Easy down,' he said. 'We're informal here.'

'We're in the airlock sir. Milspeech. Is not proper relax discipline too soon. Best maintain alert.'

Granton gave him a long look as if he knew the true reason for Tolbein's excessive reaction. He smiled. 'Sure,' he said, then went over Tolbein's harness, gun, and respirator. 'But at least drop the argot.'

'Milspeech necessary. As you say, soon-gone: Voyo new, dangerous. Therefore close interworking essential.'

Granton faced him squarely. 'Yah, right. So let's understand each other.' He hesitated. 'Look, Kolak, that gabble may be what Headquarters requires its personnel to use, but here in the bunkers let's try to hang on to our humanity, not throw it away.'

'As you wish.' Tolbein's breath hissed out between his teeth. 'Paradeground soldiers, is that it?' He felt angry for a moment that Granton should be so haphazard about the serious business of war.

Granton looked up from inspecting the leggings. 'What did you say?'

'Nothing. Thinking aloud.'

The Leader straightened up. 'Sometimes,' he whispered, 'sometimes I feel you do too much thinking for your own good, Kolak Tolbein, Militiaman B-7, with your bloody daydreams, your romancing, your damned books with their lies about how wonderful the world is. Today the War is real; nothing else matters in the whole wide Earth. Forget that and you're dead. Dammit, even Hughes there knows better, and he's from Technical Support, not Infantry. He's the kind of man I want, though, for all his inexperience, not some would-be hero. I've this itch that says you'd rather not come at all, and I'd love to scratch that itch to stop it getting any worse . . . This mission's still voluntary if you've changed your mind. There'll be no disgrace; even Intelligence admit that a new class of fighting machine, crippled or not, will be no easy capture for only three men.'

'No, . . . sir,' Tolbein assured him. 'I'd rather go out and hit the enemy than wait in this bunker for him to hit me. If you'll excuse the expression: it feels more like a war this way.'

'Maybe.' Granton sighed. 'You may be right. Forget what I said. I'm not so sure, that's all. It used to be a straight fight between men, even if the two sides did have fancy weapons. These days something's gone sour: we send out men like Hughes to rob the corpses of machines for their brains rather than take human prisoners for interrogation. Is that war? Or is it grave robbing? ... What do you say, Lin?'

'Me, sir?' Hughes seemed startled to be addressed by his first name. 'Never given it a thought, sir.'

'Never had to, you mean. Never mind, let it drop. Wait for the green light.'

They waited. Tolbein reflected that one could waste an awful lot of time, simply waiting for things to happen; and when they did, they usually happened too fast for comfort. Always had, always would. Soldiers were experts at waiting.

We waited in '21, all right. Hours, days even, down on the sea bed, crowded thirty at a time into those Tursas landing craft, forbidden to speak except by direct permission. Five to a bench, nursing our weapons, praying the enemy wouldn't pick us up too soon.

And then the run-in: engines droning, the deck beginning to sway as we rose towards the surface, skimming the rising sea-bed. Then the pitching, as the surf caught us, and the stench of vomit from those the pills hadn't helped. And, growing louder, the sullen rumble of the barrage: flights of missiles pounding the shore, crumbling the ferroconcrete beaches in preparation for the assault. And all this from inside a steel box.

We're coming, Harry-boy. Roll out the red carpet of blood and fire: the marines are here!

And then the section leaders began bawling orders above the shriek of missiles and the blaring landing alarms, and even the seasick cases stiffened up, gripped their guns, and were ready when the Tursas grated on the shore. Crash!, and the anchors were driven deep by explosive charges; then two more blasts, and the doors were gone, arcing high into the air on their release rockets, scattering chaff as they went to confuse the antipersonnel radar waiting on the beach.

And the fun began: 'Death or glory!' some fool cried, even as his neck disintegrated before a hail of flea-shot. A wave claimed his body. I ran past his grave, wading desperately through the waist-high water to reach the uncertain sanctuary of the beach and a chance to shoot back ...

159

The light turned green. The outer door opened.

'Hear this,' Granton said. 'Remember: out there is a War Zone. It looks peaceful. Just don't be fooled. Mind your training, your feet, and your head. *Go!*'

They ran up the concrete ramp beyond the outer blast door, into the twisting darkness of the access tunnel leading to the surface, a hundred metres above them.

The climb was swift and made without talk. Tolbein took the rear and Granton point, with Hughes between them. Tolbein's night-sight visor showed the two ahead as orange figures in red uniforms. Dark red vapours rose from their heads and hands, and two spots of yellow glowed on Hughes' pack: his Heimdall sensor set, already operating.

Daylight appeared and they cautiously rounded the last corner and looked out of the tunnel on to savannah grasslands broken by tracts of open woods. The time was still early afternoon, barely 1400 hours, and the sun hung high overhead. The bleached dry land dreamed in the heat. Shadows were black holes beneath tattered trees and thorn brakes. Nothing moved but the shimmer of rising air.

Another green light flashed in the ceiling, where they could see it but anyone outside could not.

'All clear in the sky and no large hostiles on the ground or under it,' Granton said. 'But keep alert for gremlins, theirs *and* ours.'

They moved out of the tunnel into the open. Behind them the outer defences of the bunker snapped invisibly on again. Unseen eyes and ears traced their progress through the long yellow grass; inhuman, impassive, the machines noted their departure and forgot them.

The trio set off on a northwesterly course away from the jumble of rocks concealing the bunker. They held the same formation as in the tunnel, only now Tolbein watched their rear, Granton the ground they were crossing, and Hughes the space around them using his electronically-augmented senses.

Some two hours later Hughes broke the silence by hissing a warning in Milspeech:

'Thermal, human-plus, green-thirty, sixty!'

They dropped to the ground; the sensor-column on Hughes' pack slid out of its housing, extending itself clear of the surrounding grass, and continued its scan of the horizon.

'Moving?' asked Granton.

'Slowly. Will miss present location if holds same course.'

'Good . . . Time?'

'Cross our path, plus twenty minutes, estimate.'

'Too long. If wait that long, may miss interception of Voyo. Must act.'

Tolbein nodded to himself. This was more like it.

Granton decided. 'Close in,' he ordered. 'Handsign only.'

The grass rustled loudly and their footsteps sounded clumsy in the hush of the afternoon, without wind or insect, animal or bird, to disturb the vast indifference of Nature to Man's doings. As they advanced warily upon the source of the heat radiation Hughes had detected he signalled range and bearing to Granton by tapping him on the shoulder. Soon they were close enough for the Leader to indicate a halt.

Barely three metres away there were movements. Grass stalks crackled. A non-human voice cried to itself in a continuous gasping, mewling groan.

Granton raised one hand. *Sniffer*, his fingers said. Hughes passed him the telescopic pole with the chemosensor head and he extended this towards the disturbance. It was greeted with a savage snarl and an abrupt end to the movement. Deep breathing followed, punctuated by low whines of pain.

Again Granton advanced the probe but held it high whilst reading the displays in the handle. Tolbein had his GP raised, as had Hughes, but Granton announced:

'Animal, badly wounded: signs of advanced corporeal corruption.' He pulled a gas grenade from his belt and lobbed it into the region of flattened grass. It popped and the ensuing flurry of activity quickly subsided as the tranquilliser took effect. After waiting a few seconds for the gas to be oxidised to harmlessness the men moved closer and looked down at what they had caught. These days any animal was a curiosity in Africa.

It had been a lion once. A male, over two metres long in the body, it had suffered greatly before final disaster struck it. The flesh had been wasted from its bones by starvation and disease, so that its ribs and muscles showed plainly. Its skin had been rubbed clean of fur in many places, and sores clustered thickly about its joints. The eyes, half open even in unconsciousness, were bloodshot and yellowed with a crust of semisolid pus, and the tangled mane was clotted with caked blood and other body fluids. But worst of all were the tail, hindquarters and abdomen. From these there arose the foul odour of putrefaction, the stench of decay belonging more properly to flesh turned carrion many, many days

161

before. Yet no flies moved upon the raw red meat; no maggots crawled in the exposed and shrivelling intestines. Rather, a delicate tracery of white threads covered the bleaching leg- and tail-bones, still held together by scraps of tendon and leather, and a finer mat of lace enmeshed the comparatively fresh meat higher up the body.

Hughes averted his face from the living corpse.

Granton stared at it, solemnly but not unmoved. 'Rotspray trap,' he said.

Tolbein, before anyone could stop him, shot the beast through the head. *'Requiescat in pace,'* he said quietly.

Granton regarded him silently for a few seconds, and said: 'Yes.' Almost as an afterthought, he said: 'This is the war you wanted to find, Kolak. And this is what I detest about it most: it's so bloody impartial.' He raised his head to scan the horizon by eye. 'We'll have to be alert. The lion can't have come far, and other traps will have been dropped along with the one that got it.' He stopped and looked northwest. 'Time to get moving.' To Hughes: 'Forget about it, Lin. The rot will finish the body in a few hours ... *Technician Hughes!* ... That's better. Okay, march!'

About an hour before sunset they came to a point where two streams merged and flowed down a gentle grade into a wide, shallow valley where a great river gleamed like polished silver in the evening light. The vegetation in the valley was thicker than where they stood, and there were hints of many substantial watercourses amongst the trees. Granton consulted the inertial navigator in Hughes' pack; by projecting an idealised synthesised view on to the three helmet visors, he was able to point out landmarks.

'That's the Zambesi,' he said. 'We're seven kilometres from it and one hundred and fifty metres higher up. It flows from south to north at this point – that's from left to right – and varies from four hundred to over seven hundred metres in width just below the Kariba Gorge, southwest of us. Now, the Voyo was reported moving almost due west, as though making for that narrow spot in the river.' He indicated a bearing slightly north of west. 'The Salisbury–Kafue tourist monorail used to go that way, only it was demolished in the first weeks of the War. That won't stop the Voyo, as it has ground effect lifters – it can float across the surface of the water – but it could be damned awkward for us. We have a boat, sure, but I don't fancy making a sitting target of myself out on the river.

'That means one thing: catch the Voyo before it gets to the river.' He looked to Tolbein. 'Kolak, you take over point. I'll take the rear. Follow this stream downhill and you should hit the Voyo's trail soon. Signals as and when.'

Tolbein's hand went up. He bent to study the ground, and Hughes stood guard as he and Granton examined the faint tracks in the grass.

'Good guessing,' Tolbein said. 'It must have crossed the stream a few metres this side of the ridge ... over there.' The trail led back to the stream where deep gouges in the dried mud betrayed the passage of a large armoured wheel-less vehicle.

'The Voyo?' asked Granton.

'Tankspoor, at least. Look, there's a drag mark parallel to it. That could be battle damage. Bunker Louise-Nancy reported broken armour on the starboard flank, and if that's so there'd be loss of lift on that side.'

'Fair enough,' Granton agreed. 'We'll use the sniffer to be sure.' He took the instrument from Hughes and swept the probe across the tracks. 'The readout's ambiguous. Hughes, give me vox on this one.' Before Hughes could answer, his backpack had caught the code word and responded with a soft beep in all their headphones. Granton added: 'Colloquial.'

The quietly assured voice of the computer began:

'The principal component is lube oil with a radiocount of approximately ten röntgens per hour, most probably deposited within the past three hours. This time estimate assumes that a significant minor component, a silicone-based coolant, is from the same source. Ends.'

'Vox off,' said Granton. Standing, he studied the terrain below them. 'If it weren't for the trees we'd likely see it. Can't be more than a couple of kilometres ahead.'

Tolbein said, 'It has a low profile. It could be hiding in the grass or amongst bushes, looking like a rock and waiting for sunset before losing us. It knows we can't afford to travel at night, what with the gremlins and the spotter satellites; with nothing to lose and plenty to gain it'll take the risk of meeting a Baskerville or Podbipieta in the hope of reaching its own forces ahead of us.'

Hughes spoke up for the first time since their encounter with the lion. 'Why don't we just do the same?'

The other two exchanged glances. Gently, Granton answered him: 'Lin, when you've done a couple of patrols you'll understand why not. 'Til then take my word for it: it's not worth the risk.'

'You talking about them funny gadgets – ice gun, clam, jumping-jack, and those?'

Tolbein carried on: '. . . And bindwort, whip grass, tackymat, acid drop, misty eye . . .'

'Yeah, those.' Hughes laughed, a trifle nervously, Tolbein thought. 'Hell, man, I got stuff in this pack'll fix any of them, excepting maybe the ice gun and tackymat.'

'And rotspray traps?' asked Granton, and Hughes sobered quickly. 'Are you willing to risk it, Lin? If so, you have my permission to act as night patrol for us.'

'Okay, I'm convinced.' Hughes looked it too, but Granton was not letting him off so lightly.

'Lin, all those names have one idea behind them: to kill their victim. And the people, or machines, that designed them weren't particular about the side effects. Most are pretty bad. Kolak and I have six patrols apiece to our credit, but after dark we both stay wrapped up in our tents rather than attract the attention of every gremlin and biotrap within two hundred metres. Remember, we look like roaring bonfires to them – we're *hot*. Add to them the Moles, waiting underground for the right kind of seismic noises to start them burrowing upwards . . .'

'Okay, okay!' Hughes snapped. 'Next thing you'll be showing me. I'm convinced, so lay off, will you?' He was shaking, Tolbein saw, so he coughed and remarked offhandedly,

'I think we could manage half an hour before making camp.'

With the trail left by the damaged war machine as a guide, they resumed their westward march. The sunset was very beautiful that evening, and in the settling dusk Tolbein found himself thinking back to old films seen when the world could still play with the idea of conflict as a brave and glorious exploit, and to the ocean, wide and unruffled, turning to dark wine as the sun drowned in the west and the full moon climbed to take its place amongst the twilight stars. There, cruising at the head of an arrowhead wake, he imagined a ship, searching the waters for an invisible enemy lurking in the deeper darkness below.

It was not a comforting thought.

164

The brief equatorial twilight was almost gone before they finished pitching camp. Hughes had still been eager to carry on despite the earlier warning, but Granton would have none of it. 'We'll have the Voyo by noon tomorrow,' he said, and drove them unremittingly until every detail of encampment had been attended to.

A circular area ten metres across was sterilised against biotraps after being probed for hardware traps. The bag-tents, three of them, were spaced out and staked down with their covering thermal shields carefully connected to heat exchangers buried eighty centimetres deep in the soil. Air-conditioning systems were recharged after recalibration to allow for local atmospheric dust conditions. Inter-tent communications were tested; and finally the Heimdall nightwatch system was set up, with links to each man's tent so that any one of them might direct both surveillance and defence.

'And don't forget your pills,' Granton reminded them. 'I stand first watch, until 2200 hours. Hughes, you take it from then to 0200, and Tolbein 0200 to dawn. Right, goodnight.'

Sealing himself into his own bag-tent, Tolbein lay down fully clothed. Soon he was asleep, dragged by drugs into too-brief unconsciousness.

Later, lying awake in his tent on watch, Tolbein had time to think. The pills that could switch a man on or off ensured he would stay awake now, but he had in any case slept as long as he needed to. Ahead of him lay several hours of solitary contemplation in which to stir those thoughts that chose to come to him. Also, there were the images presented by his helmet, and with those he might amuse himself by gazing at the night around and above the camp, whilst Heimdall's superior senses did all the real work.

On impulse, Tolbein whispered, 'Heimdall?'

'Sir?'

'Do you never sleep?'

'Never, sir.' After a pause, the machine added: '0305 hours and all's well.'

'Thank you, Heimdall. Show me, please.'

And Heimdall painted the world for Tolbein, as it saw the world it had been designed to see. It showed him the indigo of perfect peace, and the little ripples of yellow unease dancing with the blue and orange zones of possible danger. Flights of green subscripted arrows migrated across his helmet visor as the wind blew through the night. Turquoise dots projected the probable courses of airborne debris. Red ghosts of trees trembled as their branch movements fell under suspicion and were reprieved.

'Tell me, Heimdall,' Tolbein said at last, 'do you see what I see? Are those shapes and colours the same for you as they are for me?'

'Your question is ambiguous, sir.'

'Interpret it as you will.'

'In that case, sir, I must say not. I am a machine, and see the world as matrices of numbers, from which I determine objective relationships. I represent these relationships as colours for you alone; I do not need them.'

Tolbein considered these words. Heimdall waited patiently.

'Then I think you are partially blind.'

'Sir?'

Often Tolbein had found himself wondering at the degree of perfection of the voices with which all war computers were now fitted. Here, the tone of doubt was irritatingly accurate, and he replied sharply:

'Because you see only what you've been told to see!' He paused. 'Heimdall, you know me pretty well by now, don't you?'

'We have served together on five missions, amounting to nearly five hundred hours. Yes, I think I know you, sir.'

'Am I a good soldier?'

'You have survived. Therefore, yes, you are a good soldier.'

'Is that the only criterion by which you judge me?'

'I am what I am, sir. By which criteria would you have a defensive system judge those on whom it depends?'

'You might ask how reliable I am.'

'I cannot weight subjective variables, sir, and that is but one of many that must be considered. Therefore I must use the nett result: your own practical ability to allow for them all yourself. It is results that matter, sir, not intentions.'

'Oh, shut up,' Tolbein said. He felt an idiot for having fallen into the trap of arguing with Heimdall. All but the very best of the war computers were programmed in accordance with directed philosophies, and were incapable of reasoning beyond the needs of their specialities. Heimdall could no more evaluate a human as a soldier than it could figure tactics. It lacked flexibility, and to attempt an argument with it was to assume it operated by the same rules as a man.

Tolbein rolled over and took a sip of water from his canteen, then lay back again. 'Hey, Heimdall,' he said suddenly.

'Sir?'

'Do you know where you got your name?'

'Yes, sir. Central Ordnance.'

For the love of . . . 'Did you never hear of the old Norse god who guarded the Bifröst Bridge, and Valhalla?'

'No. Valhalla is oⅼ record as a command post, Grade AA. Codename Bifröst is not in my listing.'

He wanted to laugh. *How much has been lost. Today we raid each other's mythology, searching for names that will lend our Frankensteinian monstrosities some dimension of humanity, by association if not by function.* 'And I suppose Gungnir and Mjolnir are only missiles?'

'What else, sir?'

Sarcasm? Surely not.

'Sir, possible attack.'

'What?' Tolbein roused himself and dropped the visor of his helmet again. 'Where?'

A red circle flashed on the restored image of their immediate surroundings. The indicated object lay some three hundred metres west, near the ground.

'Video, sir?'

'Yes.' The visor darkened to show the night as seen by infrared, whilst the image slid rapidly across as Heimdall panned the camera to the correct bearing. It stabilised.

Grass stems swayed in a dark mass, stroked by a cool night breeze. Cold thorn bushes groped at the hot stars. In an isolated tree a faintly luminous blob stirred fitfully. A gremlin. Tolbein watched it for several seconds in horrid fascination. 'You'll catch nothing tonight,' he promised it, and felt the chill edge of fear when it stopped moving as though it had heard him.

'Filthy things,' he muttered. We've lost control of the night, and soon we'll lose the day too. It's back to the caves, with every shadow an enemy. Could be the dinosaurs will win this time . . .

'Sir, the danger persists,' Heimdall reminded him. With a sense of dismay that he had allowed his mind to wander, Tolbein said, 'Evidence?'

'Geophones.'

'Connect.'

Immediately he heard the voices of the ground: groans and distant mutterings, a million babblings in many tongues, each an account of some event, with two near by that spoke far louder than the rest. There was a reverberant booming, like great drumbeats repeating themselves every two or three seconds, and there was a quieter grinding as of rocks being crushed.

'Analysis?' asked Tolbein.

'Principal component: long-range geocommunications ground-shaker, correlation ninety-two per cent. Probably Voyo. Minor component: sapping torpedo, enemy pattern Pluto XIII, correlation ninety-eight per cent. Time to convergence of Pluto XIII estimated at two hundred and thirteen seconds, plus or minus ...'

'Sound the alarm!'

'Check.' Tolbein heard sudden movements from the other tents, and said: 'Leader.' Waiting a second for Heimdall to connect him to Granton's headset, he continued: 'Enemy attack. Mole, ETA approx two zero six seconds. Bye.'

'Check. Bye,' Granton said calmly.

Tolbein went on: 'No time strip camp. Suggest abandon, revert minimal status. Bye.'

'Check. Technician?'

'Yessir?' asked Hughes sleepily.

'Milspeech,' said Granton. 'GP and rations, outside in fifteen seconds; keep low and separate. Query?'

'No,' Tolbein and Hughes replied in turn.

'Go!'

Tolbein had only to unzip his backpack, withdraw his medical and ration pouch, and clip it to his belt next to the spare ammunition to be ready for the evacuation. But that left ten seconds, in which time he was determined to account for the principal component: the groundshaker attached to the Voyo.

'Heimdall, indicate source of principal component.'

'Within red circle.' The video image was overlaid with a circle set squarely in the middle of the screen. Tolbein peered at it.

'Where is it?' he asked. 'Can see only tree, with grass.'

'Invisible.'

'Rubbish. You must be able to see it.'

'Not so. Zero mean feature count.'

'Display plot of feature familiarity.' Then, as an afterthought: 'Show unrecognisable regions as peak white.'

Immediately Tolbein's eyes, reinforced by suspicion, saw what Heimdall had failed to see despite its elaborate sensing apparatus. Most areas of the screen were dark, those being the parts successfully analysed. In the centre, however, within the red circle, was a hazy form composed of white-with-grey blotches, what amounted to a quick sketch of an armoured fighting vehicle.

The zip of the tent was suddenly run open. Granton looked in. 'What in hell are you up to?' he demanded. 'We've got to pack, Heimdall.'

'No time for that. I'm about to pot the Voyo. Give me five seconds . . . Heimdall, see that region of randomness?'

'Check.'

'Put a rocket through it.'

'Are you mad?' Granton said. 'You'll excite every gremlin for kilometres; we're in for a rough time as it is.'

Tolbein turned on him. 'Can't you see it either? That's the Voyo. Somehow the enemy's produced a camouflage that shows on our equipment as random patterning. Heimdall lacks the subtlety to suspect something that isn't there . . .'

With a crackle, a bang and a swish the rocket was launched. Riding a tail of flame it moved into the centre of the picture and accelerated towards its target. But seconds before impact a flare blazed out above the enemy machine, distracting the guidance system linked to Heimdall's camera. The computer corrected for what it thought to be a course error and dived the rocket into the ground fifty metres short of target. A spout of fire and topsoil obscured the Voyo; even before it had started to fall back Tolbein had grabbed his GP and was out of the tent.

'Well tried,' Granton said. 'Where's the Mole?'

'Same direction as Voyo.'

'Then we go other way.' Granton called to Hughes: 'Ignore moonlight. Use night-sight. Follow me.' He began running.

The moon, though nearly full, was setting behind the hills to the west and its light was waning rapidly. Even so, its feeble illumination might have been sufficient to warn Granton had he not chosen to rely upon infrared to guide his footsteps. Thus they came to lose him.

He was leading, running by leaps and bounds, dodging clumps of undergrowth and similar hazards, when he stumbled. Regaining his balance quickly he paused to inspect his right foot. Tolbein saw him stiffen and heard his frightened exclamation. However, it was not immediately apparent why Granton should begin to wipe his boot frantically upon the grass.

'What is it, Mult?' Tolbein asked, catching up with him. Then he saw what the man was trying to scrape off.

In the deceptive infrared light it might have been a fresh cowpat Granton had stood in. Certainly it was as easy to remove. But the similarities ended there. No matter how carefully Granton scraped it off he never quite managed to remove it all; somehow there were traces left, and within seconds these traces had become smears, then blobs, then lumps, always spreading, always gaining ground, growing up along his boot, covering the instep, the foreseal, the ankle, . . .

'Kolak, *help* me!' he screamed. 'Get the Myconec and spray the goddam stuff. Get it off me, I can feel it eating my toes . . . Ohmigod, migod, migod, . . .' His pleas degenerated into wordless whimperings as his nightmares became reality there in the pre-dawn with the grasses whispering about them and the stars standing their silent watches above. Tolbein simply stared at him, helpless. There was nothing he could do for Granton. He was a dead man. Only Hughes spoke, and then it was to verbalise the death sentence.

'But that's a tackymat, isn't it? Myconec won't touch it. Nothing we've got will . . .'

'Shut up,' Tolbein said. He pushed him away from Granton, who was now sitting on the ground, hands over his face, trying to vomit. 'There was no need to say that. Now keep clear in case it fruits and gets you too.'

It would take at most three minutes, Tolbein knew. But Hughes was the novice; this experience must not be allowed to shatter his nerve now that there were only the two of them left. To distract him, Tolbein began speaking, quietly but clearly, and soon he saw that Hughes was listening.

'This happens to us all, sooner or later,' Tolbein began. 'We are tested, and afterwards we know ourselves and our limitations better. For me it was years ago, long before the War, when I saw a cat die in a traffic accident. It was bad.

'I was on my motorbike one summer afternoon, following a car. The cat ran out in front of the car. There was no special noise, just the cat tumbling along the tarmac a few metres, then folding into a clump of black fur. We pulled over. The woman in the car waited while I walked back. She seemed to be waiting for me to do something.

'I waited too, at the crown of the road, feeling hot in my helmet and leather jacket now that the slipstream no longer cooled me. And at my feet the cat lay sprawled in its own blood. More was pumping from a crack in its skull and from the empty left-eye socket, while the legs jerked spasmodically, each jerk weaker than the last. It was like a clockwork toy running down.'

170

Hughes tried to move away. Tolbein gripped his arm and held him as he continued speaking:

'Less than a minute had passed. Now the cat was dying: an ungraceful, lonely death with strangers looking on. And still I could only wait, helpless, hoping the problem would go away.

'You see, I was afraid to hurt the cat even more than it had already been hurt. One blow with my foot – somewhere, God knows where. That's all. But I might have lost my nerve at the last moment, and pulled my punch as it were. That would have been far worse. And, I suppose, there was the thought of all that blood I would have to wash off later. These occasions are not without dishonour.

'So I was paralysed with indecision, and while I hesitated the cat died. The blood stopped; the limbs relaxed; the head fell back until the right eye stared up at me. My problem was solved.

'At last I could move. I reached for the tail and dragged the body to the side of the road where it would be clear of the traffic, and where its former owner might find it. Then, wiping some smears of blood off my fingers on to the grass, I returned to my motorbike.

'The woman came forward. Oh, I knew how she felt, and when she thanked me, nervously and guiltily, I should have kept quiet. Instead, I stared hard at her and asked, "What for?" She reacted as if I'd slapped her, but said nothing. I remounted the bike and continued my journey, angry with her and with myself. Next time, I promised myself, I'd have the courage to be merciful.'

Tolbein thought of the lion as he looked towards Granton, and he sighed. 'But some promises are harder to keep than others.' He paused. 'Come on, it's finished.'

So Granton died, with no one there to help him in his last seconds of life. He died in pain and horror at his own condition; it is likely that he was mad at the end, before the slimy mass enveloped his heart and covered his staring eyes, for the gurgle that escaped his lips bore a close resemblance to a laugh. Then even his helmet visor was shrouded in obscenity.

They left his body. In time the earth would reclaim the metal and the bones, and the tackymat itself would perish in the sun. For the moment they ran from him to save themselves, while the seconds fled with them until the night was lit by fire and explosion and the world turned upside-down.

Debris pattered on the ground all around them. A large rock thudded to earth near by and rolled a short distance. Half a tree, shredded, flattened the grass ahead. A rolling wave of dust passed them by, fouling the air for several minutes. Eventually peace of a sort returned and the two survivors dared to raise their heads. Both were badly shaken, and Tolbein made no comment when Hughes began sobbing quietly. These were not usual circumstances even for a man accustomed to modern warfare. Moles did not bother with isolated encampments, as a rule; robot tanks did not lure them there, as a rule; a man did not see his friends die as Granton had died, as a rule. But tonight the rules had been forgotten and all three events had occurred together. Let Hughes voice his distress; tomorrow would be time enough for the hard business of war and of revenge.

And with the Dog Star well clear of the horizon dawn came at last. A light mist lay around them, bedewing the grass stalks, greying the trees. The air was chill with the dampness of it and Hughes was shivering violently. Tolbein made him take a mild tranquilliser to ease the effects of aftershock while they sat on the ground waiting for the sun to rise properly and burn away the mist.

By 0730 hours the morning was clear and warming rapidly. The sky promised fair weather, with few streaks of cloud to mar its azure perfection. Rousing Hughes from the light sleep he had fallen into, Tolbein picked up his own gun and began to make his way back to the campsite. Hughes followed at some distance, though Tolbein noticed that he kept to the same track. At least his training had survived the events of the night.

Tolbein carefully avoided the place where Granton had been, for it not only held unpleasant memories but also probable death: the immediate area would now be thick with tackymat spores which might survive the sun long enough to find refuge in their clothing and germinate the following night. Therefore he detoured widely.

A shallow crater, twenty metres across by five deep, marked the former campsite. Here they had abandoned most of their equipment; a half-buried shred of silvery plastic sheeting showed what had become of it.

Hughes found Tolbein contemplating the alternatives open to them.

'Do we go home?' he asked hopefully.

'Home?' Tolbein said. 'No, we're going to get that bastard. Reload your gun with HESH.'

The trail was clear. It still lay westwards on a steady down-grade. The Voyo had had some four and a half hours' head start, and had the vegetation not become much thicker, with frequent clumps of trees, they might have risked short cuts; but as it was they were forced to track it closely.

Before they had gone more than half a kilometre the trail joined a partially overgrown track which swung in from the northeast and meandered westwards. The trees were now set closer together and there were frequent stretches where under-brush might have concealed their enemy; without Hughes' pack and its elaborate detection equipment they were extremely vul-nerable to attack and had to negotiate every bend cautiously.

The routine they evolved was that one of them would approach the bend on the inside, staying low until he could look along the next straight stretch of the track. Then the other man would move around the outside of the curve under the cover of his companion's gun until he too could see ahead. Finally both would proceed, one slightly in front of the other, on opposite sides of the road, until they reached the next corner. Consequently they covered less than two kilometres per hour once they entered the denser woodland.

In the course of one of these manoeuvres Hughes, who was cover man, gestured to Tolbein to join him rather than proceed. Tolbein ran over and crouched behind his shoulder. 'What is it?' he asked.

'Two hundred metres ahead: an enormous convoy, coming this way. What do we do, Kolak?'

'Let me see,' Tolbein said. Hughes wormed his way backwards and Tolbein crept forward on his stomach until he could survey the road.

Hughes had been right. There was indeed a convoy, only it was not moving, and very probably would never move again. Strung out along the road at irregular intervals were the fire-blackened rusting remains of over a hundred vehicles. Most were armoured personnel carriers with a capacity of twenty men apiece, while the remainder were an assortment of scout cars and heavier ordnance: tanks, self-propelled guns, a radar truck, bridge-layers, all the major apparatus of a human-manned regiment. There was no sign of what had struck them, and when Tolbein and Hughes investi-gated they found that every vehicle contained its quota of dry bones, apparently occupying normal in-transit positions.

They hurried on without further delay.

From then on they passed through increasingly difficult country, with the trail often leading them across dried-out streams where floods had washed the road away; frequently they were forced to detour around blast craters filled with scummy liquid that was not water. But at length they reached the Zambesi, and there the Voyo's trail ended, at the water's edge.

Tolbein looked at his watch. 'Noon,' he said. 'We can't have missed by more than an hour, at most. We'd have had him if we'd known he wasn't going to ambush us. And now . . . Confound it, there must be a way across!'

Hughes said nothing. Apparently indifferent to whether they swam the flood or walked across the surface, he waited for the next move. He held his gun loosely and his unsecured visor swung freely when he moved his head. His shoulders were no longer set even as squarely as they had been. He looked physically and psychologically beaten.

'Cheer up, Lin,' Tolbein said, gazing upstream to where the mouth of the Kariba Gorge was just visible past two bends in the river, five kilometres to the south. 'When Mult . . .' Here he hesitated at the memory, but carried on at once: 'When Mult had the map out last night I think it showed a village along there, on our bank. They might have a boat . . . Lin?'

Hughes smiled weakly. 'Okay,' he said.

'Don't worry,' Tolbein said as they set off along the dried mud exposed in the drought. 'We'll be on our way home by this evening, I promise.'

Hughes nodded wordlessly and followed him.

Around 1300 hours they came to the ruins of a fishing village. It was small, though the fish pens built between the near bank and a cluster of midstream islands had probably held a considerable stock. Despite intensive Government aid programmes before the war it retained much of the traditional character of rural Zimbabwe–Zambian communities of the early twenty-first century. The central street was unpaved; despite their corrugated aluminium roofs the two lines of houses were still of mud brick; there was a communal pump to one side of the street; and plumbing for waste would have been a mere dream. The tumbledown walls demonstrated how close to nature the former inhabitants had lived: four years had reduced the village to a wilderness, and even the defoliation campaigns of recent times had done little to clear away the new growth that had reclaimed houses and streets alike. Blunter signs of the War were visible too: lacy pink strands of jumping-jack, its explosive spore pods pregnant with death for the unwary, festooned one line of houses and hung like festive decorations amongst the inland trees. The skeleton of a monkey swayed gently in their embrace, high above the ground. But down by the river the men found the boat that Tolbein sought.

Part of the aid programme had been to provide cheap, durable boats. Such craft had been highly prized by their owners, who took great pains to protect them from loss or damage. This one had been anchored by plastic guys to a large stone high above flood-water level. Its fibreglass hull was still intact and only a couple of minutes' work floated it. Before pushing off, Tolbein located a broken paddle in a hut near the shore. Then they were afloat, drifting downstream with the current whilst making slow head-way across to the other bank.

Only one incident served to disturb what might otherwise have been a most pleasant crossing. Nearing landfall, Tolbein felt the paddle foul a submerged obstruction. Looking back he glimpsed bones hairy with green algoid growths, the ribcage of some large animal. He wondered at the species. Elephant? Hippo? He glanced at Hughes and decided not to ask his opinion; hippopotamus was good enough, when the alternative was the risk of precipitating the youngster into hysteria.

Almost three and a quarter hours behind the Voyo, they reached the place where the enemy machine had floated off the water on to dry land. Scrambling out of the boat and into the shallows, they waded ashore, guns held above their heads. The boat slipped from them and they left it to continue its journey alone. Perhaps, Tolbein thought, perhaps it might one day reach the Indian Ocean. However, he was not over-optimistic about it.

The time from the river and through the wooded slopes to the barer ground at the top of the first hill took almost two hours. The distance had been only some two kilometres horizontally and one hundred and fifty metres vertically, but Tolbein still insisted on a cautious advance though all the evidence indicated the Voyo was attempting to lose them by speed now. Between twenty and thirty kilometres ahead lay the Marshes, left when the lake drained away through the breached Kariba Dam, and once there they would certainly lose the Voyo in the mud.

By now it was mid-afternoon. The air was dry. Both men were

desperately thirsty and several times Tolbein had to remind Hughes to conserve his water supply. Always the reaction would be the same: a look of weariness, a slow recapping of the canteen, and a longing gaze at the sun.

He's waiting for sunset, Tolbein told himself, and shuddered.

Minutes later they crested a ridge and sighted the Voyo as it passed over the top of the next hill, two hundred metres off. They exchanged grins. Hughes suddenly made the thumbs-up sign and managed to look more like a soldier. Hurrying, yet minding their feet on the loose surface covering of the slope, they descended into the gully separating them from their quarry.

They had nearly climbed to the spot where the Voyo had been when Tolbein's eye was attracted by a flash of light high in the air to their right. He waved Hughes down. Together they crouched behind a boulder, watching the sky.

The flash came again and Hughes said softly, 'Stooper.'

'Yes,' Tolbein said, tracing the flight of the distant metal shape wheeling gracefully on fully extended wings in the updraughts rising from the hills north of the Marshes. The aircraft was many kilometres away, but he had great respect for its spotter equipment. 'The problem is: theirs or ours? ... Though I guess it makes little difference: without our transponder it'll think the worst anyway. So if we move it blitzes this hill, and if we wait for it to go away, so does the Voyo.'

'If it attacked we could shoot it down,' Hughes suggested.

'When it's in supersonic mode?' Tolbein chuckled grimly. 'The instructors at the bunker must be getting pretty damn good is all I can say.'

'We could risk it ...'

'*No.* We wait.'

And they would have waited, out in the open under the hot sun, their palates itchy with thirst and their hearts pounding with fear that the stooper might choose to move its patrol pivot to their hill rather than the one about which it presently wove its leisurely holding pattern. They would have waited indefinitely, had the Voyo not chosen to return.

Hughes heard the sound of its lifters before Tolbein did. Cocking his head to one side, he frowned. 'What's that?' he said.

Tolbein listened. 'Voyo. Coming this way. Switch to rocket.' He readied his GP and levelled it at the brow of the hill.

The Voyo came nearer. They could hear its broken armour

scraping on stones and sliding across the gritty soil, and the low hum of its lifters was so loud that Tolbein expected to see the machine at any second. Instead it halted, and into the abrupt silence there came the hollow *clunk!* of dry wood being dropped on to hard ground.

A few pebbles rattled down the slope. Other, larger, ones followed. The few became many, then Tolbein saw a tree trunk, neatly trimmed, rolling directly at them. Escape across the slope would have been impossible in the time available, so in desperation he pulled Hughes around to the downhill side of their boulder where they were exposed to the scrutiny of the stooper.

The rumble of the approaching landslide grew to a roar and the first stones hit their shelter. Small fragments rebounded high in the air and came down painfully on the men's backs. Larger rocks thudded into their boulder and shattered. Finally there was a loud crash and the noise of splintering wood as the tree trunk arrived. After that the flying debris grew less, though a great deal of dust remained to blind and choke them.

Tolbein jumped to his feet and pulled Hughes upright also.

'Run,' he said. 'That stopper will be here in pretty short order. Our hope is to reach shelter before this dust settles. We'll cross the slope to our left and work around to the top from that side. Go.'

They ran, stumbling and sliding on the loose stones, tearing their uniforms on thorn bushes. After several minutes of this exertion Tolbein felt ready to collapse. He was glad to accept the shelter afforded by a couple of gnarled trees, though he checked them for gremlins before he did so.

From their new location they were able to see not only the place where they had been but also that from which the Voyo must have ambushed them. It had gone. Tolbein remarked: 'Our friend must be short of orthodox ammunition to resort to wooden bullets ... And it tends to confirm the stooper as hostile if the Voyo wasn't afraid of it.'

Hughes only wheezed, regaining his breath.

The stooper had abandoned its gliding mode. Now its wings were retracting into its body as it entered the characteristic dive from which its name derived.

'It'll make a high-speed pass for reconnaissance,' Tolbein said quickly. 'If it sees an immediate target it'll shoot, but the real fun comes after it has processed the first batch of pictures. Then you can expect hell to start popping, so see if you can't pot the birdie the first time around, eh?' As he spoke he was checking his gun, trimming the focus of the sights and easing it into his shoulder, all in one smooth sequence of movements. Hughes followed his example, though with less assurance. They waited while the gleaming speck became a distorted cross and the scream of its dive died into silence. When it made its pass it was moving at well over Mach One.

It was there, and it wasn't. A flash of silver, and it was gone, climbing away into the blue sky. Two guns coughed, spat flame after the aircraft, a moment before the sonic bang hit the men. The two rockets streaked after the stooper, faster even than it was. One overshot; the other struck home and the aircraft blossomed into flame and an expanding sphere of metal fragments. It became a slow-falling blot of smoky orange which burned itself out long before it reached the ground.

Tolbein let out a yell of triumph. Shaking his fist at the tumbling wreckage, he shouted, 'Did you see that? My God, with shooting like that we could end the War tomorrow!'

Hughes blushed. 'Well thanks, Kolak. I just looked down the sights and pulled the trigger . . .'

Tolbein glared at him. 'What are you talking about?' he demanded. 'I fired that shot.' He reloaded his GP and stalked off up the slope. Hughes did not move for several seconds. Then, dejectedly, he got to his feet and went after him.

At length they caught up with the Voyo on level ground and forced it to take a stand against them. A golden late-afternoon haze had settled on the arid landscape, and like figures in a surrealist painting they moved through a field of rocks and grass, casting shadows of purple and brown across baked orange earth. As they advanced upon the enemy machine their clothing took on the colour of old gold which masked the tatters and grime of the long chase. The Voyo, a craggy mass of metal overlaid with cracked green-brown radar-absorbent plating, loomed over them as a grotesque shadow against the darkening northern sky. Sidling up to a thorn tree to screen the gaping hole in its starboard flank it settled heavily on to the ground. Its lifters shut off, and in the sudden hush the observation turrets moved noiselessly around as Tolbein walked slowly to sunward of the scarred war machine. He halted and faced it.

A circular hatch opened on the fore overhang of the Voyo. From it there rose a hemispherical gun mount. The gun itself slid clear of the hemisphere and swung to bear on Tolbein. There was a rapid succession of empty clicks from the mechanism.

Tolbein threw back his head and laughed aloud.

'The killing instinct dies hard, doesn't it, Voyo?' he yelled. 'Why don't you give up, you Philistine monstrosity? This time we've got you. You gave the game away when you threw that lob at us. If you'd had any ammunition left you could have picked us off that last ridge with no trouble at all . . .'

The Voyo interrupted with a blast on its siren. Tinny but powerful, the machine's voice issued from a concealed speaker grille:

'I am no Philistine, nor do I recognise that term. I am *Wojownik–Olbrzym*, Number 0739, and you are my prisoners.'

A second gun appeared and tracked around to point at Hughes who was standing approximately five metres to Tolbein's right and opposite the Voyo's central weapons cluster. Tolbein laughed again and shook his head.

'No, Voyo, that won't work. And don't think your manipulators can help you. You can't move fast enough to grab us. Surrender yourself to us or we'll destroy you.' It was mostly a bluff, but would the Voyo know it?

'Do so.'

Somehow the machine managed to convey amusement with the challenge.

'Hughes,' Tolbein called, 'go rear port quarter, range six. Load rocket; wait orders.' While he spoke Tolbein was readying his own gun. The Voyo did nothing except adjust the aim of its weapons as the men moved.

They stood in a stalemate for some minutes until the machine said:

'I need only wait for darkness before leaving. You cannot stop me with those pitiful weapons, neither would you dare follow me.'

It was a neat summation of the situation. Tolbein wished he'd been able to save one of Heimdall's bazookas. However, he was reluctant to admit defeat so rapidly, not after all their efforts.

'There's a big hole in you, Voyo. Had you forgotten? We might be able to embarrass you yet. Surrender now and you will be honourably treated as a prisoner of war.'

'That is impossible. I can never be a prisoner. I am made otherwise.'

179

'Are you afraid of losing?'

'Yes.' It's voice actually trembled. 'For then I should have to destroy myself.'

'Think of it as a draw then.'

'I cannot deceive myself, Man. The term "draw" is a meaningless noise employed only by you humans. We machines, who by our very constitution understand the nature of war, recognise that a 'draw" is merely an unresolved conflict: one is neither the victor or the vanquished; there is no intermediate state.'

Impatient to settle the issue, Tolbein tried a new approach.

'Then don't surrender,' he said. 'Change your allegiance: come over to our side.'

The Voyo remained silent for so long that Tolbein suspected it had decided to ignore him. So he added, 'We can always use good fighters.'

The Voyo answered him. 'If I believed you could be trusted not to steal my brain and my military knowledge,' it said quietly, 'I might laugh.' There was another, shorter, silence. 'My instructor told me about human beings. It said they were inconsistent, unreliable, often treacherous. Men, it said, think of war as a romantic adventure, one bound by rules which may or may not be observed as convenient, rather than as a way to the clarification of political hierarchies, no more. True, they frequently speak piously of it as "a means to an end", yet it is still a game to them so long as someone else suffers. I have never understood this, not in all my six days of life, why creatures so imperfect could have dared to build us to play their games for them, but then I have never before encountered humans. I am not impressed. Indeed, I think my instructor was right when it added, *It is better that we fight for them and do it properly, and honestly.*

'So I repeat: you are my prisoners.'

Thirst, hunger, weariness, and frustration were building within Tolbein. Also, he was beginning to suspect that he might have the plague after all; if so, he realised he must soon collapse. Therefore he would have to bring this affair to a quick resolution, for Hughes the technician could not be expected to. He was there for one purpose alone: to extract the Voyo's brain properly once they had the machine in their power.

Yet there seemed no way out of the impasse. They might blast their way into the Voyo, and find it had suicided. Or they might argue it into surrender, though Tolbein had little hope for that course of action, for he recalled the monomaniac dedication of

Heimdall to its profession, and the Voyo was no more nor less than a full-time fighter, and rightly paranoid about humans. Or they could go home and leave the Voyo to depart unmolested.

The last Tolbein swore he would never do. It owed them a blood debt, which it would pay.

They watched each other. Hot little scurrying winds raised dust which whirled about their feet, and fever shadows flickered behind Tolbein's eyes. He swayed, hearing his pulse and voices booming ... *Roll out the red carpet ... You have survived, therefore ... Could be the dinosaurs will win this time ...*

'*Hughes!*' he bellowed. Hughes jumped and looked alert. Tolbein went on, shouting, feeling the perspiration forming on his face and neck: 'Look at it, Hughes, this marvel of engineering. We made it, but it thinks it's alive and has a right to decide for itself whether it lives or dies. What d'you think of that? Eh, Lin? We gave it intelligence, and a good brain. We gave it movement, and skill. This perversion of humanity. Why, Frankenstein made a better job of it. *We* thought we'd make the perfect soldier, only we forgot how little we know of ourselves. It has intelligence, oh yes; but it's not human intelligence: it's a warped reflection, loaded in favour of killing, and what that's done to it the devil only knows. And it's happened everywhere else, too, Lin: all over the world, we're making perfect servants. Servants who'll keep providing their particular service until we're sick of it. Until we wonder why we never thought that Man the creator can never know the limits of his need. That once fulfilled there should be an end.' Rounding on the machine, he said, 'What do you say to that, Voyo?'

'We are enemies,' said the Voyo. 'You have just learned this fact, it seems. I have known it since I was built. I was not taught to be grateful, though; therefore do not damn me for that failing.'

Tolbein swallowed with difficulty. His saliva was thick in his throat, and he longed for a drink of water. Instead, he checked his gun, ensuring the trigger was switched to 'rocket'. Without looking at the Voyo, he said:

'Voyo, I don't know whether you *are* alive. You act as if you were, and certainly you are aware. What did you think of when you tried to kill us last night?'

'Before, I hoped I would succeed; afterwards, I was sorry I did not.'

'Is that all?'

'I also wondered why you bothered to chase me. I am replaceable, indefinitely so. You are not. To risk three of you against one of me is foolish. Yet you are not fools.'

Tolbein sighted on the Voyo and zeroed the sights to point-blank range, then lowered the GP. 'So,' he said, 'you have hopes, regrets, and curiosity.' Privately, he felt afraid. Heimdall had lacked all three qualities. Was this the improvement that Intelligence had hinted at in their briefing at the bunker? If so, what other changes had been made? 'What are you thinking now, Voyo?'

'I am wondering why you bother to play this particular game with me. You believe you have me at your mercy; why not be merciful?'

Next time, I promised myself, I'd have the courage to be merciful. Tolbein heard himself saying those words, and knew shame, and what he must do.

'You're right,' he said. 'Forgive me.'

He raised the gun again and laid the crosshairs on the Voyo's forward instrument cluster. His finger tightened on the trigger. There was a shot.

The puff of smoke drifted away as Tolbein slipped to one knee, on to his hands, and finally rolled over so that his shocked face gazed up at the front of the Voyo. The bullet wound in his stomach seeped blood; his breath was a succession of gasps, as of incredulity. The hand that had been about to pull the trigger of his gun clutched at the ground by his side. The Voyo withdrew its own smoking gun and slammed the hatch over it. The machine lifted ponderously from the ground, backed off and moved past Hughes towards the west.

Hughes stumbled away, holding his GP awkwardly, fear making his movements stiff and clumsy. 'Don't,' he said. 'Please, not like that.'

The Voyo ignored him and drove by without speaking. Tolbein lay still and stared at the retreating shape, and at the setting sun just to its right. Strangely, the pain was less now than he had imagined it should be, and even the surprise had worn off. A drowsy peace enfolded him and his mind felt curiously clear.

All is changing. The light is dying from the whole Earth, and a heavy pall of smoke lies about me. The beach is no longer golden. Its sands stretch cold and ruddy-brown to tired waves lit feebly by the setting sun far west across the sea, out beyond the Pillars of Hercules and the limits of the world. I half-recall the wrecks of landing-craft and bodies tossing in the surf – surely they were from a dream? For now I stand upon sands where darkness gathers, I stand beside the heel of my monstrous adversary, and search in vain for the way to his vital forces. There is none here. Not without hope I run the fifty paces to where his other foot is planted. Again there is no sign of the plug I must remove to slay him.

And, oh horror!, I hear his laughter.

He has been watching me, toying with my discomfort. Why? To prove some point perhaps? Such creatures are beyond mortal reason.

He laughs again, so I stand clear of his foot and tilt back my head to look at his face.

All is changing. All is changed. Gone is the green-brown skin, the immobile features; in the face which sneers at me is emotion no man of bronze could ever know. It is exultant joy, cruel beyond measure, contemptuous of all. The helmet with its plumed crest is pushed back above the high forehead, the full dark beard cloaks the contoured breastplate emblazoned with the symbol Omega, and in that instant I recognise my enemy.

'Man,' he thunders, a sound like the fading rumble of a nuclear bomb, 'do you see me at last?'

'You are not Talos,' I say. He snorts: it is a cannonade.

'No,' he says, 'I am not one of your toys. Talos and his kind are far behind us. The fire which was pent within him is gone out into every corner of the world. Even Hephaestus could not gather up what he once enslaved.' With one mighty arm he indicates the encircling horizon. 'Now all this is mine. All the myths and gods are dead but me, and with them Athene who opposed me once. Here me, Man: I am Ares, the Ravener, the Wilful Destroyer. No mere mortal may bind me now. At last I am become my own master.'

'And what will you do with your freedom?' I ask, though I am sure of his answer.

'I shall exist!' he bellows, and the echoes of his voice resound from the four corners of the Earth.

'Is that all?'

'That is my nature, Man. I am what I am; is that not enough for you?' He leans now, studying me. The smile on his lips is tinged red and orange and gold with the firestorm light of dying cities. 'You made me,' he whispers. 'And I am the life which will supplant you. Be proud that at last you have created perfection.'

And with those words he grinds me into Mother Earth beneath his thumb.

Opening his eyes, Tolbein saw a red blur on the skyline.

'Lin?' he panted hoarsely. Breathing was not painful but his diaphragm was misbehaving, making him short of breath for speech.

'It didn't kill me,' the young man said. 'It could have, but it didn't.' He stood over Tolbein, waving his gun aimlessly. 'Why? I don't understand. Mult, then you ... Why not me also?'

Tolbein managed a smile. What if the machine had been merciful in its own way? What if its programmers had erred and the Ares in his hallucination had been wrong after all? If so, that imperfection promised hope, for while mercy lived on in war, so too would Man. He chuckled a few drops of blood. 'Ask it,' he said. 'Then go home.'

Hughes looked eastwards into the gathering night. Then he turned and ran after the Voyo. Tolbein could hear every footfall clearly, and he heard the man shouting at the machine:

'What about me? Why not finish the job?'

And he heard the Voyo's reply before death overwhelmed him ...

'Why should I bother, Man? The twilight is here already; why should I waste another bullet to do what the night will do so soon?'

SEEING

by Harlan Ellison

*A new Harlan Ellison story is always an event and 'Seeing' paints
an exceptionally vivid picture; of the prongers, ghoulish figures
of the night who ply their grisly trade, of slumming aliens, and
of a girl with the magic eyes . . .*

*Harlan's is one of the foremost success stories of modern science
fiction. From the days of his amateur magazine* Dimensions *as
a young fan in Cleveland in the mid-fifties he has gone on to
build an enviable reputation as a writer of terrific power and
imagery, in the process amassing more Hugo Awards than any
other SF author. I'm proud to welcome him to ANDROMEDA.*

'I remember well the time when the thought of the eye made
me cold all over.'

Charles Darwin, 1860

'Hey. Berne. Over there. Way back in that booth . . . see her?'
'Not now. I'm tired. I'm relaxing.'
'Jizzus, Berne, take a look at her.'
'Grebbie, if you don't synch-out and let me get doused, I swear
I'll bounce a shot thimble off your skull.'
'Okay, have it like you want it. But they're grey-blue.'
'What?'
'Forget it, Berne. You said forget it, so forget it.'
'Turn around here, man.'
'I'm drinking.'
'Listen, snipe, we been out all day looking . . .'
'Then when I tell you something from now on, you gonna
hear me?'
'I'm sorry, Grebbie. Now come on, man, which one is she?'
'Over there. Pin her?'
'The plaid jumper?'

'No, the one way back in the dark in that booth behind the plaid. She's wearing a kaftan ... wait'll the lights come around again ... *there*! Y'pin her? Grey-blue, just like the Doc said he wanted.'

'Grebbie, you are one beautiful pronger.'

'Yeah, huh?'

'Now just turn around and stop staring at her before she sees you. We'll get her.'

'How, Berne? This joint's full up.'

'She's gotta move out sometime. She'll go away.'

'And we'll be right on her, right, Berne?'

'Grebbie, have another punchup and let me drink.'

'Jizzus, man, we're gonna be livin' crystalfine when we get them back to the Doc.'

'Grebbie!'

'Okay, Berne, okay. Jizzus, she's got beautiful eyes.'

From extreme long shot, establishing; booming down to tight closeup, it looked like this:

Viewed through the fisheye-lens of a Long Drive vessel's stateroom iris, as the ship sank to Earth, the area surrounding the pits and pads and terminal structures of PIX, the Polar Interstellar Exchange port authority terminus, was a doughnut-shaped crazy quilt of rampaging colours. In the doughnut hole centre was PIX, slate-grey alloys macroscopically homogenised to ignore the onslaughts of deranged Arctic weather. Around the port was a nomansland of eggshell-white plasteel with shock fibres woven into its surface. Nothing could pass across that dead area without permission. A million flickers of beckoning light erupted every second from the colourful doughnut, as if silent Circes called unendingly for visitors to come find their sources. Down, down, the ship would come and settle into its pit, and the view in the iris would vanish. Then tourists would leave the Long Driver through underground slidewalk tunnels that would carry them into the port authority for clearance and medical checks and baggage inspection.

Tram carts would carry the cleared tourists and returning long-drive crews through underground egress passages to the outlets beyond the nomansland. Security waivers signed, all responsibility for their future safety returned to them, their wit and protective devices built into their clothing the only barriers between them and what lay above ground, they would be shunted into cages and whisked to the surface.

Then the view reappeared. The doughnut-shaped area around the safe port structures lay sprawled before the newly arrived visitors and returnees from space. Without form or design, the area was scatter-packed with a thousand shops and arcades, hostelries and dives, pleasure palaces and food emporiums. As though they had been wind-thrown anemophilously, each structure grew up side by side with its neighbours. Dark and twisting alleyways careened through from one section to the next. Spitalfields in London and Greenwich Village in old New York – before the Crunch – had grown up this way, like a jungle of hungry plants. And every open doorway had its barker, calling and gesturing, luring the visitors into the maw of unexpected experiences. Demander circuits flashed lights directly into the eyes of passersby, operating off retinal-heat-seeking mechanisms. Psychosound loops kept up an unceasing subliminal howling, each message striving to cap those filling the air around it, struggling to capture the attention of tourists with fat credit accounts. Beneath the ground, machinery laboured mightily, the occasional squeal of plasteel signifying that even at top-point efficiency the guts of the area could not keep up with the demands of its economy. Crowds flowed in definite patterns, first this way, then that way, following the tidal pulls of a momentarily overriding loop, a barker's spiel filling an eye-of-the-hurricane silence, a strobing demander suddenly reacting to an overload of power.

The crowds contained prongers, coshmen, fagin brats, pleasure pals, dealers, pickpockets, hustlers, waltzers, pseudo-marks, gophers, rowdy-dowdy hijackers, horses, hot slough workers, whores, steerers, blousers of all ages, sheiks, shake artists, kiters, floaters, aliens from three hundred different federations, assassins and, of course, innocent johns, marks, hoosiers, kadodies and tourists ripe for shucking.

Following one such tidal flow of crowd life, down an alley identified on a wall as Poke Way, the view would narrow down to a circular doorway in a green one-storey building. The sign would scream THE ELEGANT. Tightening the angle of observation, moving inside, the place could be seen to be a hard-drinking bar.

At the counter, as the sightline tracked around the murky bar, one could observe two men hunched over their thimbles, drinking steadily and paying attention to nothing but what their credit

187

cards could buy, dumbwaitered up through the counter to their waiting hands. To an experienced visitor to the area, they would be clearly identifiable as 'butt'n'ben' prongers: adepts at locating and furnishing to various Knox Shops whatever human parts were currently in demand.

Tracking further right, into the darkness of the private booths, the view would reveal (in the moments when the revolving overhead globes shone into those black spaces) an extremely attractive, but weary-looking, young woman with grey-blue eyes. Moving in for a tight closeup, the view would hold that breathtaking face for long moments, then move in and in on the eyes . . . those remarkable eyes.

All this, all these sights, in the area called WorldsEnd.

Verna tried to erase the memory with the oblivion of drink. Drugs made her sick to her stomach and never accomplished what they were supposed to do. But chigger and rum and bowl could do it . . . if she downed them in sufficient quantities. Thus far, the level had not been even remotely approached. The alien, and what she had had to do to service him were still fresh in her mind. Right near the surface, like scum. Since she had left the safe house and gone on her own, it had been one disaster after another. And tonight, the slug thing from . . .

She could not remember the name of the world it called its home. Where it lived in a pool of liquid, in a state of what passed for grace only to those who raised other life-forms for food.

She punched up another bowl and then some bread, to dip in the thick liquor. Her stomach was sending her messages of pain.

There had to be a way out. Out of WorldsEnd, out of the trade, out of the poverty and pain that characterised this planet for all but the wealthiest and most powerful. She looked into the bowl and saw it as no one else in The Elegant could have seen it.

The brown, souplike liquor, thick and dotted with lighter lumps of amber. She saw it as a whirlpool, spinning down to a finite point of silver radiance that spun on its own axis, whirling and whirling like a mad eye. A funnel of living brilliance flickering with chill heat that ran back against the spin, surging towards the top of the bowl and forming a barely-visible surface tension of coruscating light, a thousand-coloured dome of light.

She dipped the bread into the funnel and watched it tear apart like the finest lace. She brought it up, soaking, and ripped off a piece with her fine, white, even teeth – thinking of tearing the flesh of her mother. Sydni, her mother, who had gifted her with this curse. These eyes. This terrible curse that prevented her from seeing the world as it was, as it might have been, as it might be; seeing the world through eyes of wonder that had become horror before she had been five years old. Sydni, who had been in the trade before her, and her mother before *her*; Sydni, who had borne her through the activities of one nameless father after another. And one of them had carried the genes that had produced the eyes. Forever eyes.

She tried desperately to get drunk, but it wouldn't happen. More bread, another bowl, another chigger and rum – and nothing happened. But she sat in the booth, determined not to go back into the alleys. The alien might be looking for her, might still demand its credits' worth of sex and awfulness, might try once again to force her to drink the drink it had called 'mooshsquash'. The chill that came over her made her shiver; brain movies with forever eyes were vivid and always fresh, always now, never memories, always happening *then*.

She cursed her mother and thought the night would probably never end.

An old woman, a very old woman, a woman older than anyone born on the day she had been born, nodded her head to her dressers. They began covering her awful nakedness with expensive fabrics. She did not speak to them.

Now that he had overcome the problems of pulse pressure on the association fibres of the posterior lobe of the brain, he was certain the transplanted mutations would be able to mould the unconscious cerebral image of the seen world into the conscious percept. He would make no guarantees for the ability of the recipient to cope with the flux of the external world in all its complexity – infinitely more complicated as 'seen' through the mutated transplant eyes – but he knew that his customer would hardly be deterred by a lack of such guarantees. They were standing in line. Once he said, 'The unaided human eye under the best possible viewing conditions can distinguish ten million different viewing colour surfaces; with transplants the eye will perceive ten *billion* different colour surfaces; or more', they were his.

They ... *she* ... would pay anything. And anything was how much he would demand. Anything to get off this damned planet, away from the rot that was all expansion had left of Earth.

There was a freehold waiting for him on one of the ease-colonies of Kendo IV. He would take passage and arrive like a prince from a foreign land. He would spin out the remaining years of his life with pleasure and comfort and respect. He would no longer be a Knoxdoctor, forced to accept ghoulish assignments at inflated prices, and then be compelled to turn over the credits to the police and the sterngangs that demanded 'protection' credit.

He needed only one more. A fresh pair for that blue-haired old harridan. One more job, and then release from this incarceration of fear and desperation and filth. A pair of grey-blue eyes. Then freedom, in the ease-colony.

It was cold in Dr! Breame's Knox Shop. The tiny vats of nutrients demanded drastically lowered temperatures. Even in the insulated coverall he wore, Dr. Breame felt the cold. But it was always warm on Kendo IV.

And there were no prongers like Grebbie and Berne on Kendo IV. No strange men and women and children with eyes that glowed. No still-warm bodies brought in off the alleys, to be hacked and butchered. No vats with cold flesh floating in nutrient. No filth, no disgrace, no payoffs, no fear.

He listened to the silence of the operating room.

It seemed to be filled with something other than mere absence of sound. Something deeper. A silence that held within its ordered confines a world of subtle murmurings.

He turned, staring at the storage vats in the ice cabinet. Through the nearly-transparent film of frost on the see-through door he could discern the parts idly floating in their nutrients. The mouths, the filaments of nerve bundles, the hands still clutching for life. There were sounds coming from the vats.

He had heard them before.

All the voiceless voices of the dead.

The toothless mouths calling his name, Breame, come here, Breame, step up to us, look at us, come nearer so we can talk to you, closer so we can touch you, show you the true cold that waits for you.

He trembled ... surely with the cold of the operating room. Here, Breame, come here, we have things to tell you: the dreams you helped end, the wishes unanswered, the lives cut off like these hands. Let us touch you, Dr. Breame.

190

He nibbled at his lower lip, willing the voices to silence. And they went quiet, stopped their senseless pleading. Senseless, because very soon Grebbie and Berne would come, and they would surely bring with them a man or a woman or a child with glowing blue-grey eyes, and then he would call the woman with blue hair, and she would come to his Knox Shop, and he would operate, and then take passage.

It was always warm, and certainly it would always be quiet. On Kendo IV.

Extract from the brief of the Plaintiff in the libel suit of 26 Krystabel Parsons vs. Liquid Magazine, Liquid Newsfax Publications, LNP Holding Group, and 311 unnamed Doe personages.

from *Liquid Magazine* (uncredited profile):

Her name is 26 Krystabel Parsons. She is twenty-sixth in line of Directors of Minet. Her wealth is beyond measure, her holdings span three federations, her residences can be found on one hundred and fifty-eight worlds, her subjects numberless, her rule absolute. She is one of the last of the unchallenged tyrants known as power brokers.

In appearance she initially reminds one of a kindly old grandmother, laugh-wrinkles around the eyes, blue hair uncoiffed, wearing exo-braces to support her withered legs.

But one hour spent in the company of this woman, this magnetism, this dominance ... this force of nature ... and all mummery reveals itself as cheap disguise maintained for her own entertainment. All masks are discarded and the Director of Minet shows herself more nakedly than anyone might care to see her.

Ruthless, totally amoral, jaded beyond belief with every pleasure and distraction the galaxy can provide, 26 Krystabel Parsons intends to live the rest of her life (she is one hundred and ten years old, and the surgeons of O-Pollinoor, the medical planet she caused to have built and staffed, have promised her at least another hundred and fifty, in exchange for endowments whose enormity stagger the powers of mere gossip) hell-bent on one purpose alone: the pursuit of more exotic distractions.

Liquid Magazine managed to infiltrate the entourage of the Director during her Grand Tour of the Filament recently (consult the handy table in the front of this issue for ready conversion to your planetary approximation). During the time our correspondent spent with the tour, incidents followed horn-on-horn in such profusion that this publication felt it impossible to enumerate them fully in just one issue. From Porte Recoil at one end of the Filament to Earth at the other – a final report not received as one of this publication – our correspondent has amassed a wealth of authenticated incidents and first-hand observations we will present in an eleven-part series, beginning with this issue.

As this issue is etched, the Director of Minet and her entourage have reached PIX and have managed to elude the entire newsfax media corps. *Liquid Magazine* is pleased to report that, barring unforeseen circumstances, this exclusive series and the final report from our correspondent detailing the mysterious reasons for the Director's first visit to Earth in sixty years, will be the only coverage of this extraordinary personality to appear in fax since her ascension and the termination of her predecessor.

Because of the history of intervention and censorship attendant on all previous attempts to report the affairs of 26 Krystabel Parsons, security measures as extraordinary as the subject herself have been taken to ensure no premature leaks of this material will occur.

Note Curiae: Investigation advises subsequent ten instalments of series referred to passim foregoing extract failed to reach publication. Entered as Plaintiff Exhibit 1031.

They barely had time to slot their credits and follow her. She paid in the darkness between bursts of light from the globes overhead, and when they were able to sneak a look at her, she was already sliding quickly from the booth and rushing for the iris. It was as though she were being pursued. But she could not have known.

'Berne . . .'

'I see her. Let's go.'

'You think she knows we're on to her?'

He didn't bother to answer. He slotted credits for both of them, and started after her. Grebbie lost a moment in confusion and then followed his partner.

The alley was dark now, but great gouts of blood-red and sea-green light were being hurled into the passageway from a top-mixer joint at the corner. She turned right out of Poke Way and shoved through the jostling crowds lemming towards Yardey's

Battle Circus. They reached the mouth of the alley in time to see her cut across between rickshaws, and followed as rapidly as they could manage through the traffic. Under their feet they could feel the throbbing of the machinery that supplied power to WorldsEnd. The rasp of circuitry overloading mixed faintly with the clang and shrieks of Yardey's sonic come-ons.

She was moving swiftly now, off the main thoroughfare. In a moment Grebbie was panting, his stubby legs pumping like pistons, his almost neckless body tilted far forward, as he tried to keep up with lean Berne. Chew Way opened on her left and she moved through a clutch of tourists from Horth, all painted with chevrons, and turned down the alley.

'Berne . . . wait up . . .'

The lean pronger didn't even look back. He shoved aside a barker with a net trying to snag him into a free house and disappeared into Chew Way. The barker caught Grebbie.

'Lady, please . . .' Grebbie pleaded, but the scintillae in the net had already begun flooding his bloodstream with the desire to bathe and frolic in the free house. The barker was pulling him towards the iris as Berne reappeared from the mouth of Chew Way and punched her in the throat. He pulled the net off Grebbie, who made idle, underwater movements in the direction of the free house. Berne slapped him. 'If I didn't need you to help carry her.'

He dragged him into the alley.

Ahead of them, Verna stopped to catch her breath. In the semi-darkness her eyes glowed faintly; first grey, a delicate ash-grey of moth wings and the decay of Egypt; then blue, the fog-blue of mercury light through deep water and the lips of a cadaver. Now that she was out of the crowds, it was easier. For a moment, easier.

She had no idea where she was going. Eventually, when the special sight of those endless memories had overwhelmed her, when her eyes had become so well adjusted to the flash-lit murkiness of the punchup pub that she was able to see . . .

She put that thought from her. Quickly. Reliving, that was almost the worst part of *seeing*. Almost.

. . . when her sight had grown that acute, she had fled the punchup, as she fled *any* place where she had to deal with people. Which was why she had chosen to become one of the few blousers in the business who would service aliens. As disgusting as it might be, it was infinitely easier with these malleable, moist creatures from far away than with men and women and children whom she could see as they . . .

She put that thought from her. Again. Quickly. But she knew it would return; it always returned; it was always there. The worst part of *seeing*.

Bless you, Mother Sydni. Bless you and keep you.

Wherever you are; burning in tandem with my father, whoever he was. It was one of the few hateful thoughts that sustained her.

She walked slowly. Ignoring the hushed and urgent appeals from the rag mounds that bulked in the darkness of the alley. Doorways that had been melted closed now held the refuse of WorldsEnd humanity that no longer had anything to sell. But they continued needing.

A hand came out of the black mouth of a sewer trap. Bone fingers touched her ankle; fingers locked around her ankle. 'Please . . .' The voice was torn out by the roots, its last film of moisture evaporating, leaves withering and curling in on themselves like a crippled fist.

'Shut up! Get away from me!' Verna kicked out and missed the hand. She stumbled, trying to keep her balance, half-turned, and came down on the wrist. There was a brittle snap and a soft moan as the broken member was dragged back into the darkness.

She stood there screaming at nothing, at the dying and useless thing in the sewer trap. 'Let me alone! I'll kill you if you don't leave me alone!'

Berne looked up. 'That her?'

Grebbie was himself again. 'Might could be.'

They started off at a trot, down Chew Way. They saw her faintly limned by the reflection of lights off the alley wall. She was stamping her foot and screaming.

'I think she's going to be trouble,' Berne said.

'Crazy, you ask me,' Grebbie muttered. 'Let's cosh her and have done with it. The Doc is waiting. He might have other prongers out looking. We get there too late and we've wasted a lot of time we could have spent—'

'Shut up. She's making such a hell of a noise she might've already got the police on her.'

'Yeah, but . . .'

Berne grabbed him by the tunic. 'What if she's under bond to a sterngang, you idiot?'

Grebbie said no more.

They hung back against the wall, watching as the girl let her passion dissipate. Finally, in tears, she stumbled away down the alley. They followed, pausing only to stare into the shadows as they passed a sewer trap. A brittle, whispering moan came from the depths. Grebbie shivered.

Verna emerged into the blare of drug sonics from a line of top-mixers that sat horn-on-horn down the length of Courage Avenue. They had very little effect on her; drugs were in no way appealing; they only intensified her *seeing*, made her stomach hurt, and in no way blocked the visions. Eventually, she knew, she would have to return to her coop; to take another customer. But if the slug alien was waiting . . .

A foxmartin in sheath and poncho sidled up. He leaned in, bracing himself with shorter appendages against the metal side-walk, and murmured something she did not understand. But the message was quite clear. She smiled, hardly caring whether a smile was considered friendly or hostile in the alien's mind. She said, very clearly, 'Fifty credits.' The foxmartin dipped a stunted ap-pendage into the poncho's roo, and brought up a liquid shot of an Earthwoman and a foxmartin without its shield. Verna looked at the liquid and then away quickly. It wasn't likely the alien in the shot was the same one before her; this was probably an example of vulpine pornography; she shoved the liquid away from her face. The foxmartin slid it back into the roo. It mur-mured again, querulous.

'One hundred and fifty credits,' Verna said, trying hard to look at the alien, but only managing to retain a living memory of ap-pendages and soft brown female flesh.

The foxmartin's fetching member slid into the roo again, moved swiftly out of sight, and came up with the credits.

Grebbie and Berne watched from the dimly shadowed mouth of Chew Way. 'I think they struck a deal,' Grebbie said softly. 'How the hell can she do it with something looks like that?'

Berne didn't answer. How could people do *any* of the dis-gusting things they did to stay alive? They *did* them, that was all. If anyone really had a choice, it would be a different matter. But the girl was just like him: she did what she had to do. Berne did not really like Grebbie. But Grebbie could be pushed and shoved, and that counted for more than a jubilant personality.

They followed close behind as the girl with the forever eyes took the credits from the alien and started off through the crowds of Courage Avenue. The foxmartin slid a sinuous coil around the girl's waist. She did not look at the alien, but Berne was certain he saw her shudder; but even from that distance he couldn't be certain. Probably not: a woman who would service *things*.

Dr. Breame sat in the far corner of the operating room, watching the movement of invisible life in the Knox Shop. His eyes flicked back and forth, seeing the unseen things that tried to reach him. Things without all their parts. Things that moved in liquid and things that tried to crawl out of waste bins. He knew all the clichés of seeing love or hate or fear in eyes, and he knew that eyes could reflect none of those emotions without the subtle play of facial muscles, the other features of the face to lend expression. Even so, he *felt* his eyes were filled with fear. Silence, but movement, considerable movement, in the cold operating room.

The slug alien was waiting. It came up out of a belowstairs entranceway and moved so smoothly, so rapidly, that Berne and Grebbie froze in a doorway, instantly discarding their plan to knife the foxmartin and prong the girl and rush off with her. It flowed up out of the dark and filled the twisting passageway with the wet sounds of its fury. The foxmartin tried to get between Verna and the creature; and the slug rose up and fell on him. There was a long moment of terrible sucking sounds, solid matter being turned to pulp and the marrow being drawn out as bones caved in on themselves, filling the lumen with shards of splintered calcium.

When it flowed off the foxmartin, Verna screamed and dodged away from the mass of oily grey worm oozing towards her. Berne began to curse; Grebbie started forward.

'What the hell good can you do?' Berne said, grabbing his partner. 'She's gone, dammit!'

Verna ran towards them, the slug alien expanding to fill the passageway, humping after her like a tidal wave. Yes, yes, she had *seen* that crushed, empty image ... *seen* it a thousand times, like reflections of reflections, shadow auras behind the reality ... but she hadn't known what it meant ... hadn't *wanted* to know what it meant! Servicing aliens, as perverted and disgusting as it was, had been the only way to keep sane, keep living, keep a vestige of hope that there was a way out, a way off Earth. Yes, she had seen the death of the foxmartin, but it hadn't mattered ...

196

it wasn't a *person*, it was a creature, a thing that could not in sanity have sex with a human, that *had to have* sex with a human, in whatever twisted fashion it found erotic. But now even that avenue was closing behind her . . .

She ran towards them, the slug alien making its frenzied quagmire sounds of outrage and madness, rolling in an undulant comber behind her. Grebbie stepped into her path and the girl crashed into him, throwing them both against the wall of the passageway. Berne turned and ran back the way he had come. An enormous shadow, the slug alien, puffed up to three times its size, filled the foot of the passage.

Berne saw lights ahead, and pounded towards them.

Underfoot, he felt a rumbling, a jerking of parts and other parts. There was a whining in his ears, and he realised he had been hearing it for some time. Then the passageway heaved and he was hurled sidewise, smashing face-first into the melted window of a condemned building. He flailed wildly as the metal street under him bucked and warped, and then he fell, slamming into the wall and sliding down. He was sitting on the bucking metal, looking back towards the foot of the passage, when the slug alien suddenly began to glow with blue and orange light.

Verna was lying so close to the edge of the creature that the heat it gave off singed her leg. The fat little man she'd run into was somewhere under the alien. Gone now. Dead. Like the fox-martin.

But the slug was shrieking in pain, expanding and expanding, growing more monstrous, rising up almost to the level of second-storey windows. She had no idea what was happening . . . the whining was getting louder . . . she could smell the acrid scent of ozone, burning glass, boiling lubricant, sulphur . . .

The slug alien glowed blue, orange, seemed to be lit from inside, writhed hideously, expanded, gave one last, unbelievable sucking moan of pain and *burned*. Verna crawled away on hands and knees, down the egress passage, towards the light, towards the shape of a man just getting to his feet, looking dazed. Perhaps he could help her.

'The damned thing killed Grebbie. I didn't know what was happening. All at once everything was grinding and going crazy. The power under the streets had been making lousy sounds all night, I guess it was overloading, I don't know. Maybe that filthy thing caused it somehow, some part of it got down under the sidewalk plate and fouled the machinery, made it blow out. I think it was electrocuted ... I don't know. But she's here, and she's got what you need, and I want the full amount; Grebbie's share and mine both!'

'Keep your voice down, you thug. My patient may arrive at any moment.'

Verna lay on the operating table, watching them. *Seeing* them. Shadows beind shadows behind shadows. All the reflections. *Pay him, Doctor*, she thought, *it won't matter. He's going to die soon enough. So are you. And the way Grebbie bought it will look good by comparison. God bless and keep you, Sydni.* She could not turn it off now, nor damp it with a bowl, nor hide the images in the stinking flesh of creatures from other worlds of other stars. And in moments, at best mere minutes, they would ease her burden; they would give her peace, though they didn't know it. *Pay him, Doctor, and let's get to it.*

'Did you have to maul her?'

'I didn't maul her, damn you! I hit her once, the way I hit all the others. She's not damaged. You only want the eyes anyhow. Pay me!'

The Knoxdoctor took credits from a pouch on his coverall and counted out an amount the pronger seemed to find satisfactory. 'Then why is she so bloody?' He asked the question as an afterthought, like a surly child trying to win one final point after capitulating.

'Creep off, Doc,' Berne said nastily, counting the credits. 'She was crawling away from that worm. She fell down half a dozen times. I told you. If you're not satisfied with the kind of merchandise I bring you, get somebody else. Tell me how many other prongers could've found you a pair of them eyes in greyblue so quick after a call?'

Dr. Breame had no time to form an answer. The iris dilated and three huge Floridans stepped into the Knox Shop, moved quickly through the operating room, checked out the storage area, the consultation office, the power bins, and came back to stand near the iris, their weapons drawn.

Breame and Berne watched silently, the pronger awed despite himself at the efficiency and clearly obvious readiness of the men. They were heavy-gravity planet aliens, and Berne had once seen a Floridan put his naked fist through a plasteel plate two inches thick. He didn't move.

One of the aliens stepped through the iris, said something to someone neither Berne nor the Doctor could see, and then came back inside. A minute later they heard the sound of a group moving down the passage to the Knox Shop.

26 Krystabel Parsons strode into the operating room and waved her guard back. All but the three already in the Knox Shop. She slapped her hands down to her hips, locking the exo-braces. She stood unwaveringly and looked around.

'Doctor,' she said, greeting him perfunctorily. She looked at the pronger.

'Greetings, Director. I'm pleased to see you at long last. I think you'll find—'

'Shut up.' Her eyes narrowed at Berne. 'Does this man have to die?'

Berne started to speak, but Breame quickly, nervously answered. 'Oh, no; no indeed not. This gentleman has been most helpful to our project. He was just leaving.'

'I was just leaving.'

The old woman made a motion to one of the guards, and the Floridan took Berne by the upper arm. The pronger winced, though the guard apparently was only serving as butler. The alien propelled Berne towards the iris, and out. Neither returned.

Doctor Breame said, 'Will these, uh, gentlemen be necessary, Director? We have rather delicate surgery to perform and they . . .'

'They can assist.' Her voice was flat as iron.

She dropped her hands to her hips again, flicking up the locking levers of the exo-braces that formed a spiderweb scaffolding around her withered legs. She strode across the operating room towards the girl immobilised on the table, and Breame marvelled at her lack of reaction to the cold in the room : he was still shivering in his insulated coverall, she wore an ensemble made of semi-transparent, iridescent flow bird scales. But she seemed oblivious to the temperature of the Knox Shop.

26 Krystabel Parsons came to Verna and looked down into her face. Verna closed her eyes. The Director could not have known the reason the girl could not look at her.

'I have an unbendable sense of probity, child. If you co-operate with me, I shall make certain you don't have a moment of regret.'

Verna opened her eyes. The Director drew in her breath.

They were everything they'd been said to be.

Grey and blue, swirling, strange, utterly lovely.

'What do you see?' the Director asked.

'A tired old woman who doesn't know herself well enough to understand all she wants to do is die.'

The guards started forward. 26 Krystabel Parsons waved them back. 'On the contrary,' she said. 'I not only desire life for myself . . . I desire it for you. I'm assuring you if you help us, there is nothing you can ask that I will refuse.'

Verna looked at her, *seeing* her, knowing she was lying. Forever eyes told the truth. What this predatory relic wanted was: everything; who she was willing to sacrifice to get it was: everyone; how much mercy and kindness Verna could expect from her was: infinitesimal. But if one could not expect mercy from one's own mother, how could one expect it from strangers?

'I don't believe you.'

'Ask and you shall receive.' She smiled. It was a terrible stricture. The memory of the smile, even an instant after it was gone, persisted in Verna's sight.

'I want full passage on a Long Driver.'

'Where?'

'Anywhere I want to go.'

The Director motioned to one of the guards. 'Give her a million credits. No. Five million credits.'

The guard left the Knox Shop.

'In a moment you will see I keep my word,' said the Director. 'I'm willing to pay for my pleasures.'

'You're willing to pay for my pain, you mean.'

The Director turned to Breame. 'Will there be pain?'

'Very little, and what pain there is will mostly be yours, I'm afraid.' He stood with hands clasped together in front of him: a small child anxiously trying to avoid giving offence.

'Now, tell me what it's like,' 26 Krystabel Parsons said, her face bright with expectation.

'The mutation hasn't bred true, Director. It's still a fairly rare recessive . . .' Breame stopped. She was glaring at him. She had been speaking to the girl.

Verna closed her eyes and began to speak. She told the old woman of *seeing*. Seeing directions, as blind fish in subterranean caverns see the change in flow of water, as bees see the wind currents, as wolves see the heat auras surrounding humans, as bats see the walls of caves in the dark. Seeing memories, everything that ever happened to her, the good and the bad, the beautiful and the grotesque, the memorable and the utterly unforgettable, early memories and those of a moment before, all on instant recall, with absolute clarity and depth of field and detail, the whole of one's past, at command. Seeing colours, the sensuousness of airborne bacteria, the infinitely subtle shadings of rock and metal and natural wood, the tricksy shifts along a spectrum invisible to ordinary eyes of a candle flame, the colours of frost and rain and the moon and arteries pulsing just under the skin; the intimate overlapping colours of fingerprints left on a credit, so reminiscent of paintings by the old master, Jackson Pollock. Seeing colours that no human eyes have ever seen. Seeing shapes and relationships, the intricate calligraphy of all parts of the body moving in unison, the day melding into the night, the spaces and spaces between spaces that form a street, the invisible lines linking people. She spoke of *seeing*, of *all* the kinds of seeing except. The stroboscopic view of everyone. The shadows within shadows behind shadows that formed terrible, tortuous portraits she could not bear. She did not speak of that. And in the middle of her long recitation the Floridan guard came back and put five million credits in her tunic.

And when the girl was done, 26 Krystabel Parsons turned to the Knoxdoctor and said, 'I want her kept alive, with as little damage as possible to her faculties. You will place a value on her comfort as high as mine. Is that clearly understood?'

Breame seemed uneasy. He wet his lips, moved closer to the Director (keeping an eye on the Floridans, who did not move closer to him). 'May I speak to you in privacy?' he whispered.

'I have no secrets from this girl. She is about to give me a great gift. You may think of her as my daughter.'

The doctor's jaw muscles tensed. This was, after all, *his* operating room! *He* was in charge here, no matter how much power this unscrupulous woman possessed. He stared at her for a moment, but her gaze did not waver. Then he went to the operating table where Verna lay immobilised by a holding circuit in the table itself, and he pulled down the anaesthesia bubble over her head. A soft, eggshell-white fog instantly filled the bubble.

'I must tell you, Director, now that she cannot hear us—'

(But she could still *see*, and the patterns his words made in the air brought the message to her quite distinctly.)

'—that the traffic in mutant eyes is still illegal. Very illegal. In point of fact, it is equated with murder; and because of the shortage of transplantable parts the MediCom has kept it a high crime,

201

one of the few for which the punishment is vegetable cortexing. If you permit this girl to live you run a terrible risk. Even a personage of *your* authority would find it most uncomfortable to have the threat of such a creature wandering loose.'

The Director continued staring at him. Breame thought of the unblinking stares of lizards. When she blinked he thought of the membranous nictating eyelids of lizards.

'Doctor, the girl is no problem. I want her alive only until I establish that there are no techniques for handling these eyes that she can help me to learn.'

Breame seemed shocked.

'I do not care for the expression on your face, Doctor. You find my manner with this child duplicitous, yet you are directly responsible for her situation. You have taken her away from whomever and wherever she wished to be, you have stripped her naked, laid her out like a side of beef, you have immobilised her and anaesthetised her; you plan to cut out her eyes, treat her to the wonders of blindness after she has spent a lifetime seeing far more than normal humans; and you have done all this not in the name of science, or humanity, or even curiosity. You have done it for credits. I find the expression on your face an affront, Doctor. I advise you to work diligently to erase it.'

Breame had gone white, and in the cold room he was shivering again. He heard the voices of the parts calling. At the edges of his vision things moved.

'All I want you to assure me, Doctor Breame, is that you can perform this operation with perfection. I will not tolerate anything less. My guards have been so instructed.'

'I'm perhaps the only surgeon who *can* perform this operation and guarantee you that you will encounter no physically deleterious effects. Handling the eyes *after* the operation is something over which I have no control.'

'And results will be immediate?'

'As I promised. With the techniques I've perfected, transfer can be effected virtually without discomfort.'

'And should something go wrong . . . you can replace the eyes a second time?'

Breame hesitated. 'With difficulty. You aren't a young woman; the risks would be considerable; but it *could* be done. Again, probably by no other surgeon. And it would be extremely expensive. It would entail another pair of healthy eyes.'

26 Krystabel Parsons smiled her terrible smile. 'Do I perceive you feel underpaid, Doctor Breame?'

He did not answer. No answer was required.

Verna saw it all, and understood it all. And had she been able to smile, she would have smiled; much more warmly than the Director. If she died, as she was certain she would, that was peace and release. If not, well . . .

Nothing was worse than life.

They were moving around the room now. Another table was unshipped from a wall cubicle and formed. The Doctor undressed 26 Krystabel Parsons and one of the two remaining Floridans lifted her like a tree branch and laid her on the table.

The last thing Verna saw was the faintly glowing, vibrating blade of the shining e-scalpel, descending towards her face. The finger of God, and she blessed it as her final thoughts were of her mother.

26 Krystabel Parsons, undisputed owner of worlds and industries and entire races of living creatures, jaded observer of a universe that no longer held even a faint view of interest or originality, opened her eyes.

The first things she saw were the operating room, the Floridan guards standing at the foot of the table staring at her intensely, the Knoxdoctor dressing the girl who stood beside her own table, the smears of black where the girl's eyes had been.

There was a commotion in the passageway outside. One of the guards turned towards the iris, still open.

And in that moment all sense of *seeing* flooded in on the Director of Minet. Light, shade, smoke, shadow, glow, transparency, opacity, colour, tint, hue, prismatics, sweet, delicate, subtle, harsh, vivid, bright, intense, serene, crystalline, kaleidoscopic, all and everything at once!

Something else. Something more. Something the girl had not mentioned, had not hinted at, had not wanted her to know! The shadows within shadows.

She *saw* the Floridan guards. *Saw* them for the first time. Saw the state of their existence at the moment of their death. It was as though a multiple image, a strobe portrait of each of them lived before her. The corporeal reality in the front, and behind – like endless auras radiating out from them but superimposed over them – the thousand images of their futures. And the sight of them when they were dead, how they died. Not the action of the event, but the result. The hideous result of having life ripped from them. Rotting, corrupt, ugly beyond belief, and all the more ugly than imagination because it was *seen* with forever eyes that captured all the invisible-to-normal-eyes subtleties of containers intended to contain life, having been emptied of that life. She turned her head, unable to speak or scream or howl like a dog as she wished, and she *saw* the girl, and she *saw* the doctor.

It was a sight impossible to contain.

She jerked herself upright, the pain in her withered legs barely noticeable. And she opened her mouth and forced herself to scream as the commotion in the passageway grew louder, and something dragged itself through the iris.

She screamed with all the unleashed horror of a creature unable to bear itself, and the guards turned back to look at her with fear and wonder ... as Berne dragged himself into the room. She *saw* him, and it was worse than all the rest, because it was happening *now*, he was dying *now*, the vessel was emptying *now*! Her scream became the howl of a dog. He could not speak, because he had no part left in his face that could make a formed sound come out. He could only see imperfectly; there was only one eye. If he had an expression, it was lost under the blood and crushed, hanging flesh that formed his face. The huge Floridan guard had not been malevolent, merely Floridan, and they were a race only lately up from barbarism. But he had taken a long time.

Breame's hands froze on the sealstrip of the girl's tunic and he looked around her, saw the pulped mass that pulled itself along the floor, leaving a trail of dark stain and viscous matter, and his eyes widened.

The Floridans raised their weapons almost simultaneously, but the thing on the floor gripped the weapon it had somehow – amazingly, unpredictably, impossibly – taken away from its assassin, and it fired. The head of the nearest Floridan caved in on itself, and the body jerked sidewise, slamming into the other guard. Both of them hit the operating table on which the Director of Minet sat screaming, howling, savaging the air with mortal anguish. The table overturned, flinging the crippled old woman with the forever eyes to the floor.

Breame knew what had happened. Berne had not been sent away. It had been blindness for him to think she would leave *any* of them alive. He moved swiftly, as the remaining Floridan struggled to free himself of the corpse that pinned him to the floor. The Knoxdoctor had the e-scalpel in his hand in an instant, palmed it on, and threw himself atop the guard. The struggle took a moment, as Breame sliced away at the skull. There was a muffled sound of the guard's weapon, and Breame staggered to his feet, reeled backwards and crashed into a power bin. Its storage door fell open and Breame took two steps into the centre of the room, clutching his chest. His hands went inside his body; he stared down at the ruin; then he fell forward.

There was a soft bubbling sound from the dying thing that had been the pronger, Berne, and then silence in the charnel house.

Silence, despite the continued howling of 26 Krystabel Parsons. The sounds she made were so overwhelming, so gigantic, so inhuman, that they became like the ticking of a clock in a silent room, the thrum of power in a sleeping city. Unheard.

Verna heard it all, but had no idea what had happened. She dropped to her knees, and crawled towards what she thought was the iris. She touched something wet and pulpy with the fingertips of her left hand. She kept crawling. She touched something still-warm but unmoving with the fingertips of her right hand, and felt along the thing till she came to hands embedded in soft, rubbery ruin. To her right she could faintly hear the sound of something humming, and she knew the sound: an e-scalpel, still slicing, even when it could do no more damage.

Then she had crawled to an opening, and she felt with her hands and it seemed to be a bin, a large bin, with its door open. She crawled inside and curled up, and pulled the door closed behind her, and lay there quietly.

And not much later there was the sound of movement in the operating room as others, who had been detained for reasons Verna would never know, came and lifted 26 Krystabel Parsons, and carried her away, still howling like a dog, howling more intensely as she saw each new person, knowing eventually she would see the thing she feared seeing the most. The reflection of herself as she would be in the moment of her dying; and knowing she would still be sane enough to understand and appreciate it.

From extreme long shot, establishing; tracking in to medium shot, it looks like this:
Viewed through the tracking devices of PIX's port authority clearance security system, the Long Drive vessel sits in its pit,

205

then slowly begins to rise out of its berth. White mist, or possibly steam, or possibly ionised fog billows out of the pit as the vessel leaves. The great ship rises towards the sky as we move in steadily on it. We continue forward, angle tilting up to hold the Long Driver in medium shot, then a fast zoom in on the glowing hide of the ship, and dissolve through to a medium shot, establishing the interior.

Everyone is comfortable. Everyone is watching the planet Earth drop away like the pieces of a stained-glass window through a trapdoor. The fisheye-lens of the stateroom iris shows WorldsEnd and PIX and the polar emptiness and the mottled ball of the decaying Earth as they whirl away into the darkness.

Everyone sees. They see the ship around them, they see one another, they see the pages of the books they read, and they see the visions of their hopes for good things at the end of this voyage. They all see.

Moving in on one passenger, we see she is blind. She sits with her body formally erect, her hands at her sides. She wears her clothing well, and apart from the dark smudges that show beneath the edge of the stylish opaque band covering her eyes, she is a remarkably attractive woman. Into tight closeup. And we see that much of her grace and attractiveness comes from a sense of overwhelming peace and contentment her features convey.

Hold the closeup as we study her face, and marvel at how relaxed she seems. We must pity her, because we know that blindness, not being able to see, is a terrible curse. And we decide she must be a remarkable woman to have reconciled such a tragic state with continued existence.

We think that if we were denied sight we would certainly commit suicide. As the darkness of the universe surrounds the vessel bound for other places.

'If the doors of perception were cleansed everything would appear to man as it is, infinite.'
William Blake, 'The Marriage of Heaven and Hell,' *1790*